*A*NGEL *with*

a *M*ISSION

a novel

Donna Boddy

iUniverse, Inc.
Bloomington

Angel with a Mission
a novel

iUniverse books may be ordered through booksellers or by contacting:

iUniverse
1663 Liberty Drive
Bloomington, IN 47403
www.iuniverse.com
1-800-Authors (1-800-288-4677)

ISBN: 978-1-4620-1061-5 (sc)
ISBN: 978-1-4620-1059-2 (ebook)
ISBN: 978-1-4620-1060-8 (hc)

Library of Congress Control Number: 2011909313

Printed in the United States of America

iUniverse rev. date: 5/25/2011

For I know the thoughts that I think toward you, says the LORD,
thoughts of peace and not of evil, to give you a future and a hope.
Then you will call upon Me and go and pray to Me, and I will listen to you.
And you will seek Me and find Me, when you search for Me with all your heart.

Jeremiah 29:11-13 (NKJV)

ACKNOWLEDGEMENTS

I dedicate this book to the memory of my beloved grandmother, Margarethe Thomsen, who inspired me with her family stories when I was a little girl, and to my mother, Elizabeth Frazier, who encouraged me to write. Also, a special thanks to the following people who helped in so many ways as I was writing and revising this book: Maggie Nowak, a colleague and friend who helped with the editing, and Pastor Ryan Holt from First Family Church, who gave his insight and guidance for some of the spiritual passages.

Finally, I would also like to thank the following for their tremendous support during the writing, editing and publishing process: my husband, my daughter Suzanne, and my sister, Elizabeth Gregowicz, my dearest and closest friend, as well as my students at St. Joseph Grade School who challenged me to get it published.

Contents

Part I: Temptation and Transgression

Part I:
Temptation and Transgression

CHAPTER 1

Katharina

KATHARINA BRUSHED HER AUBURN TRESSES UNTIL they shone while she hummed one of her favorite songs from her role in Wagner's opera, *Das Rheingold*. The Belle Epoch decor enveloped her as her eyes traveled from the image in her Victorian oval shaped mirror to the gold floral pattern in her wall coverings. Ever since her parents had taken her to see Wagner's *The Flying Dutchman* when she was a little girl, she was smitten with the opera. She acted out the parts she favored, and memorized many of the songs. Singing was her life.

I cannot believe how much my life has changed since my first role in Hansel and Gretel, she mused. *Who knows? Perhaps one day I may even be as famous as Lilli Lehmann.*

A pensive smile crossed her face as she reveled in the resounding applause her audiences praised her with each time she stepped out onto the stage. Germany adored her.

A loud, urgent knock at her door interrupted her thoughts.

"Who's there?" Katharina asked impatiently.

"It's me, Greta. Let me in. I have some great news."

Before Kata could answer, she barged in abruptly and seated herself on the nearby settee. She smiled at Kata, as if she was about to reveal the biggest event of the century.

"Couldn't it wait until *after* the performance? I'm not quite ready and I am expected on stage any moment."

Greta emphatically placed her hands on her hips. "No, it can't,

Kata. I just talked with Director Hans Schumer, and he is working on the plans for his next great production, Wagner's *Die Feen."*

Greta leaned closer to Kata and spoke in a low, urgent tone. "You will never guess *who* he is going to star in the leading role."

"I could care less, Greta. I am *trying* to get ready for the opening act. You, on the other hand, still have two more scenes before you have to come out. Can't you tell me later?"

"No. I think you will be very interested in this—because, you see *Liebe, you* are going to be offered the lead role."

"Now I *know* you are teasing me. I can think of a number of women who he might consider first. Besides, *Herr* Schumer would have told me before he said anything to you, I am sure of it. And I *definitely* haven't been approached by him."

"I have my ways of finding things out—you know Hans is putty in my hands," Greta said in a self-confident tone. "I've been pushing him for *months* to consider you for the part of Ada. You are *perfect* for it."

"I just don't know what to make of you, Greta. You certainly can wrap *Herr* Schumer around your little finger, but this—this is just too incredible—even for you to achieve," said Kata, shaking her head.

"Mark my words, Kata. It's a part *made* for you. No one else can play Ada better than you. You have the voice and the looks for it. Before the week is out, you'll see. Hans will offer you that part."

"Look. I appreciate all that you have done for me, Greta. You are a dear friend and a wonderful roommate, but sometimes you are just too impetuous. Wouldn't it be best to let *Herr* Schumer choose who he wants rather than be pushed into such a choice *Liebe?* On the off chance that he does offer me the role, I'd much rather know he chose me because he thought of it, not you."

"Honestly, Kata, you have been like a sister to me. I have always looked out for you. I thought you would be more appreciative of my help."

With that, Greta turned and left the room almost as quickly as she had entered, leaving Kata to ponder her words. She certainly had not meant to hurt Greta's feelings, yet it bothered her that she was always meddling into Kata's life—even if she did mean well.

True, she knew that Greta was trying to be helpful, still for *Herr* Schumer to make her such an offer? That was almost unfathomable. On the other hand, Greta did seem to have an uncanny knack for making things work out the way she wanted. So what if Greta was right? Oh well, she needed to finish getting ready and let the matter rest for now. She straightened her costume, checked her make up one more time, and stepped out of her dressing room and onto the stage.

As she danced with the other flower girls, she glanced from time to time at the front row. Her eyes focused on one particular gentleman. He sat in the same seat for almost all of her shows. Each time she looked his way, he was staring intently at her. Her alone. He didn't seem to see anyone else. *Who is that gentleman? His eyes—they . . . they're piercing into my very soul. It is driving me mad! Oh, Katharina, stop it! You are being superstitious. Just focus on your performance.*

She sang with great passion, fleeing away from reality once again as she waltzed into the woods with the rest of the maidens. The stranger faded out of her thoughts . . . for the moment.

CHAPTER 2

The Courtship

FREDRIC HAD SEEN KATHARINA PERFORM A number of times. However, he fell in love with her when she starred in the opera *Das Rheingold* in 1893. Her beauty and the grace with which she moved about in her role as a flower maiden in this tale of the knights of the Grail, stirred his emotions. Her powerful, yet mellifluous mezzo-soprano voice held him captive. When she appeared on stage, Fredric lost all sense of time and space. In fact, the other members of the cast completely faded out of his mind. She was his leading lady. The show revolved around her. She was the essence of *Das Rheingold.* It existed because of Katharina.

Now, several months after that first encounter, Katharina had the leading role in the opera *Die Fien.* It was no longer his fantasy. Tonight was the premiere, and just as Greta had predicted, Hans Schumer cast Katharina as Ada, a fairy who had given up her immortality to spend her life with the mortal she loved. Fredric and his friends, the Werners, purchased front row seats for her debut. The closer he could be to Katharina, the better.

When the curtain went up and the show began, his eyes immediately searched for his diva. He studied her attentively. Katharina's soft emerald green dress and low-cut bodice accented her form and emphasized the green specks in her hazel eyes, which sparkled as her song resonated throughout the opera. Her long auburn hair, adorned with a floral wreath, flowed smoothly around her neck and shoulders, surrounding her heart-shaped face in delicate waves. Her full ruby lips enhanced each vibrato of her song.

Over the past few months, his growing desire to meet this diva wrestled with the mores of society, which made little room for relationships between the upper class and members of the arts; yet the more he attended her performances, the more he dismissed that feeling.

After all, love was a matter of the heart—not a matter of public approval in his mind. He was an independent—a freethinker and would not give way to such prejudices.

Herr Werner leaned over to his wife, whispering in her ear, "Did you notice, *Mein Schätzchen*, how captivated our young charge seems to be with Katharina?"

She offered a perceptive smile. "Yes, *Liebe*, it is rather obvious. I doubt that he is aware of anyone else in the entire opera. Perhaps we could take him back stage to meet Katharina later," *Frau* Werner suggested.

"Good idea, *Meine Liebe*. I'll suggest it to him," said *Herr* Werner.

After the show, as they were leaving the theatre, *Herr* Werner turned to Fredric and took his arm to stop him.

"*Frau* Werner and I could see that you were quite taken with the star of the show, *Fraulein* Ernst. Would you like to meet her, Fredric?" *Herr* Werner suggested with a slight knowing smile.

"You are well enough acquainted with her to arrange such a meeting?"

"Yes, quite well, as a matter of fact. We knew her parents before their tragic deaths a few years ago. They were part of the high society here in Berlin," said *Frau* Werner.

Fredric gave him a look of surprise. "You mean to tell me her family was not from . . ."

"Quite the contrary, Fredric," said *Herr* Werner. "She comes from quite an aristocratic background. Her grandmother was the daughter of an earl, actually. The opera was definitely not the life they wanted for their daughter. But Katharina would settle for nothing else. She convinced her parents that she would not be happy unless she could pursue her dream of being in the opera.

"They found it hard to refuse Katharina anything. She was their only child, and they doted on her. After she turned sixteen, she studied under Viardot and Marchisi and quickly became quite the accomplished mezzo-soprano she is today. I understand they were greatly impressed with her and encouraged her to pursue her dream."

They walked around the lobby for a while, then headed towards the corridor leading to Kata's dressing room

"Do tell me more, *Herr* Werner. I am quite interested to learn everything I can about this young lady."

"Well, her parents hoped her desire to sing would not distract her from a future marriage. They planned for her to marry into a certain family of nobility. They were close friends of a distant relative of Queen Elizabeth, Empress of Austria, Count Berthold and Countess Margarethe of Bavaria. They were working out a betrothal agreement between Katharina and their son when she announced to them that she was going to audition for a minor role in a local opera.

"She turned down such an arrangement for the opera?" Fredric asked, raising an eyebrow.

"Yes. She had her mind made up. She is quite an independent woman. Although they tried everything to dissuade her, Katharina could be very stubborn. She absolutely refused to marry and even threatened to leave home without their blessing. They couldn't bear the thought of losing her altogether, so they eventually gave in," said *Frau* Werner.

"I see," said Fredric. "So I assume her success in the art finally convinced her parents to support her in this?"

"Not at first. They still had reservations about her making this a lifetime career. They hoped that in time she would find this profession to be very grueling and come to her senses."

"Obviously that never happened."

"I think she finally won their approval when she auditioned for a part in *Märchenoper*, that fairy tale opera, you know. Not only was she successful in getting the part, but the director of the opera was so impressed with her voice, in fact, that he convinced her parents to let her continue to perform in the opera. He planned to offer her even more opportunities. They reluctantly agreed and laid aside their dream for her to marry into royalty. More than anything, they wanted her to be happy. After her first year with the opera, her confidence grew and she determined that she would make a career of it."

"What a fascinating story," remarked Fredric. "Such determination is quite rare in a woman. However, I find that quite an attractive feature." Fredric's smile created a dimple in his left cheek.

They approached her dressing room and *Herr* Werner knocked on her door. Kata opened it and greeted them.

"Heinrich . . . Edda; what a pleasant surprise!"

"Kata, I want you to meet a good friend of ours, Fredric Albers," said Heinrich.

Although still in costume, she invited the three of them in.

"How do you do, *Herr* Albers?" She put her hand out to him.

"Well, thank you," replied Fredric, bowing courteously and lightly kissing her hand.

Kata's eyes furtively studied this dashing stranger in his three-button gray frock coat and white silk evening shirt, adorned with a black silk bow tie. His fashionable black top hat enhanced his towering stature.

"Please have a seat," entreated Kata as she pointed to her settee.

"*Herr* Albers was so taken by your performance," said Heinrich, chuckling and winking at his wife, "that we felt compelled to introduce him to you."

"Now Heinrich, you've embarrassed our young protégé," Edda said, lightly tapping her husband's hand with her fan as a gentle rebuke.

"Protégé?" Kata asked. "So you are well acquainted with the Werners, I take it."

"Actually, my dear, you could say we have sort of–adopted him," explained Edda. You see, we were very close friends with his parents," she continued.

"Do tell me," Katharina remarked.

"Why yes," Heinrich added. "Fredric's parents passed away after succumbing to the terrible cholera outbreak in 1885, when he was just seventeen. Since we were his godparents and had no children of our own, we were quite happy to take him under wing."

"Heinrich has been a wonderful mentor in my life," inserted Fredric. "With his help and the recent industrial growth in Germany, I have invested most of my family's money in several chemical and agricultural factories. And so far they have proved to be extremely profitable."

"Fascinating, I am somewhat aware of this industrial revolution as they call it."

"Actually it has affected our country in a very positive way," Fredric continued. "And since the introduction of electricity, Europe has benefited substantially. Anyone with the money to invest, the ambition to work hard and the time to commit to this new industry can be financially independent in just a few years.

"Enough of this talk about the economy," Edda interrupted with a look of disapproval. "Let's stop discussing the financial state of this country and get back to why we came to visit. And it had nothing to do with such a droll subject as industry.

Heinrich stifled a smirk and winked at Fredric.

"Yes, I'm afraid such talk tends to bore my wife."

"Fredric has been a great aficionado of yours for quite some time. He expressed a desire to meet you," Edda said, appearing to ignore her husband's remark.

"Quite frankly we thought it would be a wonderful idea to get two of our dear young friends together," added Heinrich.

"I have been aware of your regular attendance at my performances," Katharina said. "It was hard to miss you sitting in the front row almost every time."

Listening to you sing is like listening to an angel. You are a very graceful and talented young lady." Fredric's deep blue eyes sparkled as he spoke.

"Now you are embarrassing me, *Herr* Albers." Kata blushed and stared down at her feet.

His voice was gentle. "Really, *Fraulein,* I don't say that lightly. I love the opera, and I have to say that I am not easily impressed, but you are quite a remarkable prima donna."

"I'm flattered by your kind words. You must be aware, though, that until this opera, I have only had minor roles. I am surprised that you even noticed me."

"Believe me, you would be quite noticeable, no matter how minor the role."

Katharina smiled coyly.

The four continued to chat for almost an hour. Fredric shared how he purposed to learn all he could about the latest inventions and how he could use them to benefit society. His knowledge belied his youth. Katharina was captivated with his determination to succeed.

Finally, she said, "I have enjoyed our visit; however, it is very late, and I need to be getting home as I have rehearsal in the morning and another performance this weekend. It was very nice getting to know you."

She looked at the Werners. "Oh, and please, come back to see me again soon, and bring this young man with you," she added, casting a demure smile in Fredric's direction.

As the three were leaving Kata's dressing room, Fredric stopped and turned around to face her. Taking her hand and holding her gaze, he asked, "I wonder if you—I mean I would be honored if you would have dinner with me tomorrow evening."

"Why, I—I don't know if. . ."

"I will be happy to invite the Werners, if you prefer we have a chaperone, *Fraulein*."

"Well, perhaps it will be all right—to have dinner, that is. I don't think there really is a need for a chaperone," she replied.

"Good. I will come by for you around 6:00 if you like."

"Yes, yes that will be a perfect time, but it would be best if you come by my flat instead, as I do not have a performance tomorrow. Greta, my roommate, will be home, so it will be just fine to come by for me there. Just a moment. I will give you my address."

She retreated into her room, scribbled her address on a piece of paper and handed it to him.

"I will see you tomorrow evening then." Tipping his hat, Fredric turned and sprinted down the hall to catch up to his friends.

* * *

Over the next several weeks, Fredric and Katharina saw each

other regularly. They dined, danced and attended concerts together almost every night that Katharina was not performing. Fredric was quite the gentleman with her, making her feel totally at ease with him. He always saw her to her door, kissed her hand, tipped his hat and left just as soon as she was safely inside her apartment.

When they were together, she felt lighthearted, like a schoolgirl again. Fredric had no doubt added a new dimension to her life, yet she wasn't sure what to call her feelings. *Love? An attraction? Friendship? Yes, it was a wonderful friendship.* She was comfortable with that word.

One evening, several months after their first meeting, when Fredric walked her to her door, she turned to him and asked,

"Would you like to come in for tea? Greta is at home, and it is still fairly early, so I see no harm inviting you in for a little while."

"I would like that," Fredric said.

They sat on the couch together, discussing trivial matters. Then, for a brief moment, they were silent. Fredric took her hands in his. He looked into her eyes and said, "Kata, it should be no surprise that I am falling in love with you. You are the most exciting woman I have ever met. I would be honored if you would agree to become my wife."

Kata stared at him for a moment, at first not reacting to his proposal. Then she responded. "Fredric, I-I don't really know what to say—I –I don't think I . . ."

Fredric interrupted her. He took her in his arms and held her close. He looked down at her, lifted her chin, then pulled her closer and kissed her eagerly and passionately on the lips.

Kata resisted at first, and then she melted in his embrace. The passion from his kiss and the fire she felt inside stirred her in a way she had never experienced before and she felt herself losing control of her emotions. Suddenly, she stopped herself, and pulled away from his embrace.

"No, Fredric. Don't do that again!" she said angrily.

His countenance suddenly took on a perplexed expression.

"I- I love you, Kata. I know you feel the same way. Please, don't fight your feelings." He reached for her again. She stiffened and resisted his attempt.

"I don't know *what* I feel, Fredric. I do have . . . feelings for you. I don't know if I am ready to call it *love*. You have to give me some time."

"Kata, I don't think you are being honest with yourself. The months we have been together . . . they've been happy ones, haven't they? Surely they must have meant something more to you than just a casual friendship."

She rose from her seat, walked across the room, and put her hands up to her face. "Yes, but that doesn't necessarily constitute love, Fredric. Love takes *time* to grow. Besides, there's my career to consider, and . . ."

"So that's it—your career is more important to you than marrying me?" Fredric retorted. "I'm sorry." His tone softened and he ran his fingers through his sandy blond hair. "I didn't mean to minimize the importance of your career. Couldn't we work that out?"

He stood up and walked over to her. He tried to put his hands on her shoulders. She pushed them away.

"No!" she exclaimed, refusing to compromise. She clenched her fists so tightly that she dug her nails into her palms until they burned from the pain. "I want you to leave now, Fredric. I have an early day tomorrow and I need my sleep," she demanded flatly.

"All right, if that is what you want," he said.

"That is what I want." She did not turn around.

Fredric picked up his hat, walked briskly to the door and let himself out, leaving Katharina standing by the window, staring out blankly.

* * *

The Damrosch Opera Company, a newly formed American opera troupe, had come to Germany on a recruitment mission, and Katharina saw an opportunity she felt that she couldn't pass up. She needed to get away and to think clearly without being entangled in a romance. Besides, this would give her a chance to expand her career. Damrosch was promising his new recruits a chance for great fame and fortune.

Katharina's singing talent and flourishing reputation quickly earned her a place with the company and she travelled all over Europe for several months. However, it just wasn't the same. Something was missing from her life.

Once Damrosch decided to take his company to the United States, she decided to leave it and return to Berlin to work for a local company once again. Besides, the idea of crossing the ocean unnerved her. There was something ominous about the deep abyss. She envisioned large ocean liners swimming about like tiny minnows, vulnerable, ready to be devoured by predatory water monsters, or gigantic waves toppling them in a single blow as if they were mere toys. When she thought about making the voyage, it sent shivers throughout her whole body.

Yet was she being honest with herself? Was this the only reason for leaving Damrosch? Something else churned deep inside of her very soul. She felt an aching, an emptiness, and for the first time in her life, the opera did not fully satisfy her needs. She traveled back in her mind to the day she had turned down Fredric's proposal. How she missed him. Had she been too hasty? Did she mistake friendship with true love?

She tried so hard to repress any feelings she had for Fredric. Still, the wonderful times that they had shared together wouldn't fade away, no matter how busy she kept herself. She had to find out, once and for all, if she was really in love with this man.

Yes, she needed to see him again. She needed to know if he was the reason she was feeling so alone and unsatisfied. She wrote him a letter.

Dear Frederic.

I know our parting was rather upsetting for both of us. Since then, I have had quite some time to think and now realize that I was not altogether honest with myself. I want to apologize for the way that I treated you. I am returning to Berlin and will be working locally. I hope you can find it in your heart to forgive me, and that you might consider meeting me for dinner one evening when I get back to Berlin.

Your friend, Kata.

When Fredric received her note, he wasted no time in responding. "You will never know how much I have missed seeing you," he said during their first dinner together following her return to Berlin.

"I had some time to think about our relationship while I was with Damrosch, and I missed you so very much as well."

Fredric took her hand, and she did not remove it. "Nothing would make me happier than if you agreed to see me again. I promise I will not rush you into a courtship. I just ask you to you give me permission to see you on occasion. You mean more to me than you can imagine."

"Yes, I would like that," she said.

At first they saw each other two or three times a month. As time passed, however, Kata's affection for Fredric grew, and she agreed to see him more often. One evening, Katharina invited Fredric for dinner with Greta as their chaperone.

After dinner, while Katharina took the dishes to the kitchen, Fredric pulled Greta aside. "Would you give me a few minutes alone with Kata? I have some very important business to discuss with her."

Greta caught on immediately. "I dare say it has little to do with "business," she said, simpering slyly at him. "I've had a little experience with romance myself, you know."

Fredric cast an omniscient grin her way. "Yes, from what Kata tells me, you have a way of breaking men's hearts."

She waved her hand to dispel his words. "Nonsense. I just haven't found the right one, yet. Something tells me that Kata has, though. She never stopped thinking about you the whole time you were apart."

"You are indeed a wise young lady. I assure you, though, that my intentions are honorable and I am not going to lose her again."

Greta excused herself. "If you don't mind, Katharina, I have to retire early, so I trust you can see Fredric out on your own?"

"Of course. We won't be very long. I have to get an early start tomorrow as well."

Before she could dismiss him for the evening, however, Fredric said, "Let's go into the parlor for a few minutes."

They sat down together on Katharina's stuffed hand-carved sofa. Fredric pulled a small box from his waistcoat, opened it and kneeled in front of her.

"Kata, you know how much I love and adore you." Patiently, he paused, giving her room to consider his words.

"Yes, and I love you, too." Her eyes sparkled as she smiled lovingly.

He opened the box, displaying a large, two-carat, Marquise diamond ring. Placing it on her finger he said, "Then marry me, *Meine Liebling*."

She gasped and her eyes grew wide. She started to speak. Before she could respond, Fredric stood up, drew her close and kissed her tenderly. She put her arms around his neck and eagerly returned his kiss. Then she pulled away slightly. "Yes, *Leipschen*. I will, with one condition," she said.

"Anything you ask."

"I want to keep working in the opera. I realize that many men might find this a difficult request. I do believe I can be a wife and a professional singer at the same time, and I want your approval in this."

"*Of course, Liebling!* I will be happy to have the most beautiful prima donna in all of Germany for my wife." He kissed her again.

After spending a little time discussing initial plans for their wedding, they parted, agreeing to continue this discussion in greater detail very soon. Fredric lightheartedly skipped back to his carriage and left for the evening, enthusiastically contemplating his future with his darling Katharina.

CHAPTER 3

Max

KATA AND FREDRIC WERE MARRIED IN the summer of 1897. They spent their honeymoon in Austria and then visited several cities along the Rhein River on their way back to Berlin, including Frankfurt, Heidelberg and Strasbourg. When they returned home, he surprised her with a large, stately home near the heart of Berlin. The seven bedroom, three-story mansion was over a quarter-century old, but Fredric had it completely renovated in the *Jugendstil* or Art Nouveau style. He had electricity and indoor plumbing installed. It boasted two large drawing rooms, two dining rooms—one could hold up to thirty guests, and the other, a smaller one, was for more intimate dining. It also included a large kitchen with servants' quarters built just behind it. Kata loved the house, but she insisted on adding some of her favorite Victorian furnishings as well.

Shortly after their honeymoon, Kata went back to work. One day as she was rehearsing, a wave of nausea and dizziness besieged her whole body. The room began to spin and she lost her balance. Another cast member standing nearby caught her before she fell to the stage.

Greta saw the whole incident and rushed over to help her. "Are you all right?"

"Y-yes, I think so. It must be the heat or something I ate, I guess." I-I don't ever remember feeling like this before."

"I think it is more than just the heat," Greta said.

"Let's call for a doctor before you even attempt to do any more today. Here, sit down." She helped get Kata to a chair, and then sent someone to get the doctor.

"Really, Greta, this is way too much of a fuss for a mere dizzy spell and a little upset stomach. I can get back up in a few minutes and I'll be just fine," insisted Katharina.

"Not if I can help it! You stay put, young lady, until the doctor gets here."

The doctor arrived about thirty minutes later, and Greta helped him get Katharina to the dressing room.

"I think what we have here is a mother-to-be," he said after he finished examining her. "I highly recommend that someone take her home for the rest of the day and let her get a good night's rest. It's still a little early to be sure, so I would like to have you come into my office next month, and I'll re-examine you to confirm my suspicions. Until then you need to take it easy and not overdo your activities. We don't want to take any unnecessary risks, do we?"

He gave Kata his card, patted her on the shoulder, walked to the door, bid the women good day and left.

Kata was in a daze. Her emotions were at war. She wasn't ready for this to be happening. *A child? Not now. How am I going to be able to manage the opera and motherhood? What will Fredric think? No, surely the doctor is mistaken. Besides, I'm in the middle of a production—I can't possibly take time out to have a baby.*

"Kata—Kata, are you listening to me?" she heard Greta say. "We need to get you home to Fredric. I know he'll be surprised to hear your news. Come, dear, let's go."

"No, no, I am not ready. I need to think about this. I don't – I'm not. . ."

"Not--what, going to have a baby?" Greta clicked her tongue. "Don't be so naïve. It's a natural part of marriage. Besides, having a baby does not mean you can never work again. It just means you need to take a little time off. Contrary to antiquated social expectations, there are other women who have been in the opera and have had children."

"Oh, you don't know Fredric very well," argued Katharina,

shaking her head in disagreement. "He will try hard to get me to stay home for good. I know him. I cannot tell him yet. I'm not ready to give up my career right now."

"Let's not jump to conclusions. Besides, Fredric agreed that you could work after your marriage, didn't he?"

"Yes, yes he did."

"Why would having a baby change things? He knows how important the opera is to you and after a reasonable length of time, I am sure that he will let you come back. You can always hire a nanny if you need to."

Kata shook her head. "You are so independent. While I enjoy having a career, I am not as progressive as you. True, at one time I thought my whole life would be wrapped up in the opera, but if I really am going to have a baby, I can't see how that can happen."

"It's about time you started standing up for yourself, Kata. If you want to work after you have your baby, then do so. Don't let old-fashioned societal mores dictate what you can and cannot do. Be a freethinker like me—I would never let a husband stand in my way of my career. Why someday, you watch and see. All women will play a larger, more important role in this world. It's inevitable. Look at the women's suffrage movement. Before too long, they will be voting and taking part in every aspect of society, mark my words."

Katharina shook her head. "That it is hard for me to believe. Not all women support the suffrage movement. No, I can't even imagine that happening in our lifetime."

* * *

When Kata and Greta arrived at the Alberses' residence, Fredric was in the drawing room, reading.

"You are home early. Is something wrong? Are you ill?"

Greta smiled at Kata as she accompanied her to the sofa and sat down beside her. "Go on, tell him."

"Tell me what? Is something wrong with you?"

Kata bit her lip. She avoided looking directly at Fredric.

"Well, I had a little dizzy spell at work, and Greta got a little excited."

"You know I had good reason to be worried. You turned pale as a ghost and almost passed out."

"I was just a bit queasy, that's all. I haven't eaten much today. Everyone is making too much of it."

"What are you not telling me?" Fredric asked.

Kata shifted in her seat uncomfortably. "Well, it's probably nothing. It's just that the doctor thinks that I may be. . ."

"Pregnant?" Fredric's eyes grew wide and his face lit up in sudden expectation.

"Now don't get excited. Nothing is definite. It is merely a guess on the doctor's part."

"Nevertheless, *Liebe,* even if it's a remote possibility, you need to take care of yourself in the meantime. Maybe you should take some time off from the opera until you know for sure."

"Nonsense, there's no need for me to stop doing what I have been used to for years. Besides, we're in the middle of a production. I can't back out now. And, even if I *am* pregnant, I still have several months that I can work, and this production will be over in about three months. I wouldn't even be showing by then, I am sure. And really, I will just be bored staying around home with nothing to do."

Fredric sighed. "That's true, it probably would frustrate you. Just promise me, that if you find out that you are pregnant, you will take some time off from the opera and take care of yourself."

"All right *Leipschen,* but I'm still not sure I *am* actually pregnant."

In April 1898, she gave birth to their first child—a son, Maximilian. Edda Werner was one of the first visitors after his birth.

"Why, you certainly can't deny he's yours, Fredric. He looks just like you," Edda commented as she held the tiny infant in her arms and cooed at him. He wrapped his little hand around her finger and yawned.

"Yes, he's going to be a charmer when he gets older, I'm sure," Kata said. She looked a bit concerned and added, "He's so tiny and weak, though. He doesn't seem to eat very much."

"I wouldn't worry too much, dear. I certainly haven't had much experience with babies, I'll admit; however, I've seen other little ones like him, and they tend to get stronger as time goes by. As for his appetite, he's a boy. That will change." Edda offered her an assuring smile.

Kata nodded. "You're probably right. I guess because little Max is our first; I tend to fret a bit. Since his birth, I've had a lot of time to think. I have decided to take some time off from the opera and stay home with him—at least until he is ready to go to school."

"That probably is a wise decision, Kata. Personally, I do not believe that motherhood and a career mix well. You know the old saying, "A woman's place is in the home. This little one will need lots of love and care, and who better to give it to him than you? A nanny can never replace a mother."

Kata chuckled lightly. "I never thought I'd feel this way, believe me. But looking at this little one that I have brought into the world makes me more aware of how dependent he will be on me, and I cannot think of leaving him with anyone. Yes, my career can be put on hold; my little Max needs his mother to be with him at all times."

Kata had built quite a reputation as a talented singer and she knew her decision would disappoint both her fans and her director. She had determined that she could always resume her career; yet she knew she couldn't replace those early years with her son.

Fredric was elated when he heard her news, of course. Even though he had agreed that Kata could work after they married, having a child changed priorities somewhat and, although he would never have insisted, he was glad she would be at home with Max.

The next few years were sheer bliss for the young couple. Fredric spoiled his family. Max was a very lovable young boy. He had his mother's beautiful auburn hair and his father's deep blue eyes and dimples. However, he was frail and often very sickly. He was always coming down with some ailment. Consequently, Kata doted over him even more. His precociousness and bubbling personality made him the center of attention wherever they went.

In the winter of 1903, after a weeklong trip at a ski resort in

Austria, Max developed a cold. It didn't seem out of the ordinary, since it was winter, and children were very susceptible to such things. Kata nursed him faithfully, and he seemed to be getting better after a few days. He insisted on going out to play in the snow. Reluctantly, she gave in.

That very night, Max complained, "Mama, I can't breed very well." He snuggled up onto his mother's lap. She put her arms around him and kissed his forehead. It felt hot.

"You mean you can't breathe?"

"That's what I said. And I'm coad."

Kata checked his temperature. He had a fever of 101.

"I'm going to call the doctor, Max. I want you to lie down on the couch while I do."

Disconcerted by his apparent relapse, she refused to take any chances with his health. Doctor Schmidt came right over.

I think it best that we have him admitted to the hospital right away," Dr. Schmidt had a grave look on his face. "We need to do some further testing."

Max tugged his mother's hand. "I don't want to go, Mama. I'm scared . . . What if I never come home?"

She knelt down and hugged him. "You will be fine, *Leipschen*; it will only be for a few days. You'll be well in no time, and then you'll come home, I promise," assured Katharina. Deep down, though, she also had reservations.

* * *

Max looked so weak and helpless as Kata looked down at her little boy, lying helpless and decrepit in his hospital bed. His delicate face was ashen and thin. He gasped for air. Blue shadows tinged his face. His tiny hands lay limply by his side. He had been in the hospital for three days, but instead of improving, he seemed to be getting worse. Kata did not leave his side. She was exhausted, and she neither slept nor ate very much at all. Her appearance suffered as well. She had developed dark circles under her eyes and she neglected to put on any make up or fix her hair.

"*Liebe*, you need rest and food. Come, let's go out for a little while and get something to eat," insisted Fredric.

She refused. "I can't leave him, Fredric. Something might happen if I do. Please, I'll be all right. You go on and get something for yourself. Just bring me some tea, and maybe a *Franzbrötchen*," she insisted.

Reluctantly, he agreed, but even though the pungent odor of bacon and the smell of freshly baked bread and steaming hot coffee wafted under his nose, he soon found he had no appetite either. He tried to eat a piece of toast. It did not go down easily, even with a glass of orange juice.

Tears welled up in his eyes as he recalled the picture of his little boy barely clinging to life under the oxygen tent. He said a prayer under his breath: *God, please make our little Max better. We can't lose him. I know I haven't talked to you or even acknowledged your existence, but if you are real, please do this for us.*"

Fredric and Kata rarely brought the subject of religion up at home. They had not attended church services since they were married, yet the present circumstances made him more open to the possibility that if there was a God, perhaps he might answer Fredric's prayer. It was worth a try, anyway. He quickly drank his coffee, ordered a pot of tea for Kata, and then brought it back to her.

When he returned to the room, the doctor was with Kata and Max. He had just finished examining Max and turned to the grieving couple. "I am afraid I don't have any encouraging news to give you. His condition is rapidly deteriorating. I'm not sure he will even make it through the night."

Fredric held his wife close as she buried her head in his chest and began to sob. He stroked her hair, trying to comfort Kata.

"Is there a specialist we can call in, Dr. Schmidt? Surely there are medical advances for this kind of thing, aren't there?" pleaded Fredric.

"I wish I could be more positive and tell you there was a magic pill or something. The truth is, he has pneumonia and to make things even more complicated, I've also discovered that he has a heart-murmur. This only makes the pneumonia harder to fight.

Unfortunately, there is little we can do right now. We don't know much about this disease, other than a type of bacteria known as *Streptococcus* causes it. Doctors Friedlander and Fränkel identified it just a few years ago. To be perfectly honest, while there's ongoing research, no cure has been found for it yet."

"Can't we contact one of these men for help?" Fredric asked. Desperation pervaded his voice. "Money isn't a problem. I'll pay anything to see my son well again," he begged.

"Well, Dr. Friedlander has passed away, and besides these men just identified the bacteria. They did not find a cure for it, and I doubt at this point that Dr. Fränkel would be able to do very much for him. His condition is quite grave," the doctor answered.

A faint groan came from Max's bed and the three turned to see him waking from his deep sleep.

"Mama, Papa . . . are you here?" Max's voice was weak, barely above a whisper.

"Yes, son, we are," replied Frederic as he grasped his son's hand. Kata was standing close to her husband as he held her around the waist. She reached over to stroke her son's forehead under the tent. It felt clammy and cold.

"I—I just had a wunerful dream," he said in a faint, yet audible voice. "I saw shiny robed men above me. They were singing in very beautiful voices . . . and then I heard a whooshing noise—I-I think it was their wings."

He took a labored breath, then paused and closed his eyes again.

"It sounds as if he is describing angels!" exclaimed Kata as she put her hand to her mouth and stifled a light cry.

"A-angels? Why would he see angels?" asked Fredric. Bewilderment clouded his face.

I—I don't know," continued Kata. "I've heard stories, but I'm not sure. It could mean we are losing him. No. I won't believe it. Please God, don't take him from us. He's—he's just a child."

She could hold back no longer. She covered her face with her hands and began to cry uncontrollably. Both the Dr. Schmidt and Fredric reached out to comfort her, when suddenly, Max opened his eyes wide, and cried out, "Look, Mama, Papa; look at that beautiful man—see the bright light around him? His face suddenly became bright and his eyes opened wide. "Oh look! . . . He's gonna take me to heaven . . . I love you . . . !"

With that, he reached up with his arms as if someone was picking him up, then he fell back and his body went limp like a rag doll. Dr. Schmidt checked his pulse and listened for a heartbeat. No response. He just shook his head and looked at the couple with a grim expression.

"*Oh no*! *He's gone*!" Kata cried. "N. . . No . . . *Don't take our son from us!"* she shouted, looking up toward the ceiling. She buried her face in her husband's chest and began to shake and cry violently and uncontrollably. Fredric held her close. Then he knelt down by his son's bed, took his Max in his arms and held him tight.

"Don't leave us, Max!" Fredric pleaded. "Come back! We love you and we need you!" It was no use. Max was gone.

Kata collapsed into the chair by her son's bed in a trance-like state. She was tired, weak, and so overcome with grief that she could not even move. Fredric did not leave Max's bedside. He looked down at his son's body, then he looked up, shook his fist to the heavens and shouted, "God, I asked you to *save* our son; instead, you *took* him from us. How could you do this? How could you take the only thing that Kata and I cherished?" He began sobbing like a baby.

The doctor tried to comfort them. It was no use. Bitterness, grief, and heartache consumed this young couple. They were oblivious to his presence. He quietly left the couple alone with their son.

A few days later, on a chilly and dreary winter morning with just a few close friends present, the couple buried their son. Both Kata and Fredric were grief-stricken. They were in a state of shock. They were inconsolable.

* * *

The first several weeks were the most difficult and trying for the young couple. They attempted to resume a normal life. Fredric went back to work; however, his emotions and actions seemed mechanical and stiff. Kata spent most of her time locked away in her room. Her friends came to visit and tried to cheer her up. Nothing worked. She was deteriorating quickly. She had lost weight and had not taken care of her physical appearance. Her eyes appeared sunken and her hair and clothing were unkempt. She lost interest in life itself.

Fredric was desperate to bring Kata back from her stupor, so he checked with some of the best doctors he knew. One finally told him to contact Johann Berber, a renowned psychologist.

He took Kata to see Dr. Berber. The man appeared to be in his forties and donned a thick, black beard, speckled with grey. His eyebrows were full and bushy, and he wore round spectacles that seemed to overshadow his small, beady eyes and gave him a scholarly look.

"She is suffering from depression," Dr. Berber said, after an initial session with her. We are just learning about this disorder. The treatment for it is still experimental; however, I think I can help her. I have spent quite a few years studying this new science known as psychology under a very knowledgeable psychologist, Dr. Josef Breuer. Have you heard of him?"

Fredric gave him a blank stare. "No. What is this science you call . . . psychology? "

"It is the science of the mind. One of the disorders of the mind is hysteria, often brought on by some traumatic event, such as your son's death. Dr. Sigmund Freud, a renowned physiologist, came up with a theory for treating this mental disorder. Today, largely due to a German psychiatrist by the name of Emil Kraepelin, many of us in the field now see this as a treatable condition known as depression."

"Is that what is wrong with Kata?" Fredric asked.

"From her symptoms, it appears to be. The patient generally experiences a sense of hopelessness, often characterized by a loss of interest in life in general.

"We are still learning about depression, but one of the causes may be a traumatic or tragic event in one's life, and the loss of your son would definitely meet those criteria. I believe we can help her with a combination of therapies."

"What kind of therapies, Doctor?"

"Well, some doctors have treated it with a type of surgical procedure known as a lobotomy. Unfortunately, this procedure has been known to change a patient's whole personality, usually for the worse. Then there are shock treatments, also known as electroconvulsive therapy, but this can bring on convulsions. Those two are rather drastic, so I prefer not to use them."

"I'm relieved. I wouldn't want to subject Kata to such barbaric treatments anyway," Fredric said with a frown.

"I am glad to hear that, because I have a less dramatic treatment I have found to be very effective."

"Well, I don't understand much about this depression or your psychology, Doctor. You do come highly recommended, and I am willing to give anything a try at this point, if it brings Kata back to me."

"Good then. I will proceed. First, she will need a change of environment and a treatment plan. I have been experimenting with the use of cathartic or talking therapy and aesthetics to treat my patients. I have a sanitarium in Dresden where my patients stay while undergoing this treatment. She will need to be there for a few weeks," Doctor Berber informed Fredric.

"A sanitarium? I thought that was a place for sick people."

"You are right. Technically, though, I believe that depression is a type of illness and I prefer to call my clinic a sanitarium rather than a mental hospital. It really is more like a resort, though. My patients stay in cottage-like dormitories that are comfortably furnished.

"The grounds are very well kept by some of the patients who love to garden. I try to find something for each of them to do that they will enjoy. That is part of the aesthetic therapy, you see."

"She enjoyed singing, but she hasn't done that ever since Max became so ill."

"We'll try to find a new interest for her, one that will take her away from her past for the time being," Dr. Berber said. "We will also introduce her to an herb I have been also experimenting with called hypericum, or St. John's Wort."

"What is that?" Fredric asked.

"Well, up to now, it has been used as a pain-killer or as an astringent on wounds. Even as early as 2000 years ago, Hippocrates had also suggested its use for 'nervous unrest,' so we have been experimenting with its use as an anti-depressant. It seems to have a positive effect in cases such as hers."

"Very well, I will put her in your hands, Doctor," said Fredric, desperately willing to do anything that would bring his Kata back to him.

"I feel confident that I can help her and will have her home in a few weeks."

Dr. Berber took Kata to Dresden and moved her into a small dormitory on the sanitarium's grounds. She had a nurse with her at all times. The process was slow at first; eventually, though, she responded well to the treatment, and in a matter of just a few weeks, just as he had promised, Kata made great improvement. By the summer of 1903, she was well enough to return home.

CHAPTER 4

A Holiday

IN THE WEEKS THAT FOLLOWED HER return home, Kata continued to improve. She had developed a new talent while in the sanitarium; she had learned to paint.

"It is wonderful to see you enjoying your new found hobby, *Liebe,"* Fredric said as he walked over to observe her painting a scene from the Rhein River. He rested his hands on her shoulders. The more he studied the scene, though, the deeper his eyebrows furrowed and the more serious his expression became.

Why has she taken such a beautiful scene and turned it into such a gloomy one? She captured the beauty of the mountains, and the river is so life-like, but why the clouds and the grey skies? It certainly adds a dreary dimension to her work. Why does she insist on paintings with such a sad and dark tone to them? Always rainy or dark. . . .And the people, they have such doleful expressions. Kata, what are you trying to say in your work?

Then he remembered Dr. Berber's words . . . *"She will use her painting as a way of dealing with her depression. But give her time. She'll eventually work through it. She's coming along very well, Herr Albers."*

Kata stopped, put her brush down and reached for Fredric's hand. "I do enjoy it, Fredric, yet I still feel so empty. I can't rid myself of that feeling no matter what I do."

"Perhaps, my love, you need more than just a painting of the Rhein. Maybe you need a vacation *on* the Rhein."

"Oh, Fredric, is that possible? We haven't been on the Rhein since our honeymoon. Could we? Her face suddenly brightened. She stood up, turned around and held Fredric tightly.

"Why, of course we can, *Leipschen.* And I could use some time off from work anyway."

"Yes, *Liebe,* you could. You have been working yourself too hard since I have been home. I've been worried about you. You look so tired, and it's as if you barely have the energy to climb into bed."

"Well, that settles it, then," said Fredric. "We will plan a holiday on the Rhein just as soon as I can turn my business over to my assistant. Give me a few weeks to prepare Deiter to take over for me and I promise that by spring at the latest, we will be off for the holiday of a lifetime."

"A cruise on the Rhein . . . How wonderful!"

"Yes, and not only a cruise around the Rhein but also through Austria and Germany as well." Fredric gave her a big grin.

Kata enthusiastically raised her arms in the air. "Oh, thank you, thank you!" She excitedly smothered him with kisses.

* * *

In February, Fredric completed the necessary arrangements to free himself up at work, then made reservations at one of the finest hotels in Vienna and purchased train tickets. Renewed energy surged inside of him as he went about working on the plans for them to go on vacation.

Fredric began to train his assistant, Deiter Zimmermann, who had proved to be a very capable and trustworthy employee, and for the next several weeks, he prepared him to take over temporarily.

Deiter was a quick study and eager to please his boss. He had an uncanny head for business. By the time they were ready to embark on their much-needed vacation, Fredric felt confident that his business would be safe with Deiter.

Fredric and Kata left for Vienna soon after Deiter's training was completed. For the next several weeks, they rekindled the flame of romance. It was a second honeymoon for the two. Fredric took Kata dancing and to several concerts and plays in Vienna. They enjoyed the best of the Vienna Opera House, and although, at first it was a little difficult for them both, they took a trip to the Alps to ski.

After this excursion, they took a train to Romania and spent a few days in a luxurious hotel by the Black Sea.

"Oh, Fredric, I don't want this to end," Kata said one afternoon as they were getting ready to attend a play. She reached up and put her arms around his neck. "I've so enjoyed being with you here. It's like when we were first married."

He wrapped his arms around her waist, pulled her close to him and kissed her tenderly, then smiled down at her.

"I know, *Mausi*, and I don't want it to end either. We can probably stay away another couple of weeks. Eventually, though, I have to get back to my factories. Staying in touch with Deiter by mail is sufficient for the present. He is doing a wonderful job, but many details will eventually demand my presence. I must get back soon."

"I do understand, and I am grateful for the time we've had, *Liebe*. Thank you so much for this wonderful holiday, I've so many great memories to take home with me." She kissed him tenderly on the lips.

The final three weeks of their vacation were unforgettable. He booked passage on a luxury cruise liner on the Danube, the second longest river in Europe, passing through nine countries, including Hungary, Austria and Germany.

One afternoon, the two of them walked out on the deck to soak in the beauty of the Rhein.

"You know, Johann Strauss was traveling on this very river when he was inspired to write one of his most famous works, *By the Beautiful Blue Danube,"* Katharina explained.

"Really? I'm impressed with your knowledge, *Mausi*."

"Yes, he wrote that celebrated song in 1867."

Just then, Fredric pointed over to the left of them. "Look Kata, over there is the place known as the Iron Gates National Park."

She looked ahead at the charcoal grey Carpathian and Balkan mountains, which form the boundary between Serbia and Romania, and they indeed resembled two iron gates allowing the Danube to flow through them.

"Oh Fredric, how breathtaking! It's a stunning scene. I will definitely have to paint this one."

They also stopped to visit some of the historic castles and museums in Hungary, Austria and Germany, as well as the splendid Benedictine monastery of Melk and the ruins of Dürrstein.

Fredric was a history aficionado and especially enjoyed this part of the trip.

"These ruins actually held the prison where the Archduke Leopold imprisoned Richard the Lion Hearted in 1192."

"Yes, I know. I am familiar with this actually, as the opera *Richard Coeur-de-lion* was all about this legend."

"Interesting, *Meine Liebe*. I had no idea there was an opera about Richard the Lion Hearted."

"Yes, there are a number of operas that cover historical events," Kata said.

They finally ended their cruise by getting off in Munich, Germany's third largest city.

After visiting many of the historical sites and museum that retold much of this history, the couple returned to their home in Berlin.

"Oh, what a wonderful holiday, Fredric. Our honeymoon was wonderful, but this trip was even more incredible. I will always cherish the incredible memories we made on this trip," reminisced Kata, as she relaxed on one of the divans in their master suite. Suitcases and boxes from their vacation lay strewn about the very large room, but it didn't matter to her. She was still reveling in all of her pleasant experiences.

She took down her hair, letting it flow freely around her face and shoulders. She had changed into a light blue satin and lace gown, which revealed the gentle curves of her body, and she gazed invitingly at her husband. Her lips parted slightly as if she was about to say something, but stopped.

Fredric sat down beside her and put his arms around her. She reached up and lovingly caressed his cheek. Gazing into his eyes, she kissed him gently.

"You have made me so very happy, *Liebe*. I will never forget these past several weeks." She released him, stood up, and sauntered towards the window. Holding the heavy green velvet curtain back, she stared absently at the ribbons of orange, gold and red, decorating the sky as the sun was setting. Fredric walked up behind her, put his arms around her waist and pulled her to him. She rested her head on his chest. He moved her long flowing tresses to one side and gently ran his hand across her neck and shoulders. He bent down and replaced his hand with his warm lips, kissing first one side of her neck, then the other. Once she was aroused, he turned her around to face him.

"You have restored my reason for living, *Liebling*," he replied. She looked up and parted her lips. He covered her mouth with his and kissed her ardently. Kata totally surrendered to him, and he picked her up and carried her to their bed.

CHAPTER 5

A Surprise for the Albers

By July, the couple returned to normal life. Fredric returned to his factories and Kata resumed managing the household and working on her paintings. Her works of art began to take on new meaning.

She put her holiday experiences on canvas by painting from memory and from the photographs that Fredric had taken with his Eastman Kodak camera. She painted scenes of the Danube, of the Iron Gate, of the Alps, and especially of life on the streets of Vienna, Budapest, and Munich.

She painted memories of the Black Sea and of the many castles they visited. This time however, her paintings were much more cheerful. Gone were the dreary and grey skies. Sunshine and clear skies had replaced them. She was in her element.

One August morning, however, Kata woke up very ill. As she attempted to get up, the room spun around and she felt nauseous and slid back onto her bed. Fredric had already left for work, so she called for her upstairs maid.

"Please, Liesel, get me a glass of water," she ordered weakly.

"Right away, *Frau* Albers," said the maid, aware that Kata was not feeling well. She hurried off to meet her mistress' request.

Kata stayed in bed for the remainder of the morning, but by early afternoon, she felt well enough to dress and go down to her studio. As she tried to work on one of her paintings, the smell of fresh paint seemed to disagree with her and waves of nausea swept over her. She grabbed her stomach and rushed to the indoor bathroom. After vomiting violently, she lay on the floor trying to recuperate. *What's happening? Did I eat something last night that didn't agree with me? I have to get back to bed.*

Liesel brought her some broth and crackers. She couldn't keep it down. When Fredric returned home that evening, Leisel alerted him to Kata's condition. "Kata," he exclaimed. "Why didn't you send for me, *Liebling*?"

"It's just a little nausea, *Schatzi*. Nothing to get excited about."

"No, Liebe. I'm not going to take any chances. I'm sending for Dr. Schmidt."

He gave her a light kiss on her forehead, spun around, then quickly left the room to dispatch a servant to fetch the family doctor. Dr. Schmidt arrived an hour later.

After he had examined her, the doctor left Kata's room to talk to Fredric, who was waiting outside their bedroom, pacing the floor anxiously.

"What did you find out?" Fredric asked the doctor.

Dr. Schmidt took off his glasses and wiped them with his handkerchief, he looked down at the polished lenses, then looked up and met Fredric's quizzical look.

"Well, she is probably going to be sick for a little while longer, I'm afraid."

"Why? What's the matter with her?" Fredric ran his fingers through his hair anxiously. She *is* going to be all right, isn't she?"

Dr. Schmidt chuckled lightly. "Oh, yes, I have no doubt she will get well. These kinds of things take a little time, though."

"What do you mean, 'these things,' Dr.? What are you not telling me?"

"It's nothing to worry about, *Herr* Albers. It's actually good news."

"Good news? That's a relief, Dr. Schmidt. Losing her would be unbearable."

"No, nothing like that—quite the contrary—you are going to a father."

"A- a father? Are you sure? I mean—we. . . "

"I think I know my business, and I couldn't be surer of anything as I am this. Your little one should be here in the spring," chortled the doctor.

"Yes, but—we assumed—it's been a long time— over five years since Max was born. We just thought we couldn't—we wouldn't be able to have any more children."

"This is not an uncommon occurrence, *Herr* Albers, people have babies all the time. I can't explain why you haven't had any others since Max, but I assure you, you are going to have a baby."

Fredric dropped into a nearby chair and stared ahead utter amazement. Dr. Smith packed his medical bag and prepared to leave.

"I gave her something to ease the morning sickness. She needs to rest and take good care of herself. Call me if you need anything else".

He excused himself and found his way to the door, while Fredric just sat in the chair, staring ahead.

Fredric's emotions were at war. He was ecstatic, yet fearful that they could lose this baby just as they lost Max. *How is she taking this? Can she handle having another child? How—what. . . do we do now?* A million questions filled his mind. He knew he needed to discuss this with Kata.

He arose and went towards the bedroom door. He hesitated just for a moment, then walked in. Kata was sitting up in the bed, with a big smile on her face.

"Oh, Fredric, did the doctor tell you the news? We're going to have another child. Isn't it wonderful? I'm so happy, *Liebe*."

She reached for his hand as he came closer. He patted hers, sat in the chair next to the bed and looked at her compassionately. Yet Kata detected a confused flicker in his eyes.

"You're worried, aren't you?"

"I can't help but feel a little concerned," Fredric said.

"It'll be all right, you'll see." She raised her hand to his face. "I think this is just what we needed to fill the void in our lives. I am beginning to believe this is a gift from God," she said.

Fredric's tone turned sharply. "God? God?—what does *God*

have to do with this? How could God be in this when *He* took our little Max?"

She tried to calm him. "*Liebe,* what I meant to say is when this little one gets here, he—or she, will help relieve us of the loss we have suffered and will give us pleasure. You wait and see." Kata squeezed his hand tightly as a way to assure him of this.

Her encouraging words seemed to help. "Perhaps you are right, Kata. A new addition to our family may be just what the *doctor* ordered."

CHAPTER 6

Martina's Debut

JUST AS THE SUMMER SURRENDERED HER warmth to the crisp fall winds, and the barren trees beckoned to the winter chill, Kata also experienced a metamorphosis. At first, her jubilant countenance enhanced her natural beauty. But by late December, as the snow began to fall and the world outside shut down, her body protested, clearly announcing the impending new birth. Her pregnancy became more obvious.

"I look so hideous, Fredric—like a large, pink elephant," Kata fretted one morning at breakfast.

"Nonsense, *Liebe.* You look even more beautiful!" Fredric looked up from his morning paper and sipped his coffee, giving Kata an admiring glance.

"Oh! You are just being kind, *Schatzi.* Look how I've expanded!"

"Actually, you look more—feminine. More womanly."

"I look so *fat!*"

"Not fat, *Leipschen.* You look like an angel carrying a child."

"Oh, Fredric, you are such an encourager. You have a way of making me feel much better about this pregnancy."

"Anytime." He winked at her playfully.

Fredric stood up, walked over to Kata, and gave her a loving hug. She relaxed in his arms.

By late January, her misgivings turned to excited anticipation. She put her newfound energy into preparing the nursery. Her mood was contagious. Fredric bought some new furniture and helped with its remodeling.

"So what are we going to name our new little one?" Fredric asked as they put the final changes on the nursery together.

"Well, if it is a boy, perhaps we should name him Karl Erich, after our fathers, or if it is a girl, Martina Elizabeth after my mother and yours." What do you think?"

"Beautiful choices, *Liebe.* They will be perfect for our baby."

* * *

The winter had a strong grip on the country getting harsher by the day, making travel almost impossible. On several occasions, the snow fell like someone vigorously shaking an overstuffed feather pillow that had burst open.

Kata was beginning to feel the toll of the extra weight of her pregnancy. She tired easily and her emotional state was fragile. She cried at the least little mishap and she got very moody if things didn't go her way.

"Oh Fredric, how much longer is this going to go on?" Kata lamented as she stared out their drawing room window.

"I can't stand it much longer. The snowdrifts are so high, that we are unable to go *anywhere.* I feel so confined!"

Fredric walked up behind her and wrapped his arms around her. Taking in the wintery scene with her, he said, "We cannot take the chance of you falling, Kata and losing our baby—or even worse, you getting sick and dying on me."

"I know you are right, but I just need to get out! I want to go shopping for our baby or visit friends, or perhaps even have friends in."

"Be patient, Kata. In just a few weeks, spring will be here and so will our baby. Then you will have the opportunity to do that."

"No, I won't! I will be confined even more when the baby gets here."

"We'll hire a nanny—then you can do everything you want to do."

"That doesn't help things right now."

Her moodiness sent Fredric into an emotional dilemma of his own. He found it a relief to be at work during this time, trying to keep from upsetting Kata unintentionally, or to avoid being the brunt of one of her demonstrative outbursts. Yet, he wanted to be there with her and help her through this trying time. He insisted that Liesel be with her at all times.

Late in March 1905, Kata woke up one morning and poked Fredric frantically. "I think I'm having contractions! Perhaps you should call the doctor."

Fredric jumped out of bed and immediately obeyed. The doctor arrived shortly after. Then the long wait began. Fredric paced the floor until he almost wore a hole in the rug. It seemed like ages to him, waiting outside their bedroom door, but after several hours, their baby arrived.

"You have a beautiful baby girl," announced the doctor. His voice sounded weary from the ordeal.

"You can see your wife now; all went very well," he said with a look that indicated he was pleased.

Fredric wasted no time. He burst through the bedroom door and ran to his wife's side. Taking Kata's hand and stroking her forehead, he looked down in wonder and amazement. The sight he beheld filled his heart with pride—his beautiful wife, holding their new daughter. And what a treasure she was, nestled peacefully in her mother's arms, tiny and pink, but not very wrinkled. A tuft of reddish brown hair adorned her head. Her eyes were shut tight. The emotions running through Fredric were almost uncontrollable. He wanted to cry, to laugh, and to shout all at once. Kata was right. This little angel filled their void. Little Martina was just what they needed.

"You can hold her if you like, Papa," said Kata.

He hesitated. "I- I might drop her if I do."

"No, you won't. Here, take her." She handed Martina to him.

At first, he was a little nervous, but in a few minutes, he got used to holding Martina in his arms. He walked around the room, holding her close and talking to her in a soothing voice. He took her little hand in his. She grasped one of his fingers, tightly wrapping her hand around it.

His eyes moistened. "What a little *Prinzessin* you are, my little Marti. You'll never want for anything. I will always be here for you, *Schätzchen.*" He doted on her for some time, then handed her back to Kata so she could feed her.

* * *

In the months that followed, Martina flourished under her parents' loving care. Her appearance was ever changing. The little tuft of hair she had at birth gave way to a beautiful crown of reddish golden waves, and her deep blue eyes, so much like her father's, sparkled with glee. She was plump and healthy—not frail like her brother had been. She had creamy skin and a typically rounded baby face.

Martina was a curious little baby who liked to explore as soon as she could crawl, which she began to do at ten months. She was content, however, to sit in her playpen while her mother painted. She loved to watch as Kata splashed bright colors on canvas, often painting pictures of clowns, puppies, and kittens for her little daughter. Kata filled Marti's room with some of these paintings. She always explained to her what she was painting, and Marti would listen intently, then giggle when her mother stopped occasionally to pick her up and give her a closer look.

Her adopted grandparents, the Werners, enjoyed spending time with her as well. Every opportunity they had, they stopped by and brought some new trinket or toy for her. One of her favorites, however, was a beautiful porcelain doll with dark blue eyes and a head of auburn hair.

"I couldn't resist," Edda said when she visited with this latest gift. "The face on this one reminded me so much of our little Marti."

"I am sure she will always treasure this, since it came from *Oma* Werner."

When Fredric came home each evening, he would seek out his little *Prinzessin*, and then put her on his knee and tell her stories or play "rocking horse" with her. The couple truly enjoyed their little Marti.

CHAPTER 7

The Winter of Discontent

In 1910, when Martina was five, Kata took her to visit a local opera house. She wanted Martina to know something about her days on the stage. She was too young to appreciate it fully yet. As they walked around opera house, something began to stir in Kata. She showed Marti the large posters of some of the great operas performed there.

"You really worked here, Mama?" Martina asked, holding on to her mother's hand and looking around the beautifully decorated lobby at its plush surroundings in wonderment.

"Yes, Marti, I really did."

The ghosts of Kata's past sprung up around her. The characters she had portrayed came alive. She imagined herself on stage as they moved closer to the orchestra pit. She remembered many of her performances. She had come so close to making it big in the opera. What if she had chosen the theatre over marriage? Then, of course, her darling Martina wouldn't even exist. No, life wouldn't have been as fulfilling.

She came back to reality when Martina tugged her hand and pointed to a large poster of the opera *Salome.*

"Were you in this one?"

"No, *Leipschen,* I wasn't. It was performed after my time. I fell in love with your Papa and stopped singing after we . . . we were married."

Kata stopped short of mentioning Max's death at this point. It wasn't the time to bring it up. After all, Marti wasn't old enough to understand; she would tell her about her deceased brother in a few years.

As her memories of the opera and her past surfaced, her expression clouded a little, and she felt a twinge. A feeling emerged within her that she couldn't quite identify. She was happy with her family and especially her little girl. She felt no regret for giving up her career for staying home and she had moved beyond the pain of the loss of her son. Having Marti had helped her to do that. She was content with her present life . . . wasn't she?

A young attendant was standing close by and approached them, interrupting Kata's thoughts. "We have extra posters of that particular production. Would your daughter like a copy?" he asked.

Kata pulled Marti a little closer to her side. "Oh, no, I don't believe. . . "

"Please, Mama!" she begged.

Marti seldom behaved in such a manner, that it took Kata by surprise. She looked helplessly at the young man.

"There is no charge. They're extra copies that have never been used. She is perfectly welcome to one," he assured Kata, as he gave Marti a wink.

"Well, I guess it will be all right, then," Kata said a bit reluctantly.

"Thank you so much, sir," Marti said as she excitedly accepted the prize from the attendant.

"Anything for a prima donna such as you, *Frau* Ernst."

"You recognize me?" She didn't correct the fact that he used her stage name and not her married name.

"Why yes. You were one of my favorite singers. Besides, your picture is in our archives. I have seen it many times."

"Mama. You were famous!" Marti exclaimed.

"Yes she was, young lady. And she was very talented!" The young man added.

"Come, Marti, we must be going. Papa will be home soon and we need to be there." She took Marti's hand and hurried out of the opera house, almost regretting that she had even come.

That evening when Fredric returned home, Martina ran to greet him. He gathered her up in his arms and gave her a bear hug. "How is my little *Prinzessin* this evening?" he asked as he brushed his hand over her curls.

"Oh Papa!" she exclaimed excitedly. "Mama and I had the most wunnerful day today. We went to the Opera house and she took me all around and showed me the stage where she used to work. It was really big! And, did you know Mama was *famous* once? "

"Really! Tell me about your visit," he said, with great interest.

Fredric tried to hide any sense of consternation he was feeling. The fear that Kata would someday want to return to the stage had occasionally haunted him, and now that fear crept back in. Surely she wouldn't want to leave their Martina in the care of a nanny, especially after losing Max. Was this trip Kata's way of rekindling an interest in her old career? Hadn't she enjoyed her life as a mother and wife so much more? After all, she had established a place with society as the wife of a highly respected and successful businessman. He thought her past was behind her. Why would she even consider returning to her former lifestyle?

Martina proceeded to tell him all about their day at the opera, and then jumped off his lap.

"Oh, I almost forgot," Martina added. "I have to show you the poster that a nice man at the opera house gave me when we were there."

She ran up to her room to retrieve the poster, and left Kata and Fredric alone.

"Why did you take her to the Opera House without telling me, Kata?" Fredric asked in an unsettled tone. "Was it because you knew I wouldn't approve?"

Kata shrugged her shoulders nonchalantly, trying to hide the fact that he was right. "I just wanted her to have a chance to see what I used to do, Fredric. That was all."

"I don't like the idea of you taking her there, Kata. She's not old enough to understand what the opera is, anyway. Couldn't you have waited until she was older?" he asked, raising his voice slightly.

"I don't know why you are getting so upset, Fredric, it was just an innocent trip, there was nothing to it. She has visited your factories, and so why shouldn't she be able to see where I used to work?"

He recanted. "Perhaps I'm overreacting a little. Just do me a favor, *Liebling*. If you decide to visit the Opera House again, would you please talk to me about it first?"

"It's not really much to worry about, Fredric. I have no intention of returning to the opera, if that's what you are worried about," she assured him.

Martina returned with the poster that she had gotten at the Opera House, so Fredric and Kata dropped the subject.

"Here, Papa. This is the poster I got today."

"Why it's very interesting, *Liebe*," remarked Fredric, looking at his daughter and smiling.

For several days after this incident, the visit lingered in Kata's memory. In her heart, she had to admit that it was not so innocent. She had opened a veritable "Pandora's Box". The ghosts continued to haunt her. She tried to bury herself in her painting, but somehow her artwork seemed to lose its appeal. It became a chore. She couldn't finish one piece of work. She grew very agitated and dissatisfied with her work.

One morning, late that summer, her old friend, Greta and former roommate stopped by for a visit.

"Why Greta, what a pleasant surprise to see you again. It's been such a long time!" Kata said as she invited her into the parlor to visit.

"I know, and I have to admit I have stayed away on purpose," Greta said.

"But why?"

"Well, you know I did all I could to convince you to stay with us after . . . you had Max. I—I just couldn't see you giving up all you had worked for."

"It was my choice—and really, I gave nothing up. I enjoyed being home with my son." Kata bit her trembling lip.

"I realize that, *Liebe,* and I am very glad you had the time that you did with him, and I know that I was wrong then."

"It's quite all right, Greta. Those years are behind us." Kata patted her friend's hand. She took a very close look at Greta. She hadn't aged very much over the years; in fact, she looked quite beautiful. The opera apparently agreed with her. She was still a tall, handsome woman with rich golden brown hair, which she kept pinned up in a loose, fashionable chignon. She had an ivory complexion and blue eyes. It was obvious that she had kept up with the latest styles. Her light blue double-breasted suit with its high empire waistline and hobble skirt, along with her matching large brimmed hat, adorned with a large dark blue plume and wide velvet ribbon, reflected the fashionable Edwardian era. Greta was quite a contrast to Kata's *Gibson Girl* mode.

"So, tell me, Greta, what have you been doing all this time?"

"Touring, singing, staying *very* busy. Actually I have been away from Berlin for quite some time. Now that I am back in town, I just had to come for a visit, especially after I heard you were at the Berlin Court Opera just recently."

Kata rolled her eyes. "My, how word gets around. And, knowing you, there is more to this visit than meets the eye," Kata said.

"Really, Kata, can't an old friend just come for a visit?"

"After so many years, just to show up suddenly? For no particular reason? Greta, we were practically sisters. I know you better than you think. So tell me, what is your *real* motive?"

"Well, perhaps there's a little more to my visit. But I'm *dying* of thirst. Can't we have some tea and catch up on the times?"

Kata had her maid make them some tea, and they went into the formal sitting room and discussed the past few years.

When Kata told her she had taken up painting as a new hobby, Greta looked at her in surprise. "I didn't know you could even draw a straight line, Kata."

A faint smile curled on Kata's lips. "Well, I took a few lessons, and have done quite well with my work. It's been mostly for relaxation and personal satisfaction."

Kata took Greta on a short tour of the house to show her more of her paintings, then the two returned to the sitting room.

"You should consider selling some of your work. You are quite an artist," said Greta.

Kata shook her head. "I don't know about that. I seem to have lost my touch lately. I haven't been able to finish any of my work in the past few weeks," she admitted to Greta, as they walked back to the sitting room.

Greta did not sit down. She placed her hands on her hips and, with an insightful expression, smiled knowingly at Kata.

"I know what your problem is, Kata. Deep down, you are homesick for the old days when we used to gad about the continent, performing together in so many wonderful operas. Why don't you come back?" she asked.

Kata took another sip of tea, then put her cup down on the end table next to the sofa and placed her hands in her lap. She chuckled and shook her head.

"That's just like you, Greta, still trying to get me to return to the 'glamour and glitz' of your world."

"Come on, Kata, you must admit that you miss it just a little," she coaxed gently and shook her finger playfully at her friend. She continued to wheedle her by reminiscing about the "good times" they had experienced and the wonderful places they had been together.

Kata raised her hands half way to shoulder height and shook her head in agreement. "All right, all right, maybe I *do* miss it a *little*, but not enough to run off every day and neglect my family—things are different for me now, Greta. Surely you can see that."

" No, I don't see that." Greta shook her head adamantly. Her eyes pierced through Kata, as if she was able to see deep into her soul, then started speaking in animated tones. It was almost as if she was performing on stage.

"I see a woman who is losing her identity in the humdrum of daily life. I see a woman who has lost the sparkle in her eye she used to get with every curtain call, when the applause permeated the whole auditorium. I see a woman who has forgotten what it was like to be her own person." Greta waved her hands about with dramatic flair as she spoke.

"Then you should also see the contentment on my face that I have to be a wife and mother," insisted Kata. "I don't want to lose what I have here. I have a wonderful husband who dotes on me, and a darling little daughter whom I adore."

"Yes, I hear you saying that, but there is something in your voice that tells me you are not being totally honest with me *or* yourself. I have several friends who are living in *both* worlds and who are very happy. Why couldn't you do the same?" Greta cajoled.

"It's high time that you return to your first love, Kata. There's no reason why you couldn't perform locally and be home every night. A new opera, *I Gioielli Della Madonna*, is opening early next year, and I have heard that there are lots of parts still available. And there are plans to build a new opera house within the next two years. That means there will be a greater opportunity for you to return to the stage."

Kata's tone became less defensive, and a pensive expression crossed her face. She paused for several seconds, then responded, "I agree that it would be a great opportunity, and I have to admit it is very tempting. . . yet I am just not sure this is the time for me to leave my family—Martina is still very young." Kata's resistance appeared to be waning, so Greta continued to persist.

" It's a wonderful time to get back into your career. You are still well remembered by many directors."

Greta could be quite stubborn when she made up her mind about something. Perhaps her friend was more intuitive than she had given her credit for and she really had discovered the main source of her discontent. Yes. Greta was right. Deep within her, she really *did* have a desire to return to the stage. Until now, however, she had not wanted to see it. She was afraid of upsetting her life as it was now. On the other hand, she recognized that her life might be adversely affected anyway if she continued to feel the way she did. She acknowledged that at least she needed to consider it—to be sure of her innermost desire. Would returning to the stage jeopardize her marriage?

Kata rose from her seat, walked behind the sofa, and grabbed hold of its back; then she faced Greta.

"Look, I know you and I had some great times together, and I miss them, too; however, I have my family to consider now. I promise I will think about this, and I will discuss it with Fredric. You need to know, though, if I *do* decide to come back to the stage, it will be with my husband's blessing."

Greta sighed. "Fine, *Liebe*, I will respect your decision. Somehow, though, I believe when you give it serious thought, you will soon realize that I am right, and then you'll make the right choice." She smiled at Kata, gave her a warm hug and took her leave.

After Greta left, Kata tried to put the conversation out of her mind. She went up to Martina's room, where she found her still napping peacefully. She gazed down at her little cherub.

How could I leave my precious little Schatzi? She is so full of life and fun to be with. She couldn't possibly understand if I left her every day in the hands of a stranger. Besides, who could possibly give her better care than I can?

She gently caressed her daughter's hair, and then quietly walked out of the room and down the hall to her studio. Once again, she tried to finish a painting she was doing of an open market day in the city that she had started a week ago. The colors were not right. She wasn't capturing what she wanted to in the bustle of the city. She put her palate and brush away, and walked over to the window and stared outside. A battle of thoughts and emotions erupted within her. *But what if Greta is right? What if the whole reason I am so discontented is that I miss the opera. . . But why now? I have a wonderful life here with my husband and my precious little girl. What is wrong with me? Why won't this feeling go away? Could I possibly go back to work now? Besides, I would need some time to practice. I have been away from the opera for some time. But then, Greta could help me with this . . . Perhaps there is a way I can balance both worlds. What will Fredric say?*

She knew how much he loved her being there when he returned home. He also was very protective of Martina. After suffering the loss of their son, he took no chances with their daughter. He liked the idea that Kata was home with her every day. No, it was not the time. She would have to get through the winter and hope that it was the season, not the circumstances that were at the root of her discontent.

CHAPTER 8

Confrontation

Autumn of 1910 delivered a change in the weather. The winds were picking up and the days were growing shorter. Martina was becoming quite a beautiful young lady. She had just started kindergarten. This was a fairly new and controversial concept in Germany. Many skeptics still thought it was an outrageous idea.

But Fredric, a true progressive, wanted his daughter to have any social and educational advantages life had to offer. This new concept was widely accepted in the United States; and, if it was good enough for America, it was good enough for Germany in his eyes.

Kata balked at first, then agreed that it might be a good thing for their daughter to get out and be around other children. Martina was so isolated, as very few of their close friends and neighbors had children, and Kata knew she needed to make friends.

Since they had made this decision, Kata began to think about the opera again. Greta called her from time to time since their last meeting to see if she had made up her mind. She wasn't about to give up on the idea of Kata coming back to work. Each time they talked, Greta seemed to kindle Kata's interest more.

One evening at dinner, Kata decided to approach Fredric with the idea.

"There's a new opera opening in Berlin, Fredric. It is set to premier early next year," she casually commented.

He looked up at her wordlessly.

"Greta has already accepted a part in it, and she says the company who is producing it is wonderful to work for."

Fredric did not respond.

"I—it pays very well." Kata began playing with the folds of her skirt, waiting for Fredric to comment.

He still said nothing, but continued to eat. He seemed to be paying little attention, or perhaps he didn't want to pay attention.

"Greta suggested that I audition for a part in it."

"Why would you want to do that, *Liebe*?" Fredric asked, in a slightly interested tone.

"Well, I've been thinking . . . with Marti going to kindergarten soon, this house can be very lonely. Besides, I am not getting any younger, and it might do me good to see if I could get a part in this production—a minor part, of course, so that I wouldn't have to be gone so much." She paused to see what his reaction would be to her proposal.

"Whether you had a major part or a minor part, *Mausi*, you would still be away from home for about the same amount of time," he reminded her. His tone elevated slightly.

"Besides, wouldn't that mean you would have to be gone for several evenings as well?" He raised an eyebrow, looking at her intently.

"Well, yes, that's true, but not *every* night, and I am just considering one opera—it's not like I am talking about being as involved as I was when we were courting," she said.

"And we don't need the money, Kata. I can buy you anything you want. You know that."

The authoritative inflection in his voice ignited a rage in Kata. The old independent streak rekindled in her. She tightened her lips into a thin line, clenched her fists and put them on her hips. Then, staring him straight in the eye, she retorted, "You can't buy me the exhilaration I get when I am before an audience performing. You can't buy me the thrill and appreciation I feel from the applause or the inspiration I get from each performance! You can't buy . . ."

Fredric interrupted her abruptly. "Our marriage doesn't give you satisfaction? Does your family not inspire you? Are you not thrilled with our little girl? What have we been to you all these years?"

Realizing that her anger merely infuriated him and made the atmosphere even tenser, she took a deep breath and forced herself to calm down.

"Of course I love you and Marti; but there's more to life than just staying home and taking care of the household. You don't understand. I can be a wife, a mother *and* an entertainer as well! You must give me that chance!"

He suddenly sprang to his feet. "No, I don't *have* to give you anything of the kind! I will *not* have a part-time wife! Either you can be my wife and Marti's mother, or you can have a career in the opera. You can't have both!" With that, Fredric furiously threw his glass, filled with his favorite cognac, across the room. As the glass shattered, he stormed out the door and up the stairs.

Kata stared in disbelief at the shards of glass and the beads of liquor as they slowly trickled across the floor. Time stood still for a moment. Fredric had never acted this way before. She tried to blink away her tears. They burst forth in torrents. She collapsed to the floor, hugged the seat of her chair and began crying hysterically. Two loves of her life were competing against each other and they held her hostage. Totally depleted after sobbing deeply for some time, Kata drifted into a troubled sleep as she lay against the chair.

* * *

Fredric trudged upstairs to his room and sat on the edge of his bed. A sinking feeling overtook him as he pondered his strong and uncontrolled response to his wife's request. He disliked his actions intensely. He knew the damage was done. He wanted her to stay home, but was that fair to her? No. He had broken his promise to her and then punished her for it. Was he making a prisoner out of her? That's not what he wanted. He slumped over the bed with remorse and put his face in his hands.

His thoughts harassed him: *What did I do? Why couldn't I just listen to her and try to see things her way for once? I have been so . . . so unreasonable. It's not as if she will be going out of the country or leaving for weeks at a time.* He knew that he owed Kata an apology.

He returned to the dining room and saw her lying against the chair like a rag doll. He now realized just how badly he had crushed his beloved with his temper tantrum. He had brutalized her with his emotional outburst and had shown her no respect. He picked her up gently and led her to the sofa in the drawing room.

As he sat holding her, he held her face up to his. "I am sorry, *Leipschen.* I was being unreasonable. I wasn't considering your feelings or my promise to you when we married." He gently kissed her forehead.

"However, if I do agree to let you do this, you must promise me that you will hire a very capable nanny for Marti. Also, I would ask you to be willing to quit if it began to affect Martina and our marriage in an adverse way," he requested.

She looked up at him, giving him a confused look. "Do you really mean it?"

"Of course, *Liebling.*"

"I promise you, if I do return to the opera, my family will always come first. Nothing will change for us, you'll see," she said. "I won't let anything come between us, including the opera. I promise."

Fredric held her in his arms and said, "I would never want to do anything that would make you so unhappy. I know how much this means to you and believe that you can be a good wife and mother and I know you will thrill your audiences as you did once before. Will you forgive me?"

She looked up at him through her swollen, tear-stained eyes and kissed his cheek. "You know that I can't stay mad at you, *Liebe.* You are my life. I won't neglect you or Martina. I will find the best nanny for our daughter, don't worry. You won't be disappointed, you'll see."

They sat holding each other for quite a while.

CHAPTER 9

Elsa

Elsa Bauer read the advertisement through tear-filled eyes:

Nanny wanted for young child. Must be unmarried, of good character, love children and be willing to live in our home. Room and board provided along with a generous stipend. One day a week off, and two weeks paid vacation annually will be allowed. References required. Call or write for appointment.

She made a note of the address and phone number that was included. This could be an answer to her prayers. Elsa had always loved children, even though she was never able to have any of her own. She knew she could be a good teacher and guide to a little child. She would be so grateful to have such an opportunity.

The young widow knew she no longer had anything to keep her in Potsdam. Even though her parents still lived here, the memories, the tragic events would continue to haunt her if she did not leave soon. She could still travel back home occasionally. Yes, she would do this. She would give her notice to the landlord, store her larger pieces of furniture with her parents and take what belongings she would need with her. She had always wanted to see Berlin. What better opportunity could she have?

Just a few weeks ago, she was sitting by her husband Stefan's side, watching him linger between life and death. He lay in a feverish state, teetering between semi-consciousness and fitful sleep. She held his hand and watched his labored breathing; her eyes tear-stained and swollen, her body sleep-deprived, and her emotions ravaged by the uncertainty of Stefan's future—her faith, however, secure in the Lord. Occasionally she took the washcloth from the basin of water and wiped his forehead with it. Although he had been ill for two weeks, he had refused to stop working. She was exhausted; nevertheless, she continued to pray under her breath for Stefan.

She cringed as she recalled how barren his room was—like the barrenness of her life right now. The image would be imprinted in her memory forever. She could still see the dingy grey walls, which held only one small, dirty window, draped with a plain white linen curtain. She remembered the black and white tile, stained over time by rust-colored dried blood spots, iodine, and carbolic acid. How she tried to blot out those smells. The acrid odors of the latter two solutions permeated the hospital. Only a small wooden cross adorned the wall above the bed. The weather was no better during that time. The cold rain pelted the glass and the strong wind caused it to rattle occasionally. How could things turned around so quickly? She and Stefan had a wonderful life together.

She met him when he started attending her father's church. They both sang in the choir and attended Sunday school together. When the two fell in love, Elsa's parents were very happy. They thought that he would make a good husband for their little Elsa. Her father, a Baptist minister, married them the next year.

They settled into a modest, yet comfortable home near her parents' rectory, in Potsdam, a city situated on the Havel River, southwest of Berlin. Stefan managed to find a job at one of the chemical factories recently built in Potsdam. The factories were poorly heated, and working conditions were extremely difficult. The foremen were often cruel and unfeeling. They had little patience for unproductive workers. They often fired workers who missed day or two of work, even if it was due to illness. There were many others ready to take his place.

Just a few weeks ago, however, Stefan developed a cough.

"Take a few days off and allow yourself to get well, *Herr* Bauer."

"It is not that easy, Doctor," Stefan told him. "Even though I have worked there a few years, my foreman won't like it if I take off a day or two."

Elsa also tried to convince him to stay home.

"You have to think of your health right now, Stefan. What is more important? This is not likely to go away without rest."

"I have no choice, Elsa. You know what will happen if I stay home even one day. I'll be fine. You'll see."

But he was not fine. In just a couple of weeks, his condition deteriorated. One morning he coughed so violently that he began spitting up blood. He was burning with fever and shivering simultaneously.

"Oh Stefan, you cannot go into work this morning," cried Elsa when she realized how sick he was. "You must stay home and rest. You have a fever."

"No, no, I can't," replied Stefan, shaking his head and struggling to sit up.

"Even if my boss understood, I can't afford to take any time off. We need the money. We're barely making it now." He said rather weakly. He managed to sit up for a brief moment, then fell back into bed.

"I don't care, *Liebe*, you are more important to me than that job. God will provide for us. I know it. Remember Matthew 6:33 tells us that when seek the Lord first, we can trust in His provision."

For twenty-five years of age, Elsa was a very wise woman with great faith. Even though Stefan was a Christian, he was also a practical man.

"God h-helps those who help themselves, Elsa." He attempted to sound strong, but his voice was fragile at best.

"That's not even in the Bible, Stefan. That's a quote from the American author, Benjamin Franklin," she said. "Papa used that in one of his sermons, remember? Besides, God is not looking for "self-reliant" men. He's looking for men who will trust in Him, and this is a time when we really need to put our trust in His provision, Stefan," she continued.

"I – I'm sorry, *Schatzi.* My faith is not as strong as yours is in these matters. God provided the job for me so I must go to work." With that, he struggled to get out of bed, continuing to cough violently, dressed himself, had some bread and tea, and then left for work.

As soon as he left the house, Elsa cried out to God, "Oh, dear Father, please look out for my Stefan. He does not know how sick he is."

Then the nightmare began. Later that day, there was a loud knock at her door. She opened it and saw one of Stefan's co-workers standing there, with his hat in his hand and looking very frantic.

"*Frau* Bauer, you must come quickly; they have taken Stefan to the hospital. He collapsed while he was working about an hour ago."

"Oh, no!" she cried covering her mouth in distress. "Of course. I'll come right away! Let me get my wrap." She quickly grabbed her woolen coat and hat, and went with the young man who had a horse and buggy waiting outside. They rushed off to the hospital.

She hurried to his room where she found the doctor examining Stefan. "What's happened to him?" Elsa put her hands to her face in shock.

She was frightened as she studied her beloved husband in disbelief. He looked so different. This strong man who normally towered over her at six feet, now appeared frail as he struggled to breathe. His ashen face and sunken blue eyes, were now surrounded by very dark circles. His blond hair was matted with sweat. He was a mere shell of a man.

The doctor tenderly held her arm and led her out of the room. He looked down at her sympathetically and said, "I'm afraid the news is not good. Your husband has developed a severe bronchial infection, complicated with the onset of pneumonia. He is suffering from pleural effusion, as well. In other words, his lungs are filling up with fluid.

"On top of that, his heart seems weak, I'm afraid. From the look of things, I suspect he's been sick for quite some time."

Elsa sadly nodded in agreement. "He's worked himself too hard. I warned him to slow down. He wouldn't listen. Can you do anything for him, Doctor?" Elsa pleaded through tear-filled eyes. "He is going to get better, isn't he?"

"I'm afraid we still don't know too much about these things. We can treat him for the symptoms. Unfortunately, there's not much else we can do for him."

"I can pray," she raised her chin and declared firmly. "I will not leave his side until he is well."

True to her promise, she stayed by his side and prayed day and night. It was to no avail. On the fifth day of his hospital stay, he passed into a deep coma and died a day later. Elsa was broken-hearted. She was tired and depleted; and although she was feeling great pain from her loss, she did not waiver in her faith. It was still strong.

After the funeral, she went home and fell to her knees. Sorrowful, yet refusing to succumb to despair, she prayed, "Lord, I don't know why you have chosen to take him home, but I do know that according to Romans 8:28, *all things work together for good to them that love God, and who are the called according to your purpose.* I know I love you and I know you have a purpose and a plan for me. No matter what, I am determined to trust you with whatever lies ahead."

No, this tragedy would not destroy her. On the contrary, she would continue to seek the Lord and His will for her future. She lost her husband, yet she hadn't lost her faith in her God. She continued to take in laundry, which helped a little, and she had enough money from Stefan's last wages to pay for her rent for the next month and to buy a few groceries. She prayed and asked God for wisdom and to give her direction on what she should do with her life.

By the middle of the next month, nothing had really come to her, and so she went to see her father and asked him for some advice. "Why don't you come and stay with your mother and me for a while? That will give you a little time to sort through things and seek the Lord."

"Papa, I know that you and Mama would let me come back home. I don't think that is God's will for my life, though. Somehow, I have to make it on my own. There is something out there that the Lord wants me to do. I'm just not sure what right now," she told him.

"I know that the Lord will not let you down, Elsa. He will show you what to do. Just trust Him. We will pray right now, *Kinder*."

With that, the two knelt together and her father prayed, "Oh Father in Heaven, we know that you do not take away without giving us something in return, so I ask that you help my dear little girl to see clearly, what you have in mind for her, and that she will walk in the direction you take her. I ask this in your son Jesus' precious name. Amen."

Her thoughts returned to the newspaper advertisement she was holding. She believed that she had received the answer to that prayer.

CHAPTER 10

The Nanny

Elsa knocked on the large oak door of the Alberses' beautiful townhouse. She had great faith that this was where the Lord was leading her. She smiled brightly when the maid opened the door.

"I'm Elsa Bauer. I am here for an interview with *Frau* Albers. May I come in?"

"Yes, of course, please do. Wait here," said the maid. She directed Elsa into the large foyer with an elaborately marbled floor. "I will get *Frau* Albers for you."

While Elsa waited, she looked around and admired the elegance of the home. The ornate gold trim and the Edwardian furnishings were beyond anything she could have imagined. The pictures on the wall around her were very colorful and appeared to illustrate city life in Berlin, scenes of the Danube and other European landmarks. A large vase with flowers adorned a small table next to the door. She stared in amazement at the electric lamp and telephone sitting atop a side table, as she had never seen such modern conveniences. Only upper-class city homes were equipped with electricity and gas, let alone had telephones. People who lived in rural areas or in the country could not afford such luxuries.

"Why hello, Elsa. Please come in," said Kata, as she walked towards the young lady and gestured for her to follow her into the drawing room.

Elsa was a lovely young woman with dark blonde wavy hair

neatly tied up in a bun, with a few little curly tendrils draping her face. She had large, blue-grey eyes and an ivory complexion. Although she was not a heavy woman, she had a large frame, but not a very large waist. She was curvy, yet she dressed modestly. She wore a long, dark brown skirt with a high-collared white blouse with long, puffy sleeves. Her rough hands made it evident that she was used to hard work.

"Can I get you some tea? You must be tired from your travel, dear. Come, sit down," said Kata in a very soothing tone. Elsa deduced that she was a kind woman, not snobbish as so many of the aristocracy could be during that era.

"Thank you, I would like that," Elsa replied, following her into the drawing room ahead.

Kata pointed to a large, green and gold striped overstuffed chair. "Sit here, my dear, and we can talk." Elsa silently obeyed and looked around the large, very tastefully decorated room. She was impressed with the well-polished oak floor, partially covered with an olive green and brown oriental rug. In the middle of the room hung a very large gold and crystal chandelier. The Victorian style chairs and sofa in the room fit in with the décor nicely.

The maid brought in silver tea set and served them tea in delicate cream-colored cups, adorned with deep pink roses.

Kata proceeded to ask Elsa questions about her family, her home life, her background and interests.

"Well, I am the daughter of a Baptist minister. My parents taught me God's Word and raised me to have a strong faith in the Lord."

Elsa sensed that Kata was a little uncomfortable with the religious tone of the conversation. That did not stop her. She was not ashamed to tell people about her Christian faith and upbringing. She had always promised God that He would come first in her life and that she would never hesitate to tell others of His great love. She felt this was the first test for her in this interview. If God wouldn't be welcome, she concluded, then neither would she.

"Oh, I see," said Kata, hesitating a little.

"I also enjoy reading," continued Elsa. "In addition to the Bible and German literature, I have read a number of British and American novels. And I love to do needlework."

"It is good to know you are well read," Kata said. "I think that will be very helpful for Martina."

"Do you have any future plans for a family of your own, Elsa?" she asked, as if she wanted to be sure that Elsa was serious about a career with them.

Elsa's countenance paled slightly as she answered. "Well, I was married for about four years, and we learned that I couldn't have children. My husband died after a brief illness about a month ago. So, to answer your question, no, I have none."

Kata's face clouded, and her eyes moistened slightly. "I am sorry for your loss. I fully understand the feeling one has when losing a loved one. You see, my husband and I lost a son just a few years ago. That was difficult, I assure you. To lose a husband would be equally devastating, I am sure."

"Yes, loss is not an easy thing, 'tis true, but God is able to help us through the tragedies of life, don't you agree?" Elsa asked.

Kata shifted slightly in her chair and responded after taking a deep breath.

"Well, I must admit that I am not really a religious woman. I do admire your faith, however. It seems to have sustained you through a very tragic time."

Kata smiled and quickly moved on to other routine questions. Finally, she stood up and said, "You definitely have many of the qualities we are looking for in a nanny. I'd like you to meet Martina, now, if you have time."

"I would love to," Elsa replied. This was very encouraging to her. If she was getting the chance to meet her daughter, then Kata must be seriously considering her.

"Wonderful. Give me a few moments and I will have her come down." Kata walked through the hallway and upstairs to get Martina.

After Kata left the room, Elsa closed her eyes, bit her lower lip, and then began to pray silently: *Lord, if this is the plan you have for me, then let it be confirmed through Martina. I know you have good plans for me and also for this family. If I can be of help to them, then open the door wide for me to get this position. Whatever happens, though, dear Father, I trust you to do your will. Thank you.*

Elsa loved the little girl the moment she saw her. She hoped even more that she would be hired.

"How do you do, *Frau* Bauer?" said Martina. She curtsied politely.

"Very well, thank you, Martina." Elsa rose and curtsied in turn.

"Are you going to be my nanny?"

"Well, now that is up to you and your mother, I suppose. I'd like to be," answered Elsa with a gracious smile.

"Can you tell stories? I really love stories."

"Oh yes, I have lots of stories I can tell you."

"And do you like to play games?"

"If you have games you like to play, I am sure I would like them as well."

Martina looked over to her mother and asked, "Mama, can Elsa read me a story?"

"Well, if Elsa doesn't mind, I am sure it will be all right," she answered.

"To be honest, I have nowhere to go, except back to the hotel, and nothing to do for the rest of the evening," said Elsa, "so it would be my pleasure to spend some time with you, Martina."

"Then it's settled. Why don't you go ahead with Marti to her room and read a couple of stories to her. She has plenty of books, and I guarantee you will not bore her by reading her favorite stories.

I have a few errands that I need to tend to, and if you will meet me back here in the drawing room in an hour, we'll talk a little more."

Elsa was pleased with the way things were going. She felt confident that if *Frau* Albers was giving her the opportunity to read to her daughter, she must seriously be considering her for the position. She felt a peace in her heart about it and knew that she would be happy with this family.

She took Martina's hand and followed her up to her room.

Martina chose several books for Elsa to read. She pulled up one of her small chairs next to Elsa, and Elsa began with two of Martina's favorites from her Grimm's fairy tale collection: *Hansel and Gretel* and *Snow White.* She told the stories with great animation and emotion, which thoroughly captivated Martina.

Martina found a few more stories she wanted her to read, and Elsa didn't mind a bit. She enjoyed telling them as much as Martina enjoyed listening to her tell them.

The hour passed so quickly, and finally she said, "I would love to stay and read to you some more, but your mother wants to meet with me again, so I had better go back to the drawing room."

"Oh, you tell such good stories, and we'd have so much fun together," Martina said. She looked up at Elsa and tugged on her hand. "Please stay, *Frau* Bauer."

"Well, *Engel*, it is in your mother's hands now," answered Elsa. *And God's,* she thought.

When they returned to the drawing room, before Kata could say a word, Martina said in a very adult-like manner, "I have made my decision and think that Elsa would be just the right nanny for me."

Kata and Elsa laughed at her declaration.

"Well, *Leibe*, if you think she is the right nanny for you, I will go along with your decision—that is, if Elsa feels the same way."

"Oh, absolutely! I would love to have the chance to be Martina's nanny and to work for you. I promise you I will care for her as if she was my very own *kinder.*"

"That settles it then. When can you start?"

"Right away if you wish."

"All right, I'll have my driver get your things from the hotel and you can move in right way. Let's have lunch and discuss the terms of your employment," said Kata.

CHAPTER 11

Back on Stage

NOW THAT THE ISSUE OF A nanny had been settled, Kata turned her attention to auditioning for the upcoming production, *I Gioielli Della Madonna.* She took a shopping day and purchased a new outfit. Since leaving the opera several years ago, Kata had not been on a serious shopping spree for clothing. Why should she? After all, she was primarily a wife and mother. Fashion did not dictate her apparel in this profession. Now of course, she needed to give careful attention to her wardrobe.

For an audition, she needed to adhere to the current vogue. Many changes had taken place in the fashion world in just a few years. Looser and lighter clothing was the mode. Waistlines were rising slightly as well. Gone were the days of corsets, excessive padding and elaborate decorations. Hats were floppy and larger and were often adorned with feathers. The hobble skirt was now the rage. Such a narrow skirt. Kata wondered how a woman could even walk in that contraption.

In a very upscale designer dress shop, she found a light green two-piece suit, trimmed in silver fox with a silver cartwheel hat, adorned with silver feathers, matching velvet reticule, and a white lace blouse. The outfit suited her still svelte figure and complimented her auburn hair and hazel eyes. She furtively admired herself in the mirror; however, after a few minutes admiration transformed into annoyance as she admitted to herself that her hair was not up to the current mode. She needed a new, more fashionable look.

She replaced her outdated *Gibson Girl* hairdo with a looser, fuller chignon, adorned with silver combs.

Next, Kata made an appointment with the director of the company, *Herr* Klein. "Come in, *Frau* Albers," he said, motioning her to enter his office. He was an older gentleman, a little on the heavy side, slightly balding with deep blue-grey eyes and a ruddy complexion. He had a cheerful expression, which put Kata at ease.

"You have wonderful credentials, and of course, as Greta has suggested, I had to interview you," said *Herr* Klein.

She rolled her eyes when he mentioned Greta. Yes, Kata had told her she was considering coming for an interview. But she didn't think Greta would---wait a minute. Yes, now she remembered; Greta knew *Herr* Klein very well. But then, who *didn't* she know in the world of opera? Of course, she would have talked to him. That was Greta's way. She should have just waited and told her *after* the interview. After all didn't she talk Hans Schumer into giving her that major role in Wagner's *Die Feen?* Oh Greta.

"I appreciate your seeing me on such a short notice and so late in the year. I know you will be starting rehearsals soon," she said.

"Yes. We haven't filled all of the parts yet, and a couple of members of the troupe have already quit, so we needed to find some replacements as soon as possible. Your timing is perfect, *Frau* Albers."

"I am glad, then," she replied.

A man who appeared to be in his early to mid-forties entered his office unannounced. Obviously, she thought, he must be close to *Herr* Klein to walk in like that.

"Excuse me Heinrich. I didn't know you had company."

"Not a problem. I was just interviewing this young lady for a part in *I Gioielli Della Madonna.*"

The gentleman bowed to Kata, raised her hand to his lips and kissed it.

"Who is this lovely young siren?"

"This is Katharina Ernst—Albers. You might remember her from just a few years ago. It was a great loss to the opera when she traded her career for marriage."

"I see you finally came to your senses, then," the gentleman said.

"I am not trading my marriage for my career," Kata insisted. "I am certain one will complement the other, *Herr*. . ."

"Forgive me," interrupted *Herr* Klein. "Let me introduce *Herr* Ignatz Waghalter to you, *Frau* Albers."

Kata smiled as if she had met an old friend.

"I have heard of you, *Herr* Waghalter. Didn't you receive the *Mendelssohn Preis* in 1902 for your performance of the *Sonata for Violin and Pianoforte in F Minor?"*

Ignatz beamed. "I am honored that you know of my accomplishment, *Frau* Albers." He bowed slightly.

"It is obvious that you have a great deal of knowledge about the opera. I would consider it a privilege to sit in on your audition, if you have no objection, *Frau* Albers."

"Please do, *Herr* Waghalter."

Kata's heart was beating with exhilaration. This was an unbelievable opportunity for her. After all, this conductor had made quite a reputation for himself in his thirty-something years. He had studied with Philipp Scharwenka, a very well known German composer and teacher. He had also worked with one of the most influential violinists of their time, Hungarian-born Joseph Joachim, who was also a close friend of Johannes Brahms. To be in such prestigious company was an honor indeed. She looked at this as a good omen of sorts.

Herr Klein gave her a script and led her to the stage. He allowed her a few minutes to look over the material. When she was ready, he returned, bringing Ignatz with him. With great ease and a resounding melodious voice, she sang with everything she had.

"Bravo! Bravo!" *Herr* Klein shouted, clapping enthusiastically at her cavatina. "Greta was right about you! I believe you are still the prima donna you once were, my dear."

Giving her a hearty standing ovation, Ignatz echoed his praise and added, "If *Herr* Klein does not hire you on the spot, *Frau* Albers, I will resign immediately as his conductor!" He smiled and gently slapped *Herr* Klein's upper back and winked at Kata.

"Well, then, it's settled. You are hired! You have great potential and I definitely want you to sign a contract with our company."

Kata was thrilled. She couldn't believe her ears. This was exactly what she had hoped for, but until this moment, she wasn't sure it could happen. "Thank you very much, *Herr* Klein," she responded in delight and fighting hard to stay composed.

"I have to be honest with you *Frau* Albers," *Herr* Klein began with a slight frown, and in a more serious tone.

"Please, call me Kata," she requested politely.

"Oh no, *Meine Leibe*, I should be thanking you and Greta." Before *Herr* Klein could continue, Ignatz took her hand, kissed it once again, and excused himself. "I hate to leave such enchanting company. However, I have work I must do, so I must take my leave for now. I certainly do look forward to working with you, though. Please, don't hesitate to ask for my help or advice if you ever need it."

"It would be my pleasure," replied Kata, almost mesmerized by the accolades and attention she had received.

"Very well. Now, as I was saying, currently there are no major roles available in *I Gioielli Della Madonna." H*owever, I am prepared to offer you a substantial part in this opera.

"We can also discuss the possibility of you being an understudy for the part of *Carmella*, and I do believe that in the future, I can almost guarantee you a more important role in one of our upcoming operas. With the opening of this new opera house, there will be more leading roles for a brilliant performer like you."

"I am very grateful for this opportunity, *Herr* Klein, and to be quite honest with *you*, I would rather have a minor role at first, in order to ease back into the industry."

"That does make perfectly good sense," *Herr* Klein said. "Can you begin rehearsing as early as next week?"

"That will be no problem."

Kata left the interview floating on a cloud. Her dream of returning to her first love, the opera, was unfolding. Things were going well for her now. She hurried home to share the news with Fredric, Martina and Elsa.

A few days later, the Alberses invited Edda and Heinrich Werner to have dinner with them. They shared Kata's news with their close friends.

"Of course while it's only a minor role, it's a good start." Kata commented to Edda during dinner.

"We are very proud of you, Kata, and have no doubt your reputation will be a boon to your future success." She patted Kata's hand.

Heinrich nodded and added, "I'm sure that once the word is out that the lovely *Fraulein* Ernst is back on stage, it will be no time before your former fans flock to hear you, and I would venture to say you have a starring role in no time." He winked at her.

Edda changed the subject for a moment. "Well, we have some rather exciting news of our own to share." A glow enveloped her face.

"What is it?" Fredric asked.

"I'm sure you remember us talking about a business associate of mine from the United States, John Astor?"

"Yes," Fredric said. "Astor is quite a well-known millionaire from the United States. I believe his family was originally from Germany. He has done business with my company, indirectly."

"I remember that. He had several inventions that were useful in the industrial world, didn't he?"

"Yes. One we tried was designed to produce gas from peat moss," Fredric said. "It worked quite well and saved us considerable money."

"Well, much of my dealings with the man were in the area of real estate. Little to do with industry, I'm afraid."

"He is a multitalented man indeed," added Edda. "Were you aware he even wrote some fiction?"

"Science fiction, actually," said Fredric. "I think it had to do with the future. Something about living on other planets in the twenty-first century. Can you imagine anything so bizarre?"

"What an imagination," said Kata. "That would be virtually impossible. I mean, men are having a difficult enough time just trying to get off the ground with those ridiculous flying machines."

Heinrich shook his head and laughed. "I agree with you, *Meine Liebe*. The thought of anyone being able to survive in outer space is just unimaginable. I am sure that's why they call it 'science fiction'."

"I don't think that is the extent of this man's notoriety. I just read somewhere about a scandal surrounding him. Didn't he recently divorce?" asked Kata.

"Yes. He did divorce his wife, Ava, just a couple of years ago, for a much younger woman, I believe," Fredric said.

"It's true, and at first, we were quite taken aback by it," said Heinrich. After all, divorce is practically unheard of, and this young lady could easily pass for his daughter."

"I understand it caused quite an uproar in New York society," said Fredric, frowning. "What was he thinking? Marriage is not something to throw away on a frivolous affair."

"Don't be so judgmental, Fredric. We don't know the whole story behind it." Kata shrugged her shoulders and took Fredric's arm.

"Perhaps Ava was very difficult to live with. Anyway, I'm not going to throw stones his way. People make mistakes and should not be condemned for it. We don't know the whole story."

"I quite agree with you," added Edda. She leaned closer to Kata and lowered her voice slightly. "As a matter of fact, I remember the first Mrs. Astor quite well. It was evident when we were around them that the couple didn't get along very well. I also heard from several other sources, mutual acquaintances, that is, that the couple had a difficult marriage and often quarreled, even in public. To make matters worse, people tell me that she was always running off on philanthropic missions of some sort. It seems to me that she neglected poor John."

"But really, to take up with an eighteen year-old. That *is* scandalous." Fredric said, shaking his head. "What is this world coming to?"

Heinrich chimed in. "Well, the whole ordeal was painful for everyone, I am sure. I hear many of his former friends have ostracized him. Regardless of the gossip, we have decided not to make any rash judgments about him. We met up with him and his young wife just recently in Paris and she seems very charming. Anyway, they have invited us to join them on a cruise in April of next year."

Edda clasped Heinrich's hand and said, "I think he's trying to get away from all of the gossip and restore his European friendships."

"Of course we saw this as a wonderful opportunity in more ways than one," Heinrich said. "Perhaps we can be some company to him, and quite frankly, this will be an adventure of a life time for us,"

Edda continued with noted excitement in her voice. "Well, at first, we weren't too sure, but then John told us about this new luxury liner, the *Titanic*. Have you heard of it?"

Fredric responded with great interest. "Yes, actually another business associate of mine, Benjamin Guggenheim, was just talking about it last week at a conference we were both attending. I believe he has booked passage on it as well."

"I understand he's quite the 'ladies' man' also. He also has a bit of a scandalous reputation." Heinrich looked at Fredric and winked.

"Well, I don't know much about that; however, he's something of an industrial genius, and he knows a great deal about this *Titanic*. It sounds like an amazing ship," said Fredric.

"To say the least," Heinrich added.

"From what *Herr* Guggenheim told me, no other ship can possibly match the eloquence of this luxurious liner. He said that it has so many amenities never experienced before in the history of ocean travel: libraries, elegant ballrooms, a Turkish bath, a full gym as well as a swimming pool."

Edda nodded and swirled her hands in the air as if to illustrate her words. "I understand it has the most expensive furnishings and elaborate décor that money could buy filled this majestic cruise ship. It even has an elevator onboard."

Kata looked at their friends and beamed. "Well, we certainly are happy for you both. I know you will have a wonderful time. We'll be looking forward to you telling us all about it."

"It has been a dream of ours for years to visit the United States and to be in on the maiden voyage of such a magnificent ship will give us memories we will cherish the rest of our lives."

Heinrich suddenly lit up. "I have an idea. Why don't you both join us?"

"Oh no, I am not stepping one foot on board any vessel that is going to cross such a gigantic body of water—no matter how luxurious it is." Kata looked horrified. "Besides, I will be quite busy with the opera."

"But, Kata, you have been on cruises before. Surely you've enjoyed them," Edda said.

"That was different. The Danube is so much smaller than the Atlantic, and the boats we were on did not look like as tiny in a large lake, as I can only imagine when I think a ship of any size on such a vast ocean. Besides on a river one can usually see land on one side or the other—and to be such a ways out in the middle of the ocean like that—what if something happened?" Kata tensed and her face reflected her sudden anxiety.

"What if suddenly the boat hit an object and sprung a leak? What if it was hundreds of miles from land? How could you possibly be rescued?"

"Oh bother, Kata," Edda said, with an air of frustration. "This boat is unsinkable. It would never happen to the Titanic. Why it's the safest mode of transportation ever invented."

Heinrich nodded in agreement, smiled at his wife and said, "The Titanic is the largest ship ever built and was designed by some of the most brilliant engineering minds. Besides, I understand that Mr. Thomas Andrews, the Irish shipbuilder who was in charge of its plans, will be onboard. I'm sure that he wouldn't even consider the voyage if he wasn't absolutely certain it was safe."

"That will be an impressive trip, I'm sure," added Fredric. "But I have to admit it would be difficult for us both to get away any time soon. Maybe another time."

Edda wasn't finished trying to convince their friends yet. She slapped her hands on her lap.

"I almost forgot to mention the famous Broadway and film actress Dorothy Gibson is also going on this voyage. It would be a wonderful opportunity for you to meet her, Kata."

Kata's ears perked up at the mention of this relatively new actress who was quickly gaining notoriety for her work in one of the most recent forms of entertainment, the silent film industry.

"Well, I have to say that would be tempting to meet Miss Gibson, but still, not tempting enough to take such a chance on the high seas. It . . . just seems too risky." Kata drew her lips into a thin line and held firm in her decision.

"We are not worried in the least. We're going to travel to Cherbourg, France in April, where we will meet the Astor's, and board her. And then it's on to America. It would be wonderful to have you with us, so if you do change your mind, please let us know. I am sure we can see that you get a booking."

"Why, thank you both. I am quite sure this would be a wonderful experience for Kata and me. There's nothing more that we would love but to be with you both on this excursion. Unfortunately, we will not be able to take advantage of this invitation. Perhaps another time," Fredric said.

"Well, we will miss having you with us as well, but when we return we will share every exciting detail of our trip with you both," Edda said.

"We will look forward to that and your safe return, of course," added Kata. An uneasy shiver rose from deep inside of her. She assumed it was her dread of the ocean, and let the foreboding feeling fade.

* * *

After their friends left for the evening, Kata and Fredric spent a little time discussing their visit with the Werners and Kata's upcoming venture.

"You know that might have been quite an opportunity for you to get over your fear of the ocean," Fredric said, as he sipped on his cognac.

"Perhaps, but I really am not ready. Let's wait and see how their voyage goes, and then maybe at a later date. Besides, I cannot think about much else right now, except preparing for my first performance in years."

"Yes, dear, that's probably so. Still, just remember you have a family to think about as well."

"I realize that, and I promise I'll not neglect you or Marti. A minor role won't take that much of my time, I'm sure." Kata attempted to reassure Fredric.

"I won't have to practice as much to begin with, unless—"

"Unless what?" Fredric asked.

"Well, it's probably nothing at all, and the chances of it happening are so remote that I really didn't want to bring it up," she said. She realized that the lid was already off the box, so the truth would have to come out now.

"You have my *full* attention," Fredric said, looking at her intently and putting his paper down for the moment.

"Well, there is a very *remote* possibility that I could be offered a chance to be the understudy for one of the lead roles—and that could mean if something happened to the lady playing this part, I could actually take over that role."

Kata looked down at her lap and fidgeted nervously in her chair, hoping that this wouldn't lead to a quarrel similar to the one they had over her announcement that she wanted to go back to the opera.

To her surprise, Fredric remained calm. "The chances of that happening are very slim, I'm sure," he said in a nonchalant tone.

"Yes, I agree with you, wholeheartedly, *Liebe*." Kata took a sigh of relief and quickly turned the discussion to their new nanny. "So what is your impression of Elsa? I haven't heard you say much about her since she's been here."

"Well, she seems qualified enough, and Marti apparently has taken to her. I think she's overly religious, though. She does like to quote Bible passages. Overall, she seems to be doing a fine job with Marti. I imagine we will just have to see how things go."

"Yes, Marti seems happy enough. Isn't that what matters?"

"I suppose so, as long as she doesn't start preaching to us," Fredric said, and he returned to reading his newspaper.

* * *

The rest of the week seemed to drag on as Kata anxiously awaited her first day of rehearsal. She spent what time she could practicing her script at home, trying to devote as much attention as possible to Marti, since she knew things would probably get hectic once she started rehearsals.

She and Elsa took Marti to the park the Friday before she started work.

"Oh, Elsa, I do appreciate what you are doing with Marti. You are a gift to us all," she commented as they strolled down the wide path winding through the park. Martina walked between the two ladies, holding a hand of each of them.

"It's my pleasure, *Frau* Albers. Your daughter is a delight to me and so easy to care for." Elsa squeezed Marti's hand and gave her an approving nod.

Martina added, "Elsa is fun to play with too. She knows all my games and she tells me great stories from her Bible as well. Mama, did you know 'bout the first two people on earth? God made a very pretty garden called Eden, then he put a man and a lady in it, an' told 'em to take care of it for him. Their names were Adam and Eve," Martina shared eagerly.

"Well, that is interesting, Marti. And yes, I remember hearing that story many years ago, too."

"Why didn't you tell it to me, Mama?" Marti asked curiously.

"Well, I guess I had forgotten about it," Kata said. After all, they're just stories made up over the years, by ancient writers, I believe."

"No, Mama," Martina insisted. "They're 'bout real people who lived a really long time ago. Elsa told me so." Did you know the story 'bout a little boy named Moses?" She didn't wait for her mother to answer. "A mean king was going to kill him, so his mother hid him in a basket and put him in the river and a beautiful Egyptian princess found him and raised him as her son."

While Kata didn't want Martina to take the stories seriously, she didn't interrupt her. She listened intently as her daughter related a few more stories that she had heard from Elsa. She would have to talk to Elsa about them in private some time.

* * *

Finally, Monday arrived and Kata got ready for her first day of rehearsals. She put on her favorite rose-colored suit, trimmed in pink taffeta ribbon and cotton lace and wore a matching pink satin blouse.

She combed her hair in a fashionable up do with loose curls flowing in the back. Then she kissed Martina goodbye and set off for her first day of work.

Her chauffeur pulled up in front of the opera house. Kata still wasn't quite used to the noise and the speed of this new motorcar Fredric had purchased, and she had to cover her head with a hat that had a thick lace veil tied under her chin in order to keep her makeup and hairdo intact. However, Fredric insisted that they use this new means of transportation whenever possible.

When she arrived at the opera house, Greta was the first to greet her. "Oh my dear, it is so good to see you! When I heard that *Herr* Klein had hired you, I was elated! It's going to be wonderful to be able to work with you again. You don't know how much I have missed our times together," she said and grabbed Kata's arm. "Come now, let's get ready for rehearsal."

Yes, and, of course, it was a complete surprise to her. Kata thought. "It will be just like the old times, I am sure," she said.

Finally, the premier performance was ready to make its debut in Berlin. Kata was excited and nervous all at once. Martina insisted that Elsa be invited, and Fredric and Kata agreed to let her join them.

The day before the premier, however, Kata decided to take Elsa on a shopping spree for a more fashionable ensemble.

"Elsa, you absolutely cannot wear any of your outdated skirts and blouses. I just won't allow it."

"But I don't have the money for a new outfit, *Frau* Albers. I am sure I can find something in my wardrobe that might be suitable."

"Suitable and fashionable are two different things, Elsa. Besides, I insist. It will be my pleasure to do this."

After trying on what seemed like hundreds of outfits, Kata finally approved of a black and red two-piece dress with a black silk bodice that began a few inches below her neck and crossed her shoulders in a straight line. She also purchased a red satin shawl to drape over her shoulders and let her borrow a pair of diamond earrings and a rose-shaped brooch.

In addition, she had her personal maid, Liesel fix Elsa's hair in a delicate chignon. Liesel was quite knowledgeable on the latest hair fashions. The transformation was amazing.

Martina gasped in delight when she saw her. "You are *beautiful*, Elsa!"

Elsa said nothing. She blushed and her gaze dropped to the floor.

"Yes, Elsa, you are quite a lovely lady," Kata agreed. "You don't have to hide behind such a drab wardrobe. You have a great deal of inner beauty, but it's perfectly acceptable to dress up once in a while and let your outer beauty show as well."

Fredric added, "We will have to watch the single men. One of them may try to snatch you up and take you away from us."

"Enough about me," Elsa said. "Look at our little *Prinzessin*."

Martina waltzed down the stairs in a red and green gingham dress her father brought her from Paris. Elsa fixed her hair in delicate ringlets and placed a large silk bow on top of her head to compliment the red in the gingham dress.

"Indeed you *do* look like a little *Prinzessin*!" Fredric exclaimed.

"Of course, Papa, that's 'cause I'm *your Prinzessin*."

"You are right, *Schatzi*." He picked her up and gave her a kiss.

When it was time for them to leave, he summoned his driver, and they rode off to watch Kata's first performance in several years.

CHAPTER 12

Disaster on the High Seas

THE FIRST MONTHS OF KATA'S RETURN to the opera were rather tedious, and the practice was repetitive. She went home thoroughly exhausted the first few nights. Within a few weeks, however, she toughened up and managed her schedule quite well. By early 1912, she had finally settled into her routine and life was going very well for Kata. She was realizing her greatest dream. Her reputation as an accomplished singer was growing, and offers for future roles were coming in from all over. She was ecstatic. That is, until the night of April 16.

Kata returned home and found Fredric slumped over in his dark burgundy and gold overstuffed chair, holding the newspaper to the side with one hand, and his other hand on his forehead, rubbing it as if he were in pain.

"Fredric, what is it? You look as if you have lost your best friend," inquired Kata as she walked up to him and put her hand on his shoulder.

"*Mein Gott! Mein Gott*!" Something very terrible has happened," he moaned as he handed her the paper without looking up.

She looked at the front page and began to tremble as she read the headlines: *Over 1300 Feared Drowned or Missing in Titanic Disaster.*

"I can't believe it! This was to be the Werner's dream voyage—now, it . . . it might have taken their lives," Kata said. She put her hands up to her face.

"We have to find out, of course. We can only hope they were among those who were rescued. I'll start checking right away," Fredric said.

Several days later, he learned the sad truth. Apparently only a little more than 700 had survived the disaster. Their friends were not among that group. Unfortunately, both went down with the ship. Fredric struggled to tell Kata the details.

"There were not enough lifeboats for everyone. The women and children were given priority for the life boats." He sighed heavily. "I learned from another friend of theirs who survived the ordeal that Edda gave her seat up to a young couple who were on their honeymoon . . . They were not going to allow the husband to get on the lifeboat with his bride." His lips quivered and tears pooled in his eyes. "Edda insisted she wanted to stay with Heinrich. She said. . . that she had a wonderful marriage and a full life. . . and wanted this young couple to have. . . a chance. . . to experience what they had. She told them she was grateful for the time she had on this earth and . . . she wanted to spend her last. . . hours. . . with the 'love of her life'."

Kata put her arms around him and wordlessly lowered her face to his shoulder. He choked back the tears, clenched his fists, and lowered his face. "It's like losing my parents all over again," sobbed Fredric. "That boat was supposed to be unsinkable!"

Unsinkable. Kata recalled the Werner's comment as they were discussing the wonders of this colossal creation several weeks ago. She tried to imagine what that terrible tragedy must have been like for their dear friends. She pictured them clinging to each other, shivering, perhaps in unquenchable fear, or maybe bravely looking to the skies in faith, ready to meet their Creator, as the unsinkable vessel was swallowed up by the liquid abyss.

Yes, it had to be a warning that people were not supposed to cross these great bodies of water. Had mankind crossed the line in with all of his latest inventions? Radios? Electricity? Automobiles? Men in flying machines? Now luxury liners like the *Titanic.* She just didn't know. Whatever it was, it only affirmed her resolve never to cross that bottomless oceanic pit.

Wordlessly, the two sank onto their divan. They wrapped themselves in each other's arms and together they despaired over the loss of their friends.

Fredric truly felt like an orphan. Now, more than ever, he was fully convinced that God didn't exist. No god that he could believe in would take so many loved ones from him. No god could be that cruel.

* * *

Time seemed to sooth the pain of the Alberses' loss and dimmed the memories of that fateful April day the world experienced the loss of the *Titanic*. Spring made way for summer to share its warmth. In just a few months, Kata's reputation as an accomplished opera star spread throughout Europe. And, although she was receiving offers from other opera companies all over the continent, she turned them down. She wanted to stay close to home. She knew Elsa was taking very good care of Martina; however, she wanted to spend as much time as she could with her daughter as well.

One day, while Kata was in her dressing room taking a break between rehearsal sessions, Greta stopped by to talk to her.

"Oh Kata, something wonderful has just happened!" She was practically out of breath. "You have a chance to perform at the Vienna Volksoper Opera House! Look! Here is your invitation from the director Hans Gregor himself! He watched you perform last winter, and he was quite taken with you. He's bringing Goethe's opera, *Claudine von Villa Bella* to Vienna early next year and he wants to give you an opportunity to audition for the lead role of *Claudine*! Isn't that great news?"

Kata raised her eyebrows. "Who gave you permission to open my mail, Greta?"

"I'm sorry; I . . . I didn't think you would mind."

"Greta, you are my dearest friend; nevertheless, at times you are very exasperating, always asserting yourself into my business like this."

"You are being much too sensitive about this whole thing. I am just looking out for you. Heaven knows you wouldn't even give this letter a second look if I hadn't read it!"

"I appreciate your wanting to see me expand my horizons. I just get rather irritated with you always chiding me when I turn down parts that I believe will take me away from home. I know you don't mean to, but sometimes you overstep your boundaries."

Greta put her arm around Kata's waist. "Kata, you know I only have your best interests at heart, and I knew this was something big when I saw the return address. I'm sorry—maybe I did go a bit far. I simply couldn't resist."

Kata snatched the letter from Greta's hand, sat down at her dressing table chair and read it for herself. She calmed down a bit.

"I—I am flattered, of course. I know it really would be quite an honor. But I just can't do it. I promised Fredric when I returned to the theatre, that I would never accept a part that would take me away from Berlin and from my family. It's *completely* out of the question." She crumpled the letter up and threw it in the trash.

Greta immediately retrieved it, took Kata by the shoulders.

"Listen—I have been patient and tried to understand when you have turned down other offers, but *this*! This one is second to none! If you get this part, why, there's no telling where your career may go. You have to do this."

"No I *don't*! *You* take it! *You* don't have a family to go home to at night, or a husband that cares about you!"

Greta stared at her in disbelief, backed up a bit. A wounded look clouded her face.

"How can you say such hurtful things to me? I—it's not fair of you to say those things because I have never married. It's not as if I haven't had suitors. It's just that . . . It's just—" She stopped in mid-sentence, turned away from Kata, covered her face and burst into tears.

Kata realized that she had cut into Greta's heart as if she had actually used a dagger. How could she have been so cruel? Greta was only interested in what was good for her, after all. Even if she *had* gone about the whole matter the wrong way, Greta was her friend—no, she was her kindred spirit. Her sister.

Kata reached out and turned Greta around, pulling her close.

She wrapped her arms around her shoulders and tried to comfort her. "I'm so sorry. I . . . I didn't mean to say those things. I was just lashing out in anger. Please—forgive me," she said in a gentle, more soothing voice.

Greta just stiffened. "You don't know how much I have envied you having a family, Kata. The times I have cried myself to sleep out of sheer loneliness. You have something that I longed for. A wonderful marriage. You and Fredric have been so happy. Yes, I have known many men, and maybe even been a bit too familiar with some . . . still, why can't *I* find what you have with Fredric?"

Maybe that's the problem. Greta is jealous. Jealous that I have a family? Is it because she doesn't have one of her own? Or maybe she wants my undivided friendship. Kata confronted those thoughts immediately.

No—that couldn't possibly be it. I've known her for years, and Greta is not a vindictive or selfish person. Bossy, meddling, pushy at times—yes, but not malicious.

"You can," she said. "You just have to wait for the right person to come along."

"But I'm getting old," Greta whined. "I'm thirty-five! Who's going to want an old spinster like me?"

"You are *not* old, dear, and you still have plenty of time to find true love," insisted Kata. "Now, back to this other matter." She picked up the letter and waved it in front of Greta. "You have to promise me that you will stop trying to get me to take these offers and that you will *never* open my mail again," Kata said adamantly.

Greta dried her eyes, wiped her nose and attempted to compose herself. "I . . . I really *do* want you to be happy. I thought this was a wonderful opportunity for you to become a great opera star. You know *Herr* Gregor has helped many an opera singer become famous." She explained, composing herself again.

"Well, I thank you for that, Greta. Besides, I'm not sure I *want* to be famous. Even though I enjoy the opera, I do not need fame. Fame doesn't always bring happiness."

"It would make *me* happy," Greta said.

"But *I'm* not *you* and I'm already very happy with what I'm doing. Look, Greta, I appreciate that you were trying to do something for me that you thought would make me happy, so please, from now on, let me determine my *own* future and happiness."

Greta said nothing. She merely nodded her head, sniffed and daintily wiped her eyes again.

"Come now, we really need to get back to rehearsals," added Kata; and the two went back to work. However, the offer in that letter tugged at Kata. She furtively retrieved the letter and tucked into her reticule.

* * *

When she returned home that evening, Kata pulled the letter out and read it again.

Why was she giving this letter a second thought? She should rip it up. After all, Fredric would <u>never</u> approve of such a thing. Secondly, it would take her away from Marti for *too* long. Besides, there's no guarantee that she would even get the part. An invitation to audition isn't the same as being chosen. And that's a long way to travel to be rejected. *But was I being very honest with Greta? Would having an opportunity to be successful and famous bring me even more happiness? Why couldn't I have both—fame and a family? No, I can't consider it; I promised Fredric I wouldn't do something like this.* She started to toss the letter away, when Fredric walked in the room.

"What do you have there, *Liebe*?"

"Oh, it's really nothing." She paused, and then reconsidered.

"Actually, that's not so. It was the cause of a big argument between Greta and me."

She told Fredric about the confrontation she and Greta had earlier that day.

"May I read your letter?" he asked.

"Why, of course, there's no harm in *reading* it. I have already made up my mind, anyway. I'm not going to respond to the invitation." She handed him the letter.

Fredric read it and then said, "I'm not sure that you should just dismiss this offer all together. It could prove to be a good experience for you—who knows?—you might become famous!" He chuckled lightly.

Kata looked at him, raising her eyebrows in surprise. "I can't believe you would change your mind like that. You know you made it very clear to me when I went back to work, that you wanted me to stay in Berlin."

"Why couldn't I change my mind? I have seen you perform. When you first went back, I guess I had forgotten how beautiful you were the very first time I saw you on the stage and how well you could sing," Fredric caressed her cheek. "Frankly, I'm very proud of you, *Schatzi*."

She was shocked at his change of heart. She took his hands and looked up at him.

"Are you telling me to answer this letter?"

"Well, let's just say, I'm not forbidding you to answer it. Like you said, you may not even get the part, but you'll never know unless you try, right?"

Kata reached up to him pulled his head down and kissed him firmly on the lips. "Oh, *Liebling*, thank you. All right then. I guess I'm just curious enough to find out—I'll answer the letter."

CHAPTER 13

Martina Learns about Jesus

Elsa and Martina were also adjusting nicely since Kata returned to the stage. They spent a great deal of time together, and Elsa was a very attentive nanny. She devoted virtually all of her time to Martina, reading to her, playing games and telling her stories from the Bible on a level she could understand. She enjoyed making the stories come alive for Martina. Martina especially loved hearing how David slew the great giant, Goliath and the how Esther saved a whole nation of people. Elsa's loving guidance greatly contributed to Martina's precociousness and remarkable wisdom for her brief seven years.

One evening, as Elsa was telling her the story about baby Jesus and how the shepherds and the wise men came to see him, bearing gifts, Martina asked her, "Is that why we get presents at Christmas?"

"Well, sort of. When we give or receive gifts at Christmas time, perhaps we could look at it as a way of remembering that God gave us the greatest gift he possibly could when he gave us his son Jesus," Elsa explained.

"I like that. The next time I get a gift, I'll think of how God gave us Jesus." Martina cocked her head, wrinkled her eyebrows and continued, "But there's something I don't understand, Elsa."

"What is that, *Engel*?"

"How was Jesus a gift to us?"

Elsa realized at that moment that Martina didn't know anything about *why* Jesus came to earth. She knew that Fredric and Kata didn't go to church, yet she hadn't given much thought to the possibility that they had never even mentioned Jesus and how he died to save man from his sin—then again, why would they have?

"Well, you see, Marti, after Adam and Eve disobeyed God in the Garden of Eden, he was very sad. He didn't want to see people die, so he revealed a way to save us. He sent his only son Jesus to die on the cross for our sins and that way we would be able to live forever."

"But I still don't understand why he had to die. Couldn't God just forgive everyone anyway?"

"That's a good question, *Kinder*. Let me explain it another way. Let's say that you did something bad, and you were going to be punished for it. Then your very best friend saw that you were going to suffer, so she stepped in and took your punishment for you. That is what Jesus did for us. He stepped in and took the punishment for us because He loved us so much. The only thing He asked us to do was to confess that we are sinners, repent of our sins, then believe in Him and ask Him to come into our heart and be our Lord and Savior."

"But how do we know if we *are* sinners?" Martina asked.

"Well, *Schatzi,* the Bible tells us that we are *all* sinners."

"But I know people who are very good—my mama is."

"Well, let me read you a very important scripture that will help you understand what God says about that."

Elsa opened her Bible and started reading Romans 3: 10–12: "As it is written, there is none righteous, no, not one: there is none that understandeth, there is one that seeketh after God. They are all gone out of the way, they are together become unprofitable; there is none that doeth good, no, not one."

Tears formed in Martina's eyes. "But what if we don't know how we have been bad?"

Elsa laughed at her naiveté and took Martina in her arms. She realized that Martina had a genuine desire to be good.

"Well, *Liebling,* we all have been born into sin, and there's not much we can do about that, but that's where the *good* news comes in. You see, God knows that. He gives us a special promise in Romans

10: verses 9 and 10: 'If we confess with our mouth the Lord Jesus, and believe in our hearts that God hath raised him from the dead, we will be saved.' "

Martina's expression changed to one of relief. "So all I have to do is tell God I'm a sinner and say I'm sorry?"

"Well, that's the beginning, anyway. You are forgiven. Then, you need to grow strong in God's Word and go to church, so you won't be tempted to fall back into sin."

"I don't think I can go to church. Mama and Papa never go—unless you can take me, Elsa. Do you think you could ask them?"

"Well, I can ask them, but I think we also need to pray that God speaks to their hearts about this as well."

"O.K. then, I want to ask Jesus into my heart. Will you help me pray?"

"Why, I'd be very happy to," Elsa replied, beaming at her proudly. She was blessed to see this little cherub, whom the Lord had placed in her care, opened her heart to Jesus. She gently took Martina's little hand in hers and said in a respectful tone, "Let's close our eyes, and you can say this prayer after me, Marti—'Jesus, I realize that I have been a sinner, I repent of my sins and I ask you to forgive me and come into my heart and be my Lord'."

Martina closed her eyes and earnestly repeated the prayer. When she was finished, her face lit up with joy and she hugged Elsa. "Oh, thank you so much, Elsa. I have Jesus in my heart now. I have to tell Mama and Papa about Jesus."

"Let's at least wait until tomorrow morning, *Leipschen*. Right now it's time for bed."

She helped Martina dress for bed, and gently tucked her in for the night. She kissed her on the forehead before leaving her to dream sweet dreams of her new Lord and Savior, Jesus.

Elsa was happy for Martina, and so grateful that she had the opportunity to pray with her. Still, she wondered how Kata and Fredric would react to her news. They seemed to resist her faith and always changed the subject when she tried to talk about the Lord with them. Nevertheless, tonight she would ask God to open their hearts to Martina's news.

That evening, Elsa prayed with even more determination, "Dear Lord, I thank you so much for the work you are doing in Marti's life and for bringing me to this family. I believe you brought me here for such a time as this, and I want to be used by you here. Please help the Albers' to understand what has happened to their daughter and to be open to her testimony. Also, please make a way for her to be able to go to church. I also ask that Katharina and Fredric come to know you as their Lord and Savior. I thank you in Jesus' precious name."

Elsa slipped into her bed and read her Bible a little while longer, taking comfort in his promises and very thankful for having a chance to lead Martina to the Lord. Her eyelids were getting heavy, so she finished reading Romans, Chapter 8, then shut her Bible and said one more prayer: "Lord, I think I finally understand how you took the tragedy in my life and turned it around for your glory. Thank you for that promise in *Romans 8:28*. You have used me to lead this precious child to you. I only hope I can lead her parents to your son Jesus also."

With those words she drifted off into a peaceful sleep, confident that no matter what trials lie ahead, God was in control. . .

CHAPTER 14

Life is full of Complications

* * *

By early July, Kata finished the operetta she had been performing in that spring, she talked to Fredric about taking a vacation to Munich in the southern part of Germany. They hadn't been in quite some time, and she really believed that it would be wonderful for the three of them to have a family vacation together. Fredric agreed and they made the necessary arrangements for their trip.

"Elsa, why don't you take this opportunity to visit your family?" Kata suggested after telling her about their upcoming vacation.

"Well, actually, I do need to go home for a while. My mother has been quite ill recently. She could use my help. I can see that she gets the rest she needs."

"That settles things, then. Take at least a couple of weeks. We'll be gone for that long, I'm sure."

Martina was thrilled as well. As much as she loved Elsa, she missed spending time with her parents. Fredric rented a large, luxurious villa in Munich, near the Isar River, which runs through Austria, Bavaria, Germany, and to the mouth of the Danube. They took Martina to see some of the most picturesque castles in all of Europe, including the famous palace Schloss-Nymphenburg, built in the 1600's.

Martina was especially impressed with the trip to the

Neuschwanstein Castle, which was just about an hour from Munich.

"This one was built in 1868 by Louis II of Bavaria. He wanted it to resemble the fairy tale castles of medieval times," Fredric explained to her.

"Wasn't he the 'Fairy Tale King,' Papa?"

"Why yes, *Schatzi*. That was because he built several fantasy castles. Some also called him the "Swan King."

"I think I could live here, Papa. It's just like the pictures in my book of Fairy Tales."

"Yes, I can understand that. It is quite an amazing place, isn't it?"

* * *

One evening during dinner in their villa, Martina decided that it was time to talk to her parents about Jesus. She had tried a few times before, but had never been very successful. They always seemed to be preoccupied with something. She wanted their full attention in this matter.

"Mama, Papa, I have something very important I want to talk to you about." She tried to sound as serious and grown up as possible.

"Yes, *Mausi?"* Fredric asked fondly.

"Well, Elsa and I were talking about Jesus," she began.

"Jesus?" Kata asked.

"Yes. You see, God sent Jesus to this earth a long time ago to save us from our sins." She continued with great authority.

They listened intently.

"God loves us too much to see us die, so he sent His son Jesus here to die on the cross for us. And when He did, Jesus took *all* of our sins with Him."

Fredric wrinkled his forehead, smiled and said, "That's a good story, Marti, but you must remember that's all the Bible is, just a book of stories written by men who thought they heard from God," he instructed her.

"No, Papa, that's not true." Martina shook her head fervently and crossed her arms. "The Bible says that every word in it is true and 'spired by God!" she insisted firmly. "I believe it, because I have Jesus in my heart now, and He's real to me too!"

Kata looked up. "*Schatzi,* we are glad that you love to hear the stories, and we know you want to believe them. I know that many people believe in Jesus, and I guess in some ways I do as well. You just need to be careful about taking those Bible stories too seriously. No one can be sure that the Bible is completely true."

"Elsa says it is!" she argued. "And I believe Elsa! She is a Christian and loves God very much!" Tears were welling up in her eyes. "And *I* am a Christian, *too*!" Martina declared emphatically.

"Enough of this nonsense, Marti," Fredric said. "I told you Elsa has been filling our daughter with these foolish religious ideas long enough, Kata. Look what it has done to her. She's actually got her believing those fairy tales from the Bible." He shot his wife a frustrated glare.

"No Papa, they are not fairy tales. Mama, I want to go to church. You've never taken me—and I want to see what it's like. Could we go, please?"

"I see no need for church, Marti," Fredric said flatly.

"You will learn all you need in school. If you want to enrich your learning, we can take you to museums. There are many other good books you can read. You don't need to fill your head with such fantasy."

"Jesus is *not* a 'fancy', Papa. You just don't know him!" She cried and excused herself from the table. She marched to her room, very disturbed that her parents didn't understand who Jesus was and what He did for them.

"I wish my Elsa was here," she sobbed. "She would know what to tell Mama and Papa."

Martina fell to her knees beside her bed and began to pray. "Oh Jesus, I'm sorry I got mad, but they just don't understand. I tried to tell them. Please help make them see what you did for them. I know you love them the same way you love me."

She took out the little Bible Elsa had bought for her and began to read the story of Jesus' birth in Luke again. She had no doubt that Jesus was her Lord and Savior. She wanted her parents to believe that too. She wept softly as she thought about them and that if something were to happen to them before they became Christians, they wouldn't be in eternity with her. She would never see them again.

Fredric and Kata retired to the villa's sitting room after Martina had gone to bed. "You must have a talk with Elsa when we get back, Kata," Fredric ordered. "It is one thing for her to read fairy tales and even Bible stories, as long as she keeps them in the proper perspective. I will *not* have her filling our daughter's mind with false hopes and trying to convince her that Jesus is a real person any more than Santa Clause is." He stood up, kissed her on the cheek and announced he was retiring for the evening.

"Good night, dear," Kata said. "I will talk to Elsa about the matter as soon as we return home."

She lingered in the sitting room long after Fredric retired, pondering what Martina had told her about Jesus. Her mind sprinted through a number of scenarios—past, present and future. She remembered hearing something very similar from a minister when she had attended church with an aunt many years ago. She hadn't thought about it in years, yet now it had come back to her.

She also thought about the chance she might have to work in Vienna next year—what an opportunity this could be for her. Then her thoughts wandered to what was going on all over Europe.

In just the past few years, world conflicts and crises erupted all around them. Tension was mounting between France, Spain and Germany. In Russia, the Socialist Revolutionary Party was on the rise, and it was rumored they were plotting an overthrow of the Russian monarchy. Many even feared the possibility that a great war might break out if things didn't improve soon.

Life is so full of complications, Kata thought. She sighed deeply as a sense of foreboding filled her. *Perhaps we do need a Savior like Jesus.* Realizing that she couldn't do much about it, and feeling worn out from travel, confrontations and sheer worry, she turned out the lights and went to bed.

CHAPTER 15

Vienna

THE ALBERSES' VACATION FLEW BY QUICKLY. Fredric and Kata carefully avoided the topic of religion while they were in Munich, hoping that Martina would forget all about it as well. They tried to fill their time with a fortnight's worth of Munich's sights and sounds. They visited every park, museum, palace and theatre that was open to the public and even the city zoo.

Kata wanted to keep Martina's mind off her infatuation with the stories of the Bible, and perhaps open her mind to the aesthetic things of the world. It worried her that her daughter was taking this whole "Jesus" thing too seriously. She and Elsa would have to discuss the matter. She liked Elsa very much, but if Elsa's religious beliefs continued to have such an effect on Martina, she might even have to consider letting her go.

When they returned home, Kata found a letter waiting for her from Vienna, Austria. Her heart started beating rapidly as she opened the envelope and read:

Dear Frau Albers,

Thank you for your prompt response to my invitation. I would consider it a pleasure if you were to audition for the Vienna Volksoper Opera's production of Claudine von Villa Bella. As you probably know, this has been a highly successful production throughout Europe, and I expect nothing less from the upcoming performance. It is a singspiel, and requires a great deal of practice and time, as it includes a number of speaking parts as well as the typical opera numbers. Ergo, I seek only the greatest talent.

You have exhibited talent at its best. While I believe that it would just be a mere formality, I would like to have you audition for the part of Claudine. I have no doubt that you will be an asset to our opera and fit the part very well.

Of course, it means that you will have to travel to Austria and that this will take you away from your family for long periods; however, I am willing to compensate you sufficiently for your sacrifice.

I wish to begin rehearsals as early as January so please make arrangements to be in Vienna no later than September 1st for an audition. The auditions will take about three days, although I am very certain that we will come to some type of agreement. I am so certain of this, in fact, that I think you should plan to find a place of residence while you are here. I would like to offer you a contract with my company.

Should you require assistance in finding a place to stay, please let me know as soon as possible, and I will see that you have help locating a suitable apartment.

Sincerely,
Herr Hans Gregor, Director,
Vienna State Opera House

She read it again to be sure of her chances of being accepted, then excitedly showed it to Fredric.

"I didn't doubt for a moment that you would get the part. It sounds like he's practically guaranteeing it, *Liebe.* I would have been upset had he not recognized your talent." He smiled and kissed her forehead and handed her back the letter.

"Oh Fredric, I *am* happy, yet I am more aware of the fact that this will separate me from my family." Her countenance clouded.

"Well, not necessarily, *Schatzi.* Actually I was so sure that you would get the part, that while we were in Munich, I made some contacts in Austria and, well, I purchased us a villa not too far from the Volksoper Opera House," he said and gave her a big grin.

She raised her eyebrows in astonishment. "Fredric, you *didn't!* How did you manage to do this without my knowing?"

"I have my ways," he answered.

Kata hugged him tightly and kissed him firmly on the lips. "You are a true *Liebling*! I can hardly wait to see it."

Fredric held her around the waist and grinned. "Whether you got the part or not, it is a great location for vacationing and I had been considering us having a residence in Austria any way. I have thought about perhaps building factories there sometime in the future. We'll take an additional two week holiday there so you have plenty of time to move in and get used to it, and Martina and I will stay with you until she needs to return for school." he said.

* * *

Elsa returned two days after the Albers family came home, and Martina was the first one to greet her. "Oh Elsa, I missed you so much!" Martina ran up to her and gave her a big hug.

"I have to tell you all about our vacation and you must tell me about yours," Martina added.

"Why, of course, *Engel.* I would love to hear about your time in Munich," Elsa answered. Leaving her luggage and coat with a servant to take up to her room, she tucked Martina's small hand in hers and together they entered the drawing room and sat down. Fredric was at work and Kata was shopping, so Elsa had some time to talk with her.

"I told Mama and Papa about Jesus," she said, lowering her head and biting her lower lip.

"You don't look that happy about it, Marti," Elsa said.

"I'm not." Martina's lower lip protruded. She tightened her fists, placed them on her hips and continued. "Papa just got furious, and Mama told me not to take the Bible stories seriously."

Tears filled her eyes as she related the whole conversation to Elsa. Elsa reached out and pulled her close. Martina dropped her arms to her lap and sniveled. A few tears fell on her dress. Elsa gently slipped her hand under Martina's chin and turned her face in her direction, but Martina did not look up.

"Did you know that even Jesus wasn't received that well by His friends and family? Actually His brother James didn't even believe that He was the Son of God until after Jesus died."

"Really?" Martina looked at Elsa in amazement. "I thought his whole family knew he was the Savior. Didn't his mother tell them?"

Elsa chuckled at Martina's childlike faith. "It wasn't quite that simple—even for Mary, I'm afraid. People in Jesus' day were just as blind to God's truths as they are today."

Then Elsa's demeanor took a more serious tone. "I didn't want to say anything, *Engel.* I was afraid they might not be as open to your news as you had hoped. Don't give up, though. Remember, we are praying for them. And even if it doesn't look like they believe in Jesus right now, that doesn't mean they never will believe. We just have to be patient."

Again, Martina dropped her face, and shrugged her shoulders in resignation. "I know," she admitted. "I just thought they would be glad to know that Jesus had died for them and that they could be forgiven. They wouldn't even let me tell them the whole story. I just want them to be in Heaven with us one day," she whined.

"And so do I, *Liebe.* So do I."

When Marti left the room, Elsa stayed behind. She stared pensively across the room. She wondered what they might say to her for leading their little girl to the Lord. She knew that Kata or Fredric, or maybe both of them would discuss this with her, and she prayed silently that the Lord would prepare her for the confrontation and give her the wisdom to know how to respond to them. But most of all, she prayed that God would give her favor and let her stay on with the family. She knew her work was not done here, and she couldn't even think about having to leave her little Marti.

Just as she had assumed, later that afternoon, while she was in her room sitting in her rocking chair, reading her Bible and while Martina was napping, she heard a knock on her door.

"Come in," she said.

Kata entered the room and sat on her bed. At first, she just made small talk, asking her about her trip home and telling her a little about their vacation. Then Kata brought up the conversation they had with Martina about Jesus.

"Elsa, I know you mean well, and I am sure you fully believe those stories in the Bible, but Fredric and I don't agree with your religious philosophy, and quite frankly, I wish you wouldn't put such ideas in Marti's head either. It could hurt her later on in life when she realizes that they are just fairy tales like *Snow White and the Seven Dwarfs.*"

Elsa bit her lip. She flushed slightly. She stifled her emotions and sighed. She looked directly into Kata's eyes.

"*Frau* Albers, did you go to church as a child?"

"Yes—yes, I did. Why?"

"Were you ever told about Jesus?"

"Yes, but that was a long time ago, and I don't think I really believed all of it anyway."

"Is it because you never personally experienced his presence?" Elsa asked.

Kata squirmed a bit, then she resumed her argument. "I . . . I don't believe *anyone* has ever *really* experienced such a thing!"

"On the contrary. Many people have, including your daughter and me. When Jesus comes into your life, He changes everything. You can't even imagine what a difference He can make in your life, if you will just let Him. He offers to forgive all of your sins and to give you a future in eternity."

Kata stiffened a little. "Now listen, Elsa," she said firmly. "I am sure you believe all of this, and I have tried to be patient and understanding. However, when it comes to Marti, I would prefer it if you would stop telling her these stories. They are just confusing her."

Elsa took Kata's hand between hers and smiled.

"I love Marti as if she was my own daughter and I would never do anything to harm her. Please understand that it's *because* I love her, I want her to know that she has the chance to live eternally with the Lord, as do you and your husband, if you will just take down that wall of unbelief and give the Lord a chance to work in your life. He offers us *all* salvation. There is *nothing* we can do to earn it; *nothing* except ask him to forgive us and to be our Lord and Savior. It's a *free gift! Jesus* paid the price for us!'"

Elsa continued. "It's a very simple message and it's truth—not mere stories."

Kata's eyes glistening slightly. She didn't say a word. She just looked at Elsa with a serious look on her face.

This bolstered Elsa's courage. She knew Kata was pondering her words and might have responded, except at that instant, Martina walked in.

"Mama, did you come to welcome Elsa home?" She jumped up in her mother's lap and gave her a big hug.

"Yes, Marti, I did," Kata replied with a smile and kissed her little daughter on the top of her head. She took Martina's hand and left the room with her, but her mind was wrapped around the conversation she and Elsa just had. *Could there really be something to what Elsa was saying? She was so sure of herself.* Kata stored Elsa's words deep inside of her soul. Perhaps she would reconsider her ideas about God. Just not now.

* * *

Kata fell in love with the spacious villa from the day the family arrived, barely three weeks before her interview. Fredric apologized for its size.

Kata put her arm around his waist and reassured him, "This is just perfect, *Liebe.* We certainly don't need more than six bedrooms. After all, most of the time, with the exception of the servants, I will be by myself, except when you, Elsa and Marti come for visits. The other rooms will be more than sufficient for guests, I'm sure."

She looked down to admire the polished oak floors that gleamed between the Persian rugs scattered about. Then she took a tour of her new home. Each room boasted a fireplace large enough to keep them warm in spite of the high ceilings. She was surprised to see how spacious the living room was. It could easily accommodate fifty people if she wanted to entertain, she thought. Yet she appreciated the cozy feeling that rose from deep within her as she entered the much smaller family den, with its flocked wallpaper, inviting brocaded, overstuffed chairs and matching divan. She knew that once she hung a few of her paintings from Germany, she would feel at home here.

Finally, September 1st arrived and, not surprisingly, she sailed through her audition. *Herr* Gregor was very pleased with her performance. He was not a young man, but his appearance was quite striking. He had dark brown hair, graying at the temples, dark blue eyes that sparkled when he smiled, a square chin and a well-trimmed mustache. Kata estimated that he was around fifty or fifty-five.

"You are indeed my pick for Claudine," he exclaimed enthusiastically. "I hope you have settled in my dear, because we will be starting rehearsals within the next month, and I want to make sure you can devote your time to this."

"Of course *Herr* Gregor," she answered, trying to contain her joy. "As a matter of fact, my husband purchased a villa not far from here and I have been living there for a couple of weeks."

"Wonderful! Then I'll expect to see you here first thing January second."

As they were finishing their conversation, to Kata's tremendous surprise, Greta walked into the auditorium. Kata's eyes grew wide with amazement. "Greta! Wha—what are *you* doing here?" she asked with astonishment.

Greta just laughed. "Well, you see, I had also planned to audition for the part of Lucinde, Claudine's cousin, when I heard you were being seriously considered. I wanted to work with my best friend again. I didn't tell you because I wanted to surprise you—and from the look on your face, apparently I was successful." She chuckled as she hugged her dear friend.

Hans Gregor watched the two for a moment as they completed their greeting, then said, "Yes. I have chosen her for that very part, so you two will be working together a great deal. I agreed not to say a word to you, as I'm a soft one when it comes to surprises." He grinned at the success of her plan and winked at Greta.

And when it comes to Greta's 'influence,' I'm sure you were not hard to convince, Kata thought. "Where are you staying, Greta?" she inquired.

"I found a hotel nearby."

"That just *won't* do. You get your things after we finish here and come home with me. We have *plenty* of room, and it will get very lonely in that big house with just the servants and me when Fredric and Marti leave."

Greta didn't argue. When the auditions were over that day, both of the women had parts in *Claudine von Villa Bella.* Although she did not have the lead role, Greta was content to be a *comprimario.* She was happy enough being with her best friend again.

That evening the two had much to discuss. Fredric retired early and they reminisced into the early hours of the morning. They knew that when the holiday was over, they would have little time for rest.

Their vacation was over almost as quickly as it had begun. Fredric, Elsa and Martina bid a tearful goodbye to Kata and left for home. With the exception of a few servants, she was alone. She decided not to dwell on the emptiness she felt inside, seeing her family leave. Instead, she would put her energy into planning for the upcoming rehearsals. Besides, Greta would be returning in another week, and she had agreed to stay with her for a while. She would help to fill that void. Kata filled the next few days shopping, practicing her music and writing to her family. Although her letters were brief, she made sure she always expressed her love for them:

Dear Fredric and Marti,

Even though it has just been a couple of days, how my heart aches to see you both. It is so hard to be separated like this. While Greta will be good company, it will not be the same without you both here.

In just two more days, I go to work. I have been practicing my role daily. The servants have had to put up with my incessant singing, day and night, I'm afraid.

I do hope you will be able to get away for a few days next month and visit. I miss you all terribly.

Your loving wife and mother.

* * *

With six weeks of rehearsals completed, and the production going very well, Hans did not wish to wear his cast out before the performance began, so he gave everyone a two-week break at the middle of October. Kata decided to go home to be with her family. She took the train to Berlin, caught a taxicab and then drove up their long driveway, eager to see Fredric and Martina.

"Mama! Mama! You're home!" Martina, now a spunky nine-year-old, rushed to the door to meet her, giving her an enthusiastic hug.

"Yes, *Meine Liebe,"* cooed Katharina as she scooped her daughter into her arms. She pushed Martina's long golden curly locks out of her face, and kissed her on her forehead.

"I wanted to surprise you all. I had to come home as soon as my show was finished. I have missed you so much," she continued.

"I missed you very much, too, Mama."

"I have something for you, *Schatzi."*

"A present?"

"Of course, I *always* bring you a surprise, don't I?"

True to form, she pulled a small box out of her reticule, beautifully wrapped in pink paper with a silver bow around it. Martina squealed with delight as her mother set her down to devour the package. Her eyes twinkled brightly and when she smiled, dimples like her father's creased her cheeks.

When she opened the little box, she did not see the usual souvenir she was accustomed to receiving. Instead, she discovered a beautiful heart-shaped gold locket inside, etched with diamond chips that formed her initials, *M.A.* Inside the locket, she found a wedding photo of her parents.

"Oh Mama, it's beautiful!" she exclaimed.

"I thought it would make you happy and that it would be a good way to share with you the love that your father and I feel for one another, and for you."

"I have to go show it to Elsa," said Martina. She broke free from her mother's arms and ran off.

When Fredric came home that evening, he greeted Kata with a loving kiss.

"I missed you both so much," she said. "I only wish there was some way I could keep up my demanding schedule and have my family with me."

"I've missed you too, *Liebe.*" Fredric caressed her in his arms and kissed her softly on the lips.

"Perhaps we can all spend the summer together. I'll try to come for a few weeks when Martina visits you."

Kata planned to spend most of her time with her daughter while Fredric was at work, and then share her evenings with him. She, Martina and Elsa took some time to go shopping to buy new clothes. They had great fun shopping, talking, walking through the park and visiting the zoo.

"I can see that you are doing a marvelous job with Martina. She seems so happy, even though I have had to be away from her," Kata said as she and Elsa drank tea together one afternoon while Martina napped.

"She's quite a precocious young lady. She does miss you, and gets very excited when she receives your letters. She has a lot of faith as well, and prays for you every night."

Surprisingly, Kata didn't get alarmed over this. In fact, she was actually glad to hear that. Her attitude was changing. She was grateful that Martina had relied on some kind of faith to help her during their separation.

Perhaps I should consider this concept of "faith" and "prayer" a bit more seriously, Kata thought. There were so many times when she had been alone that she yearned for something to fill that void. *Could that "something" be Jesus?*

* * *

The night before she had to return to Austria, Fredric told Kata they needed to discuss something of importance.

"It has been good to have you home, *Liebe,"* he said, holding her close.

"I've enjoyed this time with you as well, *Schatzi*, and I do hate to leave so soon. Hans has another major role for me in his next opera."

"I've been giving quite a bit of thought to our situation, Kata." Fredric took her hand, and led her to the parlor and motioned for her to sit down next to him.

"Since we have been apart, I have had great deal of time to think. I can't help but wonder if we made the right decision about things," he continued.

"What do you mean?" Kata couldn't miss his troubled expression.

"Well, Elsa does a fine job with Marti, and the staff in general is doing well, but it is still not the same as having you here to oversee things."

"I come home as often as possible, Fredric, and when I'm here I spend time with the staff going over any problems or concerns they might have."

"Yes, I know you do. I'm still concerned, though."

"About what, then?"

"Well, when you were home, even when you were working, you were home every evening, so you kept the household intact. I know the staff does a wonderful job, don't misunderstand, but in your absence, they seem to lack the leadership and organization you give to them."

"So what are you suggesting?"

Fredric's countenance softened slightly. "I know you are in your element, Kata, and I am not going to force you to give up your career. I just think we need at least to consider hiring a housekeeper, if you choose to keep up this lifestyle."

A housekeeper. Why hadn't she thought of that? Of course. Maybe that would be the perfect solution to their problem.

"All right, that might be a good idea. I don't want to give up what I have worked so hard for right now. I'm finally at the pinnacle of my career. It would crush me to quit at this point."

"I understand, Kata, and, well, actually, I've already put an advertisement in newspapers here in Berlin and in surrounding cities. I'm glad that you are at least open-minded about the idea."

"Well, it *might* solve the problem. We can certainly give it a try," Kata said. Yet something still needled her about this decision. Was she compromising her family for her career? Would hiring a housekeeper be a threatening force? No, absolutely not. After all, many well-to-do families hired housekeepers. Besides, Fredric brought up the idea. He understood how important the opera was to her. Yes. It was the right thing to do. After all, she wasn't giving up her position as wife and mother. She was merely getting assistance—just as Fredric had an assistant in his work.

"I just have one request, though, Fredric."

"What is that?"

"I want to be consulted before you make a final decision in hiring a housekeeper."

"Of course, dear. I have no problem with that."

CHAPTER 16

Changes in Administration

"AHA! THIS IS WHAT I HAVE been looking for," the young woman cried. She read the newspaper advertisement again.

Experienced housekeeper needed for prominent family in Berlin. Must have experience and reliable references. One day off per week, two weeks off per year. Please contact Fredric Albers.

An address was included.

Fredric Albers, she mused. He's quite well off. No, he's more than just well off. Why, he's a multimillionaire! He owns all of those factories. And, isn't his wife out of the country? Of course. She's the famous Katharina Ernst Albers. She doesn't deserve that man. He deserves someone who . . . can be there to meet his needs. Yes, I'll answer this one. I'm exactly what he—they need.

Griselda cast a smug grin, took out a pen and sat down immediately to write a letter to *Herr* Albers. She was the only child of a middle class farmer in Bavaria. Her father spoiled her, giving in to her every wish. Her mother, on the other hand, tried to discipline her and give her some boundaries, but she was a frail and sickly woman. She was never strong enough to resist Griselda's stubborn will and temper tantrums. It was easier to give in. Consequently, Griselda ruled the household from a very young age. She knew how to get her way. She treated everyone around her as if they were inferior to her, and she fantasized about being a great lady some day and having immense wealth.

Her mother passed away when she was twenty, and she took advantage of her father's grief. She was all he had left, and he did all he could to make her happy. Feigning depression over the loss of her mother, she convinced him that she was inconsolable and manipulated him into indulging her every whim.

She insisted that he buy her the latest and best of fashions. It took every bit of money he had, and eventually ruined him. He died a pauper and left her with the farm, except he had mortgaged it for all it was worth to pay for her expensive lifestyle. When she realized he left her penniless, instead of mourning her father's death, she was angry with him for not providing for her. She knew she had to find a way to move up in society. She was not satisfied with marrying any one from the middle class. No, she was determined to marry someone with money.

At last, she found her opportunity. Once she heard back from *Herr* Albers, it was just a matter of insuring she had the proper credentials, and letting her charm work its course. *Let me see . . . how am I to get those papers? Ah, yes . . . Uncle Rudolf. He owns a lucrative business. He'll help. After all, doesn't he want this rattrap of a farm? Better to give it to him than to try to take care of it by myself. Besides, he doesn't need to know that it's about to go back to the creditors. It's a worthless old farm. I'll let him think he's getting a bargain in exchange for printing up a set of believable documents and references for me. He's always been an easy touch. Considering he gets that rascal of a son of his out of scrapes all the time. Yes. He can do this for me.*

She convinced her Uncle to pay a little extra for the farm. In addition, she collected enough money from him to pay for travel expenses and an attractive new outfit for her interview with *Herr* Albers. Her attire had to be respectable, yet alluring. She had to be sure he hired her on the spot.

* * *

Just a few days before Christmas, Fredric, Martina and Elsa traveled to Vienna to spend the holidays with Kata. The opening night of *Claudine von Villa Bella* was still a few months away, but the cast were given a month off as after New Year's, rehearsals would become even more intense. Fredric had a nine-foot Christmas tree delivered, and he had the servants set it up in the family den. Elsa, Marti and Kata all pitched in to decorate it. Greta returned to Berlin to visit with family and friends for the holidays.

Marti decided to make one more plea to her parents to go to church. "Mama, Papa, I have only one Christmas wish this year."

"What's that, Marti?" Kata asked.

"Please take me to a Christmas Eve service."

"Well, perhaps we could go once."

"Oh that would be *wonderful!* Papa will you come too?"

"I don't know about that, *Mausi.* Maybe you, Elsa and your mother should go," said Fredric.

"Please? Just this once? We're going to be apart for so long. This would be such a splendid present for me."

Kata chimed in. "Fredric, let's take her. She has a point. Besides, a Christmas Eve service might be a great way to celebrate the holiday this year."

Fredric shrugged his shoulders in resignation. "Oh, all right. If it means that much to you *Mausi.* But only this once. Don't get any ideas that we will make this a habit."

"Thank you! Thank you both so much!" She hugged them both and ran to tell Elsa.

The church they chose was the biggest that Marti had ever seen. It had a very large steeple and numerous stained glass windows lined each side of the sanctuary. The altar was adorned with candles, Christmas greenery and flowers, and a large Nativity was set up in the center back of the altar. They found a pew about half way from the front. The organist played many of the Christmas carols that Kata remembered as a child. A feeling of warmth passed over her as she listened to them. The service was not a disappointment to any of them.

Elsa and Martina were both happy that they had come and loved the way the minister told the Christmas story. He took it right from the book of Luke and just as Elsa had done so many Christmases before this, he made it sound so real. Fredric appreciated that the minister kept his message brief. Kata listened closely to his version of the Christmas story. Perhaps there was some truth to it after all.

On their last evening together, once Elsa had taken Martina to get her ready for bed, Fredric and Kata spent a little time sitting on their divan together in the parlor, just holding each other.

"This vacation has sped by so quickly. I cannot believe that you all have to leave in the morning. I will miss you so."

"And we miss you, *Liebling."* Perhaps after this production, you might reconsider and come back to Germany," Fredric said as he held Kata in his arms.

"I will definitely give that serious consideration. I assume it will all depend on what opportunities lay ahead for me here. However, I will definitely look for something closer to home, if possible." She kissed him tenderly. "I don't like neglecting my family like this, and yet this opera has opened the door to my becoming an international star of the stage." Her eyes sparkled as she mused the possibility."

Fredric kissed the top of Kata's head. "I know how important your career is to you, and will try to be patient. After all, your happiness is very important to me, *Liebe."*

Kata caressed Fredric's cheek. "I do appreciate that. You have been more than considerate. I know most husbands would have never agreed to the sacrifices you have made for me. I am so lucky to have such an understanding husband."

"I will do my best to always be understanding, my dear, dear Kata, but I have to admit, I miss holding you in my arms and having you close to me every night." He drew her close and began to kiss her passionately. She returned his ardor. He pulled her up to her feet and led her upstairs to their bedroom.

The next morning, Kata accompanied her family to the train station. "This is so hard, Fredric. I love what I am doing, but I miss you both so."

"And we will miss you as well."

She knelt down and hugged Marti. "And you, *Mausi,* take good care of your Papa. Try to be brave for all of us."

Marti's eyes filled with tears as she kissed her mother goodbye. "Come home soon, please, Mama. I don't like you being gone so much."

"I will, *Shatzi,* I will." She hugged her daughter tightly and kissed the top of her head.

They kissed each other one more time, and then Fredric, Martina and Elsa departed. Kata's heart sunk as the train pulled out of the station. A deep sense of foreboding crept into her thoughts, yet she passed it off as the sadness of seeing her family leaving.

* * *

A few days after they returned home, a number of applicants' letters began flowing in for the position of housekeeper. One particular letter especially caught his attention. He looked over the letter from a *Fraulein* Oblander. Her credentials impressed him. She had also included a photograph of herself. The beauty of this woman caught him off guard. Her eyes drew him in, and her smile captivated him. He couldn't seem to put it down. Was he attracted to this incredible creature? No. It was impossible. Of course not. True, he did admire a beautiful face—most men would. He knew that there was no other woman for him but his beautiful *prima donna.* Yet, her qualifications were undeniably impeccable. There certainly would be no harm in an interview. With that, he wrote a brief note to the young lady, encouraging her to apply for the position.

* * *

"How do you do, *Herr* Albers? I am *Fraulein* Oblander and am here in response to your letter," Griselda said when the maid showed her into Fredric's parlor to meet him.

"A pleasure to meet you, *Fraulein,*" he said.

Griselda noticed that he was studying her very thoroughly. His expression made it quite clear to her that he liked what he saw. She had fiery red hair and big blue eyes. Her complexion and figure were flawless, complemented by a fitted green velvet suit, with a V-neck, allowing her creamy skin to be exposed just enough, without showing cleavage. Her lips formed an enticing smile as she took off a glove to allow him to take her hand.

"Why, thank you, sir. I appreciate you seeing me so soon after receiving my letter."

"Well, tell me about yourself," Fredric said, briefly looking over her papers again.

She wasted no time in convincing him that she was extremely capable of taking care of a household, feeding him a series of rehearsed details, which bolstered her experience. She beguiled him with her manners.

"My mother died when I was quite young, and my father sent me to householder school, where I learned to take over mother's duties quite well."

She produced documents her uncle had forged showing that she graduated from a prestigious finishing school.

"He had a large farm, and I managed the household staff for him."

"So you have a great deal of experience in managing a staff, then?"

"Why yes. Unfortunately, a few years later, my father became gravely ill." She sniffled and wiped away a tear with her handkerchief.

"Please, have a seat." Fredric showed her to a nearby chair to allow her the opportunity to compose herself.

"I nursed him faithfully for the next several months, and then he . . . he joined my mother." She conjured up a few tears to make her grief over the loss of her parents credible.

"I am so sorry for your loss."

"Well, I knew that I would need to continue to support myself as it took almost all of my father's estate to pay for his medical expenses, and I had to mortgage the farm."

Fredric listened as she continued her story.

"I worked for a couple in our town for the next two years. Here are my references from them." She handed him the false documents.

"But they moved to Switzerland. I had no desire to leave

Germany, so I needed to find employment elsewhere. Then I saw your advertisement in our local paper."

He read the references from "the couple" and was very impressed. The document stated that Griselda *was quite well organized and managed their household with the utmost integrity and efficiency imaginable.*

"Well, it sounds as if you may be exactly what we are looking for; however, I do need to contact my wife and consult with her first, you understand," Fredric said.

This would not do. She had to have this job *now*. She couldn't take the chance that his wife might object. Griselda had to act quickly. She started to tremble. She held her handkerchief up to her lips as if to stifle a cry.

"Oh! I assumed from your letter that you might hire me right away. I . . . I had only enough money to travel here, and I do not have a place to stay this evening. I would be happy to work a day or two for you if you would give me the chance; then if you were not satisfied, you could send me on my way with enough wages to get me back home."

Fredric's eyes met hers. She could tell that he had fallen for her brilliant scheme. She read his expression and knew that it would impossible for him to refuse her plea. A woman left to fend for herself in the city, alone and penniless? What would that do to the reputation of an upstanding businessman like himself? She knew she had him where she wanted him.

"I certainly cannot let you out on the street on a cold wintery night like this with no place to go. Perhaps I could hire you temporarily—for at least a day or two anyway. After all, I need a housekeeper, and you need a place to stay. We can certainly give it a try, and if things don't work out, I will be happy to at least pay you for your time and for your fare back home."

Oh, it would work out all right. She was sure of that. Once she had her foot in the door, she knew she could win Fredric's complete approval, and then he could convince Kata that she was the best choice for a housekeeper. Men were easy prey.

* * *

Over the next few weeks, Griselda managed to secure her position in the Albers' household.

She proved that she was well organized, and she seemed to take charge quite easily. She went out of her way to impress her new employer. She attended to his every need when he returned home at night; she saw that he had his coffee, his pipe and his newspaper, and his cognac. She made sure his dinner was exactly as he liked it and that his clothes and shoes were laid out each morning.

"I have to say, you have proved yourself over and over. I am impressed with your abilities to run this household."

"Why thank you, *Herr* Albers. I find taking care of your household very fulfilling. You have an easy staff to work with."

"You have my complete confidence, *Fraulein.*"

Now that he had decided to make Griselda's employment permanent, Fredric realized that he had better write a letter to Kata, soon, explaining his decision to hire Griselda without consulting her first.

. . . The poor young lady was virtually homeless. Besides, she had such impeccable references and she is quite capable of running the house in your absence. I know you will understand and I think you will be very satisfied with her, Schatzi.

Love, Fredric.

When Kata received the letter, she was disturbed. While she trusted his judgment, she had some reservations. She couldn't explain her feelings. Intuitively, she felt she needed to make a trip home and form her own opinion.

Dear Fredric,

I trust you made your decision with the best of intentions, but I still would like to meet this young lady myself. I am planning to make a brief trip home between shows, next week. At that point, I hope that you will give me an opportunity to

make a determination of my own about this new housekeeper. Please remember, you did agree to consider my opinion, so should I determine she is not suitable, I hope you will respect my wishes to let her go.
Love, Kata

She asked Hans for two weeks off to take care of a family emergency. "That will be no problem," he said. We still have another nine weeks before opening night, and you know your part very well. Take the time you need."

She arrived home within a few days of writing her letter to Fredric. Griselda met her at the door.

"Good afternoon, *Frau* Albers. We have been expecting you," said Griselda in a pleasant tone. "Here let me help you with your things," she offered and took her coat and luggage.

"Thank you so much."

"I asked the cook to prepare you a light lunch to hold you over until dinner. I hope you don't mind." Griselda was very cordial and seemed to be doing all she could to make Kata comfortable after her long trip. For that, Kata was grateful.

"I appreciate it, but I think more than having lunch, I need to lie down for a bit, until Martina gets home from school. You can have the cook put my lunch up until later."

"Quite understandable, Ma'am. I will have the servants take your bags upstairs after you have a chance to rest."

"Thank you, *Fraulein.* If you will excuse me, I need to lie down for a bit."

Kata went to her room and stretched out on her bed. She was depleted after the long trip from Vienna. Despite her fatigue, her mind stayed focused on her meeting with *Fraulein* Oblander. She thought she was polite enough, but there was something unsettling about this woman. Something in her eyes. The way she looked at Kata. Almost like. . . No. She was just exhausted. That surely was clouding her first encounter with this new housekeeper. Yes, that had to be it. Nothing in the woman's mannerisms gave her any pause for alarm. She fell asleep.

She was awakened by a loud, "Mama!" Martina burst into her room and jumped on the bed beside her.

"Oh, Marti, don't do that. You almost gave me a heart attack, waking me up that way."

"I'm sorry—I just was so excited to hear you were home. I had to come right away to see you. I couldn't wait."

"And I'm glad to see you as well. She hugged her daughter tightly. So tell me what you have been doing since my last visit."

"Well, I've been going to school every day. I really love it, and I am making high marks," Martina said with an excited grin. "I have made so many new friends, and they love to hear stories about my "opera singer mama."

"Well, I am glad you are doing so well, *Liebe.* I am sure that Elsa has been a big help with your schoolwork in my absence. Then Kata inquired, "Speaking of Elsa, where is she?"

"She's in her room, I think. I haven't gone to see her yet—you were my first priority."

"Priority. What a big word for an eight-year old."

"Yes, I know. Elsa has been helping me with my vocabulary. She says it's good to know grownup words like that."

Kata kissed the top of Martina's head. "Yes, *Mausi,* it probably is."

After Martina filled her in with the rest of the latest news, the two went downstairs together and found Elsa. She had hoped Elsa or Martina might have mentioned how the new housekeeper was doing. But neither said a word. Nothing positive or negative. She thought it best just to observe things a bit before making any judgment about this new employee.

Griselda was rather cool and aloof towards the other servants in the house; however, Kata was aware that she was very organized and seemed to have everything under control. She decided that perhaps she was just her way of exercising authority and maintaining a sense of professionalism.

After the first few days of being home, though, it was very evident Griselda was used to having her way, even if it clashed with Kata's ideas. Kata had planned a small dinner party for some friends of theirs and was working on the menu with the head cook. Griselda walked in on the conversation:

"I think we should have *Roulade*, served with red cabbage, *spaetzle*, potato dumplings and *weinkraut*. Let's serve a good wine with it as well," Kata was telling her, when Griselda interrupted:

"Pardon me, *Frau* Albers, but I don't think you should serve both the *spaetzle* and the potato dumplings at the same meal. You are putting too much starch in the menu. And I would highly suggest Veal Cordon Bleu for entertaining rather that a common dish like *Roulade*—that is . . . if you want to make the right impression on your guests."

Kata stared at her. "Griselda, I appreciate your suggestions; however, may I remind you that when I am here, I make the decisions, and I have made up my mind as to what will be served."

"Very well, madam." She raised her chin in noticeable indignation and walked stiffly out of the room.

"That woman is just too bossy at times," muttered Berta, their cook, shaking her head in disgust.

"In what way?" asked Kata, very interested to hear what the cook had to say.

"Oh, nothing, Madam," said Berta, almost looking as if she had said too much already and trying to take back her words. "I guess I—I mean that we are not used to having anyone tell us what to do other than you and *Herr* Albers. It is just taking some getting used to, that's all."

Berta quickly changed the subject and asked, "Which wine would you like us to serve, a Riesling or a sparkling Rosé, perhaps?"

After completing her plans with the cook, Kata left the kitchen, somewhat disconcerted over her conversation with Griselda. She was not used to someone taking over her duties, and the idea that a mere servant would contradict her decisions made it even worse. She discussed the matter with Fredric that evening.

"Leibe, I think you are making too much over this." Fredric tried to put her mind at ease when they had retired for the night. "Remember, you have been gone for quite some time and Griselda has been used to taking care of such details. I am sure she didn't

mean anything by it." He patted her hand and then drew her close to him.

"Well, maybe. . . It's just that. . . there was an air of animosity in her voice I found very unsettling. Also, I think Berta is a little intimidated by her. And you know she is not *easily* intimidated."

"If it makes you feel any better, I will have a little talk with Griselda about it." He kissed her on the forehead, and then turned over and went to sleep.

Kata tried to put it out of her mind. Her encounter with Griselda embedded itself deep into her subconscious. She had a rather fitful sleep that night and woke up very tired the next morning. She slept in later than usual. When she got up, Fredric had already left. She dressed and went into the dining room for her morning tea and toast. Griselda walked in as she was eating. While she spoke politely to Kata, she had a distant look on her face.

"Forgive me *Frau* Albers for yesterday, but please understand that in your absence I have been running the household, so naturally, I assumed you would still want my advice in such matters."

Kata noticed slight contrition on Griselda's part.

"Well, thank you, Griselda. I am sure you meant well. On the other hand, I am not used to a housekeeper, and I have been doing quite well for myself for many years, so when I am home, I would appreciate it if you will defer to me," she said firmly.

She saw Griselda stiffen a bit and detected a flicker in her eyes. Nevertheless, she answered, "Yes, Madam. I will try to remember that in the future." Griselda turned around and left the room, not waiting for Kata to say anything else.

Kata was concerned that Griselda might be a troubling force to contend with and wasn't sure how she was going to handle it. Yet she seemed to be doing a very good job of managing the household and Fredric seemed satisfied with her work. Perhaps it was just a matter of adjusting.

For the next week, they didn't cross paths much at all. Griselda stayed out of her way as much as possible, and Kata was relieved. She assumed it was because Fredric had probably already talked to her. Her vacation was over before she knew it, and Kata had to return to

Vienna to finish rehearsals for the upcoming debut of *Claudine von Villa Bella* in April.

Martina held her tightly, and trying to be courageous, she fought back tears. "I'll be praying for you, Mama," she said. "I can hardly wait to be with you again this summer."

"Me too, *Liebling*. Time will go quickly, you'll see." She kissed her little girl goodbye and left.

Even though she was anxious to get back to the stage, there was something disquieting about leaving this time. She brushed it off, deciding that it was just the fact that she had to be separated again, and now she was leaving her entire household in the hands of a stranger.

After Kata had returned to Vienna, Griselda once again assumed control of the Albers' household, but she wasn't satisfied the way things were. She already decided before she arrived, that one day the Albers' household would be hers. She also knew that Katharina did not trust her, so she had to act quickly before Katharina talked Fredric into letting her go. She had to have a staff that answered only to her and one that would be instrumental in her plot. She decided to work on Fredric to increase her authority. Shortly after Katharina left, she asked to talk with Fredric.

"*Herr* Albers, I hope you have been satisfied with my work thus far," she said in a seductive tone. It did its magic.

"Very much so, *Fraulein* Oblander. He studied her in a way that might have made a young lady nervous, but it merely encouraged Griselda. "You are exactly what this house needs. I don't worry about anything here at home when I am gone."

"Then, I hope you won't mind . . . if I make a request of you."

"What is that?"

"I believe it would be beneficial to you and *Frau* Albers if I have complete authority over the household staff. You both have so much to take care of, and the home should be the least of your worries. I would hope that by now, my talents have been enough to convince you to trust me with . . . certain decisions that are in the best interest of everyone."

Fredric smiled knowingly. "You mean that you wish to take care of any necessary employing or firing of staff?"

"Why yes. I have learned what you prefer in your staff now, and I have been aware of some . . . inadequacies, so to speak. I believe that I can resolve them, if you leave it to me. I assure you, I will keep everything running with the utmost efficiency."

"Well, it certainly would relieve us of a tremendous burden, and you have indeed proved that you are responsible and skilled enough to manage the household."

"I assure you that I will run it as my own," Griselda said with confidence exuding from her tone. And that is just what she intended to do.

"There would be only one exception, if I agreed."

"What is that?"

"Elsa."

"Elsa?" This bothered Griselda somewhat. Elsa was already agitating her.

"You see, *Frau* Albers hired Elsa, and Martina is in her complete charge. With her mother gone so much, she has grown so close to Elsa. I would not want to interfere with their relationship in any way, and I know that Kata is satisfied that Elsa is good for Martina . . . though at times she can be rather overbearing with her religious ideas."

"Yes, I can see that." Griselda tried to act nonchalant about it, but deep down this woman irritated her. She talked about Jesus all of the time. She was always quoting the Bible, and that's the last thing Griselda wanted to hear. Sermons from the Bible. Was it that she chiseled away at her conscience? No. Elsa was just a nuisance. But if this were the only exception Fredric made, she would have to live with it. After all, she did not want the added burden of a child to look after, and Martina seemed quite taken with her. If Elsa and Martina kept her out of her way, she would have to concede to this, at least for now. . .

Griselda made it clear to every other member of the staff, however, that she was in control and if they did not adhere to her wishes completely, she could—and would fire them on the spot. After getting Fredric's complete approval, if any employee gave her the slightest opposition, she made their lives miserable with her demanding, temperamental behavior.

A few of the servants rebelled and quit. That, of course, was of no consequence to Griselda. She merely hired new ones who were loyal to her from the start. Actually, she had hoped that all of the domestic help who did not see her as completely in charge *would* quit. That would make her job easier. Once she had the staff under her complete control, it was time to work on Fredric. When he was around, she turned on all of her charm and looked for any opportunity she could to capture his interest. Madam Katharina was not around to keep her from luring him into her trap. And woe to anyone who stood in her way.

At first, the task proved very difficult. Fredric worked long hours, and when he was home, he usually spent his free time with his daughter, and writing letters to Kata. Afterwards, he slipped away to his room most evenings before Griselda had a chance to get his attention. She realized that she had to battle his devotion to his family. But that was not going to stop her. She knew how to use her wit and pour on the charm when it came to men. She would bide her time. She would find the opportunity to be alone with him.

CHAPTER 17

A Royal Visit

THE PRODUCTION OPENED ON SCHEDULE IN early April of 1913, and it was a great success. Kata outdid herself as Claudine. The reviews were good to her. In fact, her reputation as one of the most outstanding mezzo-sopranos in modern opera history reached the royal palace. In April, she heard that the Archduke Francis Ferdinand, and his wife, Sophie, the Princess of Hohenberg were going to attend one of her performances. Of course, she was very nervous about this piece of news.

"Meine Gütt! I can't believe they are coming to see me! I'm not sure what to do," Kata told Greta when she heard they were coming.

"They will *love* you. Just be yourself," she said.

Herr Gregor also encouraged her. "You are one of my finest prima donnas ever, Katharina. They will see you as the shining star that you are. Just relax."

"I appreciate your confidence in me. But the royal family—I don't ever recall having royalty attend one of my performances," she said.

"Everything will be just fine, you'll see," he said.

Indeed, it was fine. The royal couple *loved* her and insisted on meeting her after the show. Hans led them back to Kata's dressing room after the performance. The Archduke was tall and slightly overweight. He had deep blue eyes, an oval face and a thick mustache. Princess Sophie was not necessarily beautiful, but she had a sweet countenance about her. She had big brown eyes and wore her hair in a fashionable upsweep. Her lovely warm smile and friendly handshake put Kata at ease right away.

"It is a pleasure to make your acquaintance, my dear," said the Princess.

They were both very friendly and carried on a warm conversation, asking her about her family, her career and interests. She soon felt very comfortable with the royal pair.

"I am honored that you wanted to visit me, Your Majesties," Kata said.

"Oh, please, don't be so formal," Princess Sophie replied. "I do not like titles. You know, Francis only became Archduke because his father didn't want the position after his cousin, Prince Rudolf, had –well, you know, committed suicide."

"I am aware of that, Princess. And I am sorry for your family's loss. In any case, you both have been given that honor now."

Princess Sophie quickly changed the subject. "I understand you also come from a distinguished family. Yet you chose a career with the opera?"

"Yes, you are correct in your assumption, but titles mean nothing to me. I would not have been happy in any other station of life."

"I see. Well, you certainly have earned quite a reputation as a diva," said Sophie.

"We thoroughly enjoyed your performance, *Frau* Albers," added the Archduke.

"Thank you so much for your kind words. I was not sure how I would be received when I returned to the opera, or if many people would even remember me."

"You do yourself an injustice, my dear," replied the Archduke. "Your reputation never faded in the eyes of your public. I think you were highly missed all those years."

"I agree," added the Princess. "You are very popular among the royalty as well as the common class."

"Well, I did work hard to earn that reputation," Katharina admitted. "But there are times I feel that I don't really belong to either category. I've experienced quite a bit of prejudice from both at times. There are many from my parents' circle of friends who have never forgiven me for abandoning my status in life for such a profession as the opera."

"I think I understand how you feel, Katharina. You know, I've also experienced a great deal of discrimination as well. Franz's family never considered me to be a suitable choice for him."

"I don't understand why. You are also from nobility, isn't that true?"

"Yes. Despite that fact, however, for one to be accepted by his family, one has to be from the House of Hapsburg. Of course, my family was not part of any ruling dynasty. To make matters worse, I was the lady-in-waiting to the Archduchess Isabella."

"Everyone naturally assumed that Franz would marry her daughter, Marie. However, when they learned that he had fallen in love with me, I was released from my position and Franz was ordered by his uncle Franz Josef, to stop seeing me immediately."

Francis added to Sophie's statement. "Yes, but of course I refused. Nothing was going to stop me from marrying my dear sweet Sophie. I wouldn't have been happy with anyone else. Finally, after many a heated argument with my uncle, he reluctantly gave us permission to marry."

"Well, thank goodness he finally saw how important it was for you to marry the woman you loved."

"But at great cost to him, unfortunately," Sophie said.

"Yes, I never fully had his blessing. He made me sign an agreement that she could not share my rank or privileges, including riding with me in the royal carriage. That was extremely petty of him."

"Nor could any of our children be heirs to the throne." Sophie said.

"How cruel."

"To make matters worse, Franz refused to attend our wedding," Sophie said.

"You certainly paid quite a price for love, then."

"In the end, despite the harsh stipulations, it was worth it. We are very happy together." Sophie gave Francis a loving glance.

"Royalty can be very complicated. I guess that is one of the things I found distasteful about my heritage," Kata said.

"I resented being told who I had to marry. I'm a firm believer that marriage should be based on love, and love should be something from the heart, not some arrangement made by uninterested parties who are just looking for the proper breeding."

"Well, we certainly did get off the subject, my dear. I thought we would be discussing you and your experiences with the opera—not our heritages," said Sophie, "but it was wonderful to meet someone who understands how I feel."

"I agree. It's good to meet someone who knows the prejudices society imposes on people like you and me."

"Well, it has been a delight to meet you, Katharina, and to spend time with you," Sophie said. "But we really must take our leave, as much as I would love to spend hours talking with you."

"Yes, unfortunately we have other pressing obligations to attend to. Perhaps some time in the future, we could have you perform for us at the Palace?" the Archduke requested.

"It would be my pleasure," said Kata, curtseying politely.

The couple left and Kata reminisced over their visit. She had been aware of the instability in the Austrian Monarchy and that a great deal of tension existed between the Archduke and his uncle. However, she never had heard the whole story behind it. Politics never interested her. Of course, she never expected to have a conversation with the Archduke Ferdinand and Princess Sophie. They were indeed a very interesting and accepting couple.

*   *   *

CHAPTER 18

The Cat Strikes

IN THE LATE SPRING OF 1913, Elsa and Martina traveled to Vienna. After they boarded the train and settled in for the long trip, Martina exclaimed, "I can't believe we are going to get to spend a full six weeks with Mama, Elsa. We'll have such wonderful time!"

"Oh yes, *Engel*, I agree," said Elsa. "The change will do us all good."

Elsa was also looking forward to the trip, but for another reason. They needed to get away from the oppression that had permeated the house since Griselda's arrival. There was something unsettling about this woman. Elsa did not feel peaceful when she was around her. She was creating havoc in the Albers' home. So many of the Alberses' loyal servants had left because of her and their replacements were completely obedient to Griselda—either out of fear or because they sympathized with her.

She knew that Griselda did not like her and would do her best to get rid of her if she could. It was evident that she felt threatened by her Christian beliefs and influence on Martina.

Elsa looked out the window as the train sped out of the city and thought about the first time she experienced Griselda's opposition to the message of salvation and to Jesus.

It was the first week after Griselda had arrived. She found Elsa reading the Bible while she was enjoying some free time in the drawing room.

She shook her head and challenged Elsa. "How can you read that ridiculous book?"

"It is not ridiculous. It is God's inspired Word," Elsa said.

"What's inspiring about a book of fables?"

"God's Word is truth, not fable, Griselda."

"It's full of gibberish!"

"Have you ever read it?"

"No. Nor do I intend to."

Elsa shook her head. "Perhaps you would have a greater understanding of how much God loves us if you had. He loved us so much that He sent his only Son to die for us in order that we might have eternal life."

Griselda rebuffed her. "My uncle tried to force that same nonsense on my parents. My father would not allow it, thank goodness. Religion is a man-made idea designed to control unsuspecting victims and browbeat them into submission. So don't try to persuade me about that God nonsense."

"I have more important things to do with my time than wasting it on going to church or reading such foolishness. It seems that you could make better use of yours as well, Elsa," she continued.

Then Elsa recalled another volatile incident involving Martina. Griselda caught Elsa reading the Bible to Martina. She tried to interfere.

"Really, Martina, you shouldn't be spending so much time on those fairy tales. Elsa, you need to be reading her from more meaningful and educational works, instead of trying to warp her mind with that phony religion."

Martina immediately retorted. "Elsa can read whatever she likes to me, and the Bible is very meaningful!" She exclaimed, putting her hands on her sides.

"You had better watch your tongue with me young lady, or I will have to have a talk with your father," Griselda scolded in a very sharp tone.

Martina moved towards Elsa, and Elsa pulled her close. "Leave her alone, Griselda. She is not in your charge. She is my responsibility," she said in an even but firm tone.

"That can change, Elsa, so be careful," Griselda warned, pointing a threatening finger in her direction.

"I am fully aware of *Herr* Albers' views on religion, and I have no doubt it would take little to convince him that you are teaching his daughter heresy! Just watch your step!"

Elsa stared in Griselda's direction. She decided not to snap back. She remembered Matthew 5:44: *But I say to you, love your enemies, bless them that curse you, do good to them that hate you, and pray for them which spitefully use you, and persecute you.*

While she wasn't sure she could ever love this woman, she knew she had to pray for her and ask the Lord to fill her with his love for Griselda. She took Martina's hand and said, "Let's take a walk *Schatzi*." She led her past Griselda, who was looking as if she was fuming inside.

Yes, this was a break they both badly needed. Elsa just hoped that in their absence Griselda would not make any more drastic changes. Surely, there was a limit to what *Herr* Albers would allow.

When Martina and Elsa arrived at the villa, Kata rushed out to greet them. She hugged them both.

"It is so good to see you two!" she exclaimed. "Come in and let's get you settled."

* * *

Events were taking a different turn back in Berlin. Now the stage was set for Griselda to move ahead with her diabolical plot. Things were about to change in her favor. After Elsa and Martina had left, Griselda knew she had an open door to secure her future with Fredric for good. She had to work quickly. She knew her window of opportunity was a narrow one, and she had to strike while she had the advantage she needed.

Now that the household was in her full control and no one was there to stop her, she emphatically resolved to turn Fredric's head and to steal his heart. Like a lioness contemplating her prey, she began to stalk him, looking for the right time to make her move. Fredric, who had turned against God after the death of his son, had neither understanding nor knowledge of the Bible; consequently, he had no spiritual armor with which to fight. He did not realize that he was about to meet the woman of Proverbs 5:3-5—that immoral woman *whose lips drop as an honeycomb, and her mouth is smoother than oil: But her end is bitter as wormwood, sharp as a two-edged sword. Her feet go down to death; her steps take hold on hell.*

Since Kata had been away for so long, Griselda knew he was quite vulnerable. She knew men's weaknesses and how to use them for her advantages. She would take her plan in stages, carefully moving forward, like a cat tracking her quarry.

First, Griselda changed the way she dressed. There was no need to hide behind her domestic garb now. Elsa and Martina were not there to observe her and the servants were under her complete control.

She wore alluring dresses when Fredric was home. She always made sure she wore low-cut, tight-fitting bodices that emphasized her figure and colors that accentuated her beautiful red hair and piercing blue eyes. She quickly learned that Fredric had a weakness for redheads. That was a plus in her corner. Once she discovered he was being more attentive, complimenting her on how lovely she looked, she made her next move.

"I can't help but notice you seem quite lonely, eating by yourself each night, now that Martina and Katharina are both gone," she said one evening before dinner. "Would you like some company tonight?" Griselda said with a lilt in her voice.

At first he hesitated, then he studied her and said, "Why, that would be rather nice, *Fraulein* Oblander. I would enjoy your company."

His gaze made it very clear to her that he was seeing her in a completely different way than just a housekeeper. She followed his stare and noticed that he was searching her curves, her bodice, her full lips and large blue eyes. She offered him an alluring smile. From his expression, she knew that he enjoyed every detail he observed. She was making progress. It was going to be easier than she first expected.

"I would be quite happy to join you any evening you need someone to talk to—just until Martina returns, of course. Besides, I get quite lonely myself." She lowered her eyes slightly, and her mouth formed a pouty expression.

"I certainly don't see any harm in it. Actually, I have been starved for the company." He smiled. She would make sure he never felt alone while she was around. She planned to satisfy his "appetite" in more than one way. She would also see to it that he was always in an affable mood. She ordered a bottle of his favorite cognac at each meal, and kept his glass full.

By the third night, she accompanied him into the drawing room. She walked over to the fireplace, warmed her hands, and wrapped her arms together as if to warm herself.

"I hope you don't mind my joining you tonight. It is so much warmer in the drawing room than in my parlor."

"Of course," he said. "You are welcome to join me anytime." His guard was down. Not only did she have his confidence, but now she also had his friendship.

She subtly took on more of a wife's role than that of a housekeeper, discussing the each day's activities with him. She pretended to have a great interest in his work, and she catered to his every need. She increased his cognac a little each night in an attempt to get him to relax and drop his guard. She had to be sure that he would be vulnerable to her charms. It was working. Each night they stayed a little longer in the drawing room. One evening as she was getting ready to leave, Fredric stopped her.

"You don't have to go yet, do you, Griselda?" He evidently had consumed a little more cognac than usual. He talked a bit slower, he seemed more relaxed, and he took her arm. She didn't resist.

"Why no, Fredric, I'll stay as long as you like," she said.

"Good." He reached up and brushed a curl away from her face. She smiled and looked into his eyes.

"Thank you, Fredric." He didn't correct her use of his first name.

"You know that Katharina's absence has been difficult for me," he said, appearing to be somewhat woozy from the liquor.

"I-I don't mean to sound forward, but you have been a great friend to me lately, taking very good care of my home and keeping me company after your long hours of work. I do appreciate that."

He gave a slight gesture as if he wanted to say more; then he hesitated.

This is the moment I've been waiting for, she thought. She moved closer to him, looked into his eyes and parted her lips seductively.

"I know you have been lonely, Fredric." She took his hand and leaned in closer towards him, beckoning him with her entire body.

Tonight he was taking the bait. He didn't back away. She saw desire and eagerness in him. She felt his eyes searching her curvaceous figure. She looked up at him with an inviting look. He pulled her closer and entered her trap; but she was not done with her "cat and mouse" game yet. She pulled away to "tease" him just a little longer. She sensed his frustration and savored the power she had over him.

"Fredric, something has been bothering me and I've wanted to talk to you about it for some time. Can I be candid with you?"

"Yes, Griselda, you have my attention," he responded huskily. "What is it?"

She turned away, hiding her cunning smile from him. Then she swirled around again so he could see her trembling lips and tear-filled eyes.

"It has been hard on me to watch you come home to this empty house night after night. I just can't believe that your wife could be so—so. . . Oh, I am sorry. I have overstepped my boundaries."

He put his arms around her and drew her to him. She didn't resist.

"No, no, it's all right. I know you don't mean to think negatively of Kata. She is just trying to make a name for herself. I understand that."

Griselda feigned anger. She wrenched herself from him, knowing that since he had felt the warmth of her body, and her curvaceous form, he was eager to play his part in her plan.

"Make a name for herself when she has *your* name? When you have given her a luxurious home and everything that she could possibly want? I can't understand a woman who would neglect such a wonderful man like you. That's the last thing I would do if I was fortunate enough to have such a kind, loving, handsome husband who adored me so much—something I would give *anything* to have." She stopped, leaned against him, put her head on his shoulder, and began to sob.

"I . . . I didn't know you felt this way, Griselda."

He pulled her head up gently and ran his hand along her cheek to dry her tears. He looked at her amorously and put his arms around her waist, holding her close once again. At that instant, she reached up, slipped her arms around his neck and kissed him passionately—then suddenly pulled away in feigned shock.

"Oh! I am so sorry, Fredric. I—I don't know what happened. I . . . I—" She stopped in mid-sentence and whirled around to leave. He caught her arm and pressed his body against hers even tighter. His lips covered her mouth. She felt his heat and passion. Her body was a magnet to his. His heart was pounding against her chest.

By the intensity of his caresses, she knew that she had vanquished him. He looked up for a moment. "You are right, Griselda. I am lonely and you are so . . . exciting!" Secure in his embrace she reached up to her head with one hand and let her hair down until it flowed about her shoulders. He ran his fingers through it and lingered, gazing at her beauty. Then he picked her up in his arms and carried her upstairs. Fredric had succumbed to her sinful scheme.

CHAPTER 19

Regrets

THE TIME WAS SPEEDING BY VERY quickly for Elsa, Kata and Martina. During Kata's days off, she took Elsa and Martina all around Vienna to see the sights. They were having a great time together.

However, Kata grew more concerned as the weeks passed. She hadn't received a letter from Fredric since Elsa and Martina had arrived. He told her that he planned to come to visit her. To her chagrin, she had no idea when that might be. Each time she tried to call home, Griselda answered and she made excuses as to why he couldn't come to the phone. She tried his office. Each time she called there, he was at one of the other factories. She soon realized it was futile to reach him at work. She called home once again.

"I'm so sorry you keep missing him, *Frau* Albers," Griselda said cordially. "He has been working very long hours. Why most evenings I don't even see him."

"Very well then. Please ask him to call me as soon as he gets this message."

"Of course. I will see that he returns your call the next time I see him. He has just been so busy, that I rarely see him."

She hung up and a diabolical expression washed over her face, complimented by an evil barb. *It's quite true, my dear Katharina. He is working long hours into the night—with me. He will always be too busy to take your calls,* Griselda mused slyly. *And, it's just a matter of time before he will forget about you altogether, if I have anything to say about it.*

"Oh, Elsa, I am so worried that Fredric is working himself to death. I haven't heard a word from him in over a month. I am not sure what I should do. I am about to start a new production, so I can't possibly leave," she said.

"That does seem strange, *Frau* Albers. I don't recall him putting in long hours when we were home, but then he loved spending his evenings with Martina. Perhaps he is trying to work ahead so he can take off more time to visit and to spend more time with you," she said.

"Yes, that's probably it I'm sure you are right, Elsa." Kata's face brightened a little. "I'll try to be patient a little longer. I'll write him another letter and encourage him to come as soon as possible."

She went back to her den, pulled out a pen and paper from her roll-top desk and began to write:

Dearest Fredric.

It has been several weeks since I have heard from you. I have called several times, and Griselda tells me that you are either still at work or have gone to bed. I am concerned that you're not taking care of yourself. I hope that you are all right and are just working too hard in order to make time for a vacation. I am concerned about you, Liebe.

Please, take some time off and come stay with me for a week or two. You have sufficient trained staff to run your business for a little while, and heaven knows that Griselda is capable enough to run the household. Please write to me very soon and let me know your plans. I love you and miss you so.

Your loving wife.

Kata

She mailed the letter, knowing that he probably wouldn't get it for about a week, and then it would take at least another week before she would hear anything. She decided to try to get her mind off her worries and accept Elsa's plausible explanation of the situation.

* * *

Griselda insisted on moving into Fredric's bedroom after the first week of their affair.

Fredric hesitated. "*Liebe,* this could get back to Kata if one of the servants decides to write to her."

"You worry too much, Fredric. They are loyal to me. Besides, it would be much more obvious if I were traipsing back and forth from your room to mine, don't you think?"

She didn't give him a chance to answer. She wrapped her arms around him, kissed him fervently and dispelled his fears.

"You're right, of course," he admitted, kissing her again and running his hands through her hair. Passion and her lovemaking skills had so consumed him, that he found it hard to refuse her anything. It had bothered him at first, but he had sunk so low in his sin that his conscience was seared and he was oblivious to it. He made excuses for his behavior. *After all,* he thought, *most men of my social standing are keeping mistresses today.* Besides, in his mind, Griselda filled a need that Kata had failed to meet. It was her fault that he had given in to this fiery mistress.

Kata's latest letter arrived the following week. Fredric was home when it came, and was very disturbed when he read it. He was puzzled about Kata's sudden turnabout. Perhaps she was having regrets for neglecting him. This only confused his feelings towards Kata. He had to find out where he stood, beyond any doubt. He brought it up to Griselda that evening as they were lying in bed together.

"I think I need to take a couple of weeks and go to Austria. Kata has asked me to come for a short visit. I don't want to give her any reason to suspect things are not right between us, you understand."

Griselda gave him a surprised look.

"*No* Fredric! Please don't leave me *now!* We are just getting to know each other so well," she pleaded. She rolled over, pressed her body into his and put her arms around him, making sure he felt her passion. She brushed her lips over his ear and then whispered in a seductive tone, "Don't go yet. Give us a few more weeks. Wait until Elsa and Martina return and let's enjoy our time alone while we have it."

She outlined his face with her finger. "You know she will get so involved with her work that she will forget all about you again. Look how long it took for her to write this letter, *Liebling,*" she said, caressing his chest. Her words were like dripping honey to him. She pulled him closer and kissed him with such fervor that he forgot his brief change of heart. She was a goddess to him—his *Venus*. He melted into her embrace and fell prey to her manipulation.

"Perhaps it can wait a little longer." Fredric placed the letter on the table, and the two became enraptured in their passion.

Since he had decided not to go to Austria, he had to answer her letter. He knew he had to come up with a good excuse. One sin had led to another, he had not only had committed adultery; but now he was about to deceive Kata as to why he had not come to Vienna. A few days later, he sat down and answered her letter:

Dear Kata,

Please forgive me for not writing or calling lately. I have been so busy with the factories. My assistant recently resigned, causing me to have to work long hours. I have been very exhausted and have had little time to do anything but come home and sleep. Thank goodness for Griselda. She has held our household affairs together so well. We have nothing to worry about with her in charge.

I have more bad news. I am afraid my plans to come to Vienna will have to be postponed until I can find someone as competent as Deiter was and train him.

Please be patient with me. I'll come to Vienna as soon as possible. Give my regrets to Martina. Tell her I love her and miss her as well.

Love, Fredric.

For an instant, he felt a twinge of remorse as he read his letter, but quickly dismissed it when Griselda sauntered in, sat beside him, and put her arms around his neck. He let her read the letter before he sealed it, and she was satisfied that she had Fredric in her power. She kissed him demandingly. He let himself surrender to her. She quickly erased his regrets.

* * *

While Elsa and Martina were still with Kata, Greta came to visit again. She had returned to Berlin after the close of *Claudine von Villa Bella.* She had had some news she wanted to share with her dearest and oldest friend.

Once she settled in, after Elsa had taken Martina to bed, Kata and Greta spent time catching up on news from Berlin and talking about Kata's new opera. Kata studied her friend's face. Her countenance glowed and her eyes had a sparkle that Elsa hadn't seen before. There was an excitement in the tone of her voice and she seemed a bit more animated than normal. After Elsa had taken Martina up to her room to get her ready for bed, she and Greta sat together in the parlor.

"Is there something you want to tell me?" she asked with a curious expression.

"Why would you say that?"

"How long have we been friends? You are very transparent, dear. So let me hear what you are *dying* to tell me."

"All right," Greta said in a placating tone. Her eyes were bright and her face was aglow. "I guess you will find out sooner or later, but I really wanted to be sure of this before I told you. You know that very dashing baritone in *Claudine. . . ?* The one who played the part of my lover, Rugantino?" Greta asked.

"Karl Schneider?"

"Yes," Greta nodded.

Kata recalled the handsome man who played the father of one of the characters in the opera. He was the only baritone in the opera, actually, and he was hard to miss. His Italian and German roots were physically evident. He had jet-black hair and a light olive complexion. His chin donned a handsome cleft and his jet-black flashing eyes often made the ladies swoon when he performed.

"I do remember him." Kata said with a grin. "He was perfect for the part of the dashing outlaw who fell in love with Lucinde."

"Only to admit later that he was the long lost brother of Claudine's lover, Carlos, a member of the Italian nobility," Greta finished with a blissful grin.

"I am assuming by the look on your face, that perhaps a romance has blossomed between the two of you?"

Greta blushed and smiled coyly. "Actually, it was not hard for us to be lovers in the opera. You see, we were. . . well, we have been seeing one another for the past several weeks. And…now, our relationship has taken a very serious turn."

"Oh my, Greta; are you sure this is not just another one of your *rendezvous?*"

"Oh no, *Liebe*, really. I have never felt this way about any man before—and he has been the perfect gentleman the whole time we have been seeing one another—courting."

"Courting. That is quite encouraging. I don't think I've heard you use that term when referring to your 'gentlemen' friends before."

"I—I guess you are right. Until now, I haven't considered anyone as seriously as I have Karl."

"Well, then, I am happy you have found someone. Didn't I tell you that you were still young enough to fall in love?" Kata asked in a motherly tone.

Greta nodded. "You did; although, I really didn't think it could happen. Oh Kata, he is the sweetest, kindest man I have ever known, and he seems to adore me." Greta clasped her hands together and spun around. "I think, for the first time in my life, I understand what it is to really be in love."

Kata just looked at her thirty-something friend and shook her head. *Falling in love. Well that is a novel idea for her. Love does strange things to a person. And Greta is acting so giddy. I've never seen her like this before. She must be in love.*

"You know I want nothing but the best for you. Tell me, what do you know about him? Until we worked together, we had never met him." Kata queried.

"That's true, but I know so much more about him now. I also understand why he didn't want anyone to know much about his background. He has mainly worked in Italian Operas until he performed in *Claudine von Villa Bella*. He saw this as a chance to expand his career. Also, he wanted to travel and break away from his family ties."

"The irony is that while Karl was playing his part, he, too, was living a double life. You see, like his character, Rugantino, he was also from a very wealthy family."

"Do tell me," said Kata, with a look of wonder on her face.

"His mother is from Spain and is a distant relative of Alfonso XIII. She's a second or third cousin, or something that. That makes him royalty, you know." She smiled proudly and continued.

"His father is a well-to-do businessman in Munich and owns several companies in Germany and Spain. Karl had been under great pressure from his father to leave the opera and become a partner in his business. He has always been wary of marriage because his family was fairly well known throughout all of Spain, so he always felt that the young ladies who pursued him were more interested in his wealth."

"Well, he does have quite an interesting past," Kata said.

"Yes, he does. When we started seeing one another, I had no idea of his background or family history. He doesn't throw his money around, and it wasn't until last week that he told me all of this," she said. "Oh Kata, is it possible that I have finally found 'my true love'?"

"Anything's possible, dear." Kata laughed again, quite entertained by Greta's definite infatuation with her new beau.

Greta's effervescence suddenly changed as she dropped her eyes and a shadow of sadness passed over her.

"What's so difficult about this whole matter, is that if we do marry, I will have to move away. That probably means we may never see each other again. I'm not sure how to handle that."

"Your happiness means more to me than anything else in the world. So, you handle it with no regrets," said Kata.

CHAPTER 20

A World Turned Upside Down

GRETA AND KARL'S RELATIONSHIP GREW SERIOUS very quickly. In fact, just weeks after they began to court, he asked her to marry him. She told him she would give him an answer at the end of the month.

"Oh Kata," Greta sighed one day as they were resting after rehearsals. "It's such a big step for me. I would never have thought I would be considering marriage—especially after so short of a courtship. Tell me how you felt after Fredric proposed to you. Were you this undecided?"

"Of course, Greta. Don't you remember how I demanded he leave the first time he asked me, and then I ran away for several months? As much as I felt close to Fredric, I wouldn't admit to myself I was in love with him."

Greta chuckled lightly. "Oh, that's right. I remember now. It seems like a lifetime ago. You were a muddle of emotions."

Kata tapped her hand gently. "You know, marriage *is* a big step. A woman has to be absolutely sure before making a lifetime commitment. Your feelings are perfectly normal. If you *didn't* feel nervous or have some misgivings, I probably would worry about you."

Just a few days later, Greta floated in the door waving a very noticeable two-karat diamond ring in Kata's direction.

"It's official! I accepted! "

"I am so happy for you," cried Kata. She hugged her friend tightly as she tried to fight back a flood of tears.

"We are getting married July 15."

"That's rather soon, isn't it?"

"Yes, but Verdi has offered Karl a major role in an Italian opera, in Milan at the end of the year. He has to be there no later than August 15, so if we are to have any time for a honeymoon, then we have to move quickly."

"We're going to have a quick ceremony here in Vienna, with just a few close friends, and I want you to be my matron of honor, if you will."

Kata's eyes widened and she put her hands up to her mouth. "Of course, I would be thrilled to be there for you!"

"*Wunderbar*!" exclaimed Greta. "You can help me with my plans then. We must get started right away—there's little time."

"You know I will help any way that I can."

Greta continued to ramble on about her plans as if she was in a world of her own.

"After the wedding here, we will be leaving right away for Munich. His family wants us to have another ceremony with them, and then of course, we must travel to Italy as Karl wants to get settled in before he starts working."

"Well that makes good sense," Kata said.

"We will spend a couple of weeks in Rome for our honeymoon." Greta whirled around and clasped her hands together. "Oh Kata, I'm so excited. It's hard to believe I'm really going to get married!"

The two worked together planning the wedding, arranging all of the details, and before they knew it, July 15 had crept up on them. The ceremony was simple, yet poignant. About seventy-five guests attended, including many of their friends from the Vienna Opera Company. Kata watched her friend sachet down the aisle in her white satin gown trimmed in lace and pearls. The gown had an empire waist adorned with lace and ribbon. The narrow skirt flowed to her ankles, and the sleeves bloused at the shoulders and tapered at the arms. Her train was long and graceful.

Kate felt as if she were watching her friend perform in her finest role in the operetta of her dreams. *She deserves a wonderful life with Karl. Many would consider her worldly, and she certainly can be very forward and meddlesome, but she has been the best friend anyone could want. I will miss her.* Kata thought. Her eyes moistened with happiness for her dearest and closest friend.

Greta and Kata spent their last moments together saying tearful goodbyes.

"I will miss you terribly, but more than anything, I want you to be happy. We have had our moments, and at times, I must admit, you have been exasperating, but you have always been like a sister to me. Before Fredric and I were married, you were my only family." Sentiment and sadness filled Kata's tone.

"And you were mine, Kata. I will never forget you no matter where I am in the world," sniffed Greta.

"All right, now enough of this," Kata said. "Write to me every chance you get." Tears streamed down their eyes as they hugged each other firmly, and parted company. Greta and her new husband left that evening for Munich.

* * *

During the last few days of their stay in Vienna, Martina was depressed. She realized that her time with her mother was going to be over soon. She had to return to Berlin in order to get ready for school.

Kata's heart also saddened. She had enjoyed a wonderful holiday with Martina and Elsa, but she was so disappointed that Fredric was unable to come to visit. However, she had received his letter and it was enough to convince her that things were just too hectic for him to get away. There was no point in trying to go home, either. He just wouldn't have any time for her, she reasoned. Besides, her current role was going to consume so much of her time that there would hardly be any left for him, even if he were able to come in the next couple of weeks. It was probably best to postpone their time together until the holidays.

Elsa and Martina planned to leave for Berlin the end of that same week. Their last day together was more like a funeral. Kata went with them to the train station, but she found this to be one of the hardest moments of her life.

"Please come home soon, Mama," said Martina, fighting back tears. "Papa and I miss you so much when we're apart."

"I will be home by Christmas, *Schatzi,* don't worry." She kissed her daughter goodbye and hugged Elsa. Kata's homesickness surfaced even before Elsa and Martina departed. She ached to return to Berlin, but she knew she had a few more weeks before she completed her next production. Yes, it would at least be until December before she could be with her family again.

She turned to Elsa and took her hand. "Thank you so much for being such a wonderful companion to Martina—and to me these past several weeks."

"I have enjoyed your company as well. It has been a wonderful break from—"

"From what?"

"Oh, nothing. It's just that we miss having you at home. Things are not the same without you there."

Martina and Elsa climbed aboard the train and found their seats. They waived through the window. Kata watched the train pull out and began to cry. A part of her heart went with them.

On her way home, she reflected on their visit. During this trip, Elsa had spoken to her on several occasions about her faith. Kata, although, still resisting total surrender, mulled over their discussions. For the first time since she had known Elsa, she paid closer attention to her ideas about salvation. She found herself more open to this Jesus. Was it because she was lonely? Perhaps the emptiness of her life in Austria added to her interest. On the other hand, she was much too busy for religion right now. Besides, would God accept her as she was? Didn't she need to straighten out her life before she could ask Him to forgive her sins? *Perhaps one day I will make a commitment to Jesus, but I'm just not quite ready,* she thought.

* * *

When Elsa and Martina arrived home, Elsa detected almost immediately things were different. The maid met them at the door and looked very somber. After they had unpacked and come down to the living room, Elsa discovered the source of the change. Griselda. They found her sitting on the sofa in the main drawing room, looking very regal and in command. Elsa could see right away she exuded more authority; more so than when they left. She also was dressed more elegantly. Her dress was not that of a typical housekeeper, but rather one that the lady of the house would wear. She donned an emerald green crimson silk and taffeta ensemble, with an empire waist and a low V-neck bodice.

She had on a pair of diamond drop earrings and a matching necklace. Elsa knew that Griselda couldn't possibly have purchased her outfit on her salary. Something had happened while they were away. She didn't dare to speculate, but she feared the worst.

"Martina, I would like you to go to your room while I talk with Elsa for a few moments," Griselda said sternly.

At first, Martina balked, but Elsa told her to go ahead. She deduced that she and Griselda might have a confrontation, and she did not want Martina to be present.

"I trust you had a good visit with Katharina," Griselda said, in a somewhat pleasant voice.

The fact that she used *Frau* Albers' first name alarmed Elsa. She just nodded and said, "Yes, it was quite a pleasant trip."

"Well, that's good," Griselda said coolly. She stood up and sauntered close to Elsa. "Now there are few things we need to discuss." She paused, raised her chin in a haughty manner and continued. "Things are different around here, and if you know what's good for you *and* for Martina, you will accept the changes without question."

It was one thing for Griselda to threaten her, but to include Martina in her warning was another. She tried to contain herself at first. "Let's leave Martina out of this, Griselda. What exactly *have* you been up to since we have been away?" Elsa demanded calmly, but firmly.

"First of all, you need to understand that *I* am in charge here and have the full support of Fredric to do what I need to do to run his household *and* to take care of his daughter!" She glared at Elsa as if she were challenging her to protest.

"Also, before you say a word, let me make it very clear, there's *nothing* you can do to change that." Griselda's face took on an evil twist, and her eyes glared in victory as she raised an eyebrow. Elsa instinctively knew she should not challenge her. Her whole demeanor alarmed Elsa. Griselda continued, still not giving Elsa a chance to respond.

"Fredric and I are in love," Griselda announced proudly. "He has agreed to divorce Kata and marry me." Her lips broke into a wicked smile. She appeared to be enjoying the shocked look on Elsa's face. Elsa shuddered as if she were facing Jezebel herself. "He loves *Frau* Albers and would *never* do anything to hurt her!" Elsa exclaimed in disbelief.

"That's where you are wrong. *Katharina* has hurt *Fredric*! For weeks now, Fredric has been despondent. He has often come home in such a state of depression. It breaks my heart to see him that way." Griselda feigned sympathy for him as she sniffed and dabbed a manufactured tear from her eye and continued her story: "He needed a woman to be . . . here for him. *She* neglected him. He was lonely, and so . . . he reached out to me, and. . . Well . . . I consoled him." Griselda shrugged and partially raised her arms in resignation. "My heart broke for this poor soul. *I* am the one who has seen him through this very difficult time, and naturally, one thing led to another . . . and we fell in love."

Elsa knew that this was a lie. What could this woman possibly know about love? Let alone a broken heart—if Fredric really was broken hearted, which she highly doubted. Yes, she may have seduced Fredric in a moment of weakness, but love? *Never!*

"You *harlot*!" shouted Elsa, losing her temper. "How *dare* you come into this house and tear this family apart? You may think you have gotten away with something, but someday you will have to answer to God for your actions!"

Griselda merely laughed coldheartedly. "You delude yourself if you believe that a *god* will make any difference here. I have to answer to no one but Fredric, and believe me; he's quite satisfied with *anything* I do."

"No! I don't believe you! I will have a talk with *Herr* Albers about this right away."

Griselda slowly circled around her like a tiger circling her prey. "I would think carefully about discussing this with Fredric. I could easily convince him to let you go as I've already done with so many others who carried their loyalty for Katharina too far. Fredric knows how you tell his daughter those ridiculous Bible stories and it wouldn't take much to convince him how damaging they might be to her later in life. I am warning you, watch your step, or you won't be here to care for Martina much longer. I'll see to that!" Griselda boasted vehemently.

Elsa made no attempt to move. She just studied Griselda in disbelief. She couldn't believe this *Jezebel* had torn her little family apart.

"But I am not without feeling, Elsa," continued Griselda. "I know that Martina loves you, and quite frankly, she still needs a nanny—especially to get her through this difficult time, so I am willing to *allow* you stay on—for the time being. Besides—believe me I really don't want to be bothered with a brat child."

Then, Griselda abruptly turned on her heel and faced Elsa, shaking a warning finger at her. "Let me be perfectly clear, though. If you give me *any* problems, I won't hesitate to see that little hooligan is sent off to some boarding school miles from here and you are sent packing back to wherever you came from."

How dare she call Martina such names! . . . If only Fredric could hear her now. He would think otherwise about this temptress. Elsa fumed inside, yet she knew that if Griselda had seduced Fredric, she would stop at nothing now to have her way. She couldn't take a chance of losing her job. Someone needed to protect Martina. How would her Marti and Katharina get through this? She knew that Griselda could care less about Martina and would stop at nothing to destroy her life.

"All right, Griselda, I'll stay out of your way, but I am asking you to leave Martina in my care."

"I'll agree to that for now, but I warn you, *don't* cross me! If you do *anything* that even makes me *suspect* your interference, I assure you, Elsa, you will be sent packing!" she said sharply.

She wanted to let Kata know what was going on, but she wasn't too sure it would do any good at this point. Her only hope now was that Fredric might be able to see her for who she really was and turn from his sin.

Elsa went to her room and prayed, "Dear Lord, please give me wisdom in this situation. Please protect Martina and Katharina from this woman, and help *Herr* Albers to open his eyes and see how he has been so deceived."

She continued praying fervently for some time, and with great effort to hide her consternation from Martina, she went into her room to help her get ready for bed.

For the next few weeks, Elsa managed to avoid Griselda most of the time. She worked hard to keep Martina from seeing what was happening.

Fredric spent at least a couple of hours each evening with his daughter, and, although Griselda was extremely jealous of their relationship, she appeared to go along with it. She reluctantly went out of her way to encourage Fredric to give as much time as he could to his daughter, and she was especially nice to Martina as well—at least when he was around. Otherwise, she didn't pay much attention at all to her. She would bide her time, then after they were married, she would work on getting him to agree to send Martina off to boarding school.

Fredric was civil to Elsa and left his daughter's care completely in her hands. She sensed Griselda was definitely gaining control over him. Griselda did not hide her affections for him in front of the staff, especially since she had browbeaten Elsa into staying out of her way.

Elsa was aware that Griselda was sharing Fredric's bedroom, as she was blatantly open about it. She was disgusted with their adulterous behavior, yet she was helpless to do anything except pray. She did that faithfully. She continually asked the Lord to shield Martina from what was going on, and she was pleased to see that Martina appeared oblivious to her father's and Griselda's relationship. Fredric must have warned Griselda not to let Martina know yet, but she knew that was temporary. Eventually the sin would be exposed and the whole family would be greatly affected by it. Griselda had her claws in Fredric and was determined that he would be hers alone very soon.

* * *

By August, Fredric started having misgivings about Kata coming home and finding out about his affair. He didn't want the confrontation in the household. Nevertheless, Griselda would not stop chiding him to confront Kata with the truth.

"You have to tell her about us. I am not going to live like this much longer. If you truly love me, you must take a stand. Will it be Katharina or me?"

"Be patient a little longer, *Liebe,*" he said. "We've been married too many years for me just to tell her in a letter or even on the telephone. I owe her that much."

"Very well, but you cannot keep putting this off. Make up your mind who you want to be with." She drew close to him, took his arms and put them around her waist, then rested her head on his shoulder. "If you really love me, you won't let this go on any longer. Either you tell her as soon as possible or I walk out of your life forever."

"That's not fair, Griselda. You know I love you . . . I'm just not sure if this is the right time to break such a thing to her."

"If you don't act before long, I'll have no choice but to leave," she pouted.

Griselda put her arms around his neck. "It's you I want, and I won't share you any longer. I have much more to offer you."

The ecstasy of the moment weakened his will as she kissed his neck and ran her fingers through his hair, then caressed his cheek. His desire for her outweighed his apprehensions, and he returned her passion with great ardor.

"All right, I'll go," he conceded. "I'll leave first thing next week." He left as soon as he could make arrangements at work.

* * *

Throughout the train ride to Vienna, Fredric was miserable. He was in turmoil. His mind and body waged war against each other. Griselda now had a firm hold on him. She was an addiction. He couldn't help himself. This fiery redhead held his soul captive. She knew how to play with his heart.

Yet occasionally, when he came to his senses, he knew he was wrong. This would break both Kata's and Martina's heart. But he couldn't stop himself. He was in too deep now. Even if he wanted to change his mind, his marriage would be over. Griselda threatened to tell Kata about their affair if Fredric didn't. Physically and emotionally, this woman had entrapped him in their adulterous affair; there was no turning back for him.

What had he become? No. He needed to look at the whole picture. It wasn't entirely his fault. After all, hadn't Kata abandoned the marriage in her zeal to pursue this career? Hadn't she been the one to shirk her responsibility to him? Yes. He was justified. He deserved more than Kata could give him. After all, Griselda had filled the void in his life. She had earned his love. Kata had thrown it away.

But confronting Kata was another thing. This news would crush her. How was he going to face her? He had no choice. Things had gone too far. He had to get this over with. His marriage was over either way.

* * *

"Oh Fredric, what a surprise!" Kata exclaimed. She hugged him and said, "I wasn't expecting you, since I was coming home in just a few weeks!"

Fredric stiffened. He didn't return her hug. His face was pale and he just stood in the foyer for a minute, then he spoke with hesitation in his voice, acting as if he didn't know if he wanted to come in or to run in the other direction.

"I'm—I can't stay long, but I had to come and see you in person," he said solemnly. She drew back. Something was not right. She tried to keep her composure. "Come in," she said, looking at him with great apprehension. She tried to read his thoughts.

"Let's talk in the living room." She beckoned him towards the large, opulently furnished room and he followed her, saying nothing until they sat down. He did not take off his coat and hat. His morose expression and somber demeanor alarmed Kata.

"Please tell me it's not Martina, *Liebe,"* she said.

"No, that's not it. She's just fine." His tone was brisk and distant.

She sat down and folded her hands in her lap, looking at him in nervous anticipation. He remained standing. There was no show of affection from him. He didn't even give her a kiss on the cheek.

"Then, what is it? You don't seem like yourself at all." She knew it had to be something very serious for him to come to Vienna, and not plan to stay.

"I—we—well, you know that we have been apart for a very long time, Kata. And yes, something has happened, but I'm not quite sure how to tell you."

A wave of trepidation enveloped her. Her heart pounded and she thought it was going to leap into her throat. She could almost imagine what he was going to say, yet she hoped she was wrong. "Just tell me, Fredric. Is—is there someone else?"

She did not want to say those words, but considering his behavior, that seemed an obvious conclusion. He just stood there, looking down. His silence spoke volumes. *That must be it. He hasn't called or written in weeks. It's another woman!* Why hadn't she read the signs before now? Had she been so caught up in her own world that she couldn't have seen this coming? Tears formed in her eyes and she looked at him for confirmation, one way or the other. Only seconds ticked away before he responded, yet it seemed like eons to her.

"Yes . . . there is." He released a long sigh.

She froze. Suddenly she felt queasy. Her whole body felt as if it were on fire. "Who is she?" Kata asked, trying to keep her composure.

"It's. . . Griselda." His response was flat and final.

"*Griselda?* Griselda, your *housekeeper?* You and *Griselda* have been carrying on in *our* home in my absence?"

Her mood went from shock to rage. It would have been less painful if he had thrust a dagger into her heart. She stormed up to him, and began beating his chest, and screaming loudly, "You – you *adulterer*! You *scoundrel*! How could you do this to me—and to your *daughter*?" she cried.

He grabbed her wrists to protect himself. "It's not all my fault, Kata. You haven't been home in weeks. What was I supposed to do, be a monk the rest of my life?" he assailed. "You are not married to *me*, you are married to your *career*! I need a *wife*! I want a woman who will be with me every night!"

She jerked herself from his grasp and glared at him angrily. How *dare* he even insinuate that this was *her* fault. She returned the blame.

"You agreed to my doing this, Fredric; in fact you even *encouraged* me to take this contract. You bought this villa, and never gave me the slightest hint that you were dissatisfied with our life the way it was! You *deceived* me!" she cried as she turned from him and hid her face in her hands. "How could you?" she railed.

He looked at her and for a brief moment, she hoped that he might soften and admit he was wrong, but instead she saw the anger and determination return to his eyes.

"It's over, Kata. I don't know what else to say to you. I am sorry, but it's *over*. You have your career and I have our daughter."

She backed away and glared at him incredulously. "You—*what?*" "You can't take Martina from me. I will *not* have her living in the same house with that—that *harlot*! I'm coming home for her at once!" she demanded.

He pressed his lips into a thin line and said firmly, "You don't have a choice in the matter. You know the law—the husband has the right of custody of his children. Besides, you have no time to fit her into your life. I'm sure you will be doing quite a bit of traveling, and that is not much of a life for a child. I can give her everything she needs as well as the stability of a home."

He paused, and then walked towards the door. "I will be filing for divorce as soon as I return home. I will allow her to visit you briefly in the next two weeks. I know our daughter will want to see you as soon as she finds out what has happened, and I will allow you to have an opportunity to discuss this new living arrangement with her as well. You can keep this villa, and I will provide a stipend for you, but you may *not* have Martina."

With that, he stormed out and left her in staring at the doorway in total shock.

It was bad enough to discover that she had lost Fredric, but to lose Martina was inconceivable. She couldn't begin to imagine life without her daughter. Nor did she want to. She knew that Fredric was right about the law, and no amount of money to hire a lawyer would change that. She slumped down on her couch and burst into a torrent of tears. She couldn't believe what had just happened. The emotions she experienced the night Max died stirred within her once again, only this was even worse.

In an instant, she had lost everything: her home, her husband, and her daughter. She was devastated. An icy feeling permeated her very being. Her heart had been ripped out and she felt hollow. She had no one. Even her best friend had moved away. How could she go on?

She relived the last several months repeatedly in her mind. She had to confront her part in all of this. How could she have been so blind not to see this coming? She had become so wrapped up in her career that she *had* neglected her family. Now she was paying the price. Her whole world had turned upside down. She could never forgive his adulterous affair, but she realized that Fredric was right about one thing: she had to take her part of the blame for letting it happen.

The night wore on very slowly as Kata lay on her couch in a nightmarish fog. Her body was a dead weight. She couldn't move. She had cried until she could cry no more. She was numb. This whole evening was surreal. It just couldn't be real. Would she wake up to find out she had just had a terrible nightmare? No, it had happened, all right. All feeling and emotion drained out of her.

Fredric returned to his hotel room. He, too, felt empty. He lay in bed and couldn't sleep. The truth caught up with him. He knew that he was caught in an inescapable web of sin and adultery. He thought about his confrontation with Kata and realized he had crossed a line and couldn't go back. In that moment, a wave of remorse washed over him. He had just sold his soul to the devil, and her name was Griselda.

Part II:
The Power Of Redemption

CHAPTER 21

New Beginnings and Adjustments

MARTINA WAS NO MORE RECEPTIVE TO the news than Kata had been. She refused to accept that her mother was never coming home. Fredric had tried to be as gentle as possible when he broke the news to her about the divorce. It didn't help. She was heartbroken. She cried and begged her father to change his mind.

"I know you don't understand, *Mausi,* but it really is for the best. Your mother and I—"

"No Papa," Martina interrupted. "I see more than you think. It's Griselda. She's the reason you and Mama are getting a divorce. I don't like her. She's mean and hateful! She doesn't treat anybody nice—especially my Elsa." She crossed her arms and lowered her head. Tears filled her eyes. "She'll never take the place of Mama—never!"

Martina protruded her lower lip and stomped her foot.

"You're just upset because of the divorce. You're being too harsh on Griselda. I don't expect you to accept her like you do your mama, and I promise you will have many opportunities to visit her. You can still spend some of your holidays and half of your summers with your mother, but you will live here with Griselda and me," he said. "You just need to get to know her better."

"I don't *want* to get to know her better. I hate her! And she doesn't like me either."

Martina remained closed. She refused to look at her father. He continued. "Our lives have taken different paths. Your mother has her life in Austria, and I have my life here—with you and Griselda. I'm sorry, Marti, but we can't go back to the way things were. It's too late for us. You must accept the fact that Griselda is your stepmother," he said firmly. He put his arm on Martina's shoulder and said in a gentler tone, "I hope in time you'll learn to accept her."

"I never will!" Martina pushed his hand away and left the room in a huff. She ran up to her room and fell on her bed. Tears were streaming down her red-hot cheeks. She would not accept this woman as her stepmother no matter what her father said. Even though she was a child, she was not blind. Since her father's return from Vienna, Griselda flaunted her relationship with Fredric, even in front of Martina.

She was angry. She was angry with her father for not seeing the person Griselda really was and for taking up with her. She was also angry with herself for not being able to stop Griselda from taking her Papa away from her Mama. She was even angry with God. Now the only person she had to turn to was her Elsa. Elsa was the only one who understood her heartache. She loved her parents, but they hadn't even considered her feelings in all of this.

Elsa heard Martina crying as she passed by her room, so she turned around and entered. She sat down on the bed next to Martina and pulled her into her arms. She kissed her forehead, and after giving her a few moments to calm down, she said in a soothing voice, "It's not your fault, Marti. Grownups fall into temptation and make mistakes just like children—and sometimes those mistakes are very serious. Without having the Lord to guide them, they can easily lose their way."

"They are both lost. They're not acting like grownups at all. It's all Griselda's fault. I hate her, and I will *never* care for her—no matter what Papa says!" A flurry of emotion burst out in the form of sobs and deep gasps as she leaned against Elsa for comfort.

Elsa held her tighter. "Hate is a very strong emotion, and as Christians we need to be very careful of allowing it to enter our hearts, even when someone has hurt us."

"I-I can't help it! She stole my papa, and now he is going to marry her! She'll make my life so hard! She doesn't love Papa. She doesn't like anybody but herself. How could God let this happen to us?"

"We can't blame God. He hurts too. He doesn't like to see his children in such pain."

"He must really be in pain over this, then," Martina said, tearfully. I don't know why He can't just make everything the way it was again. Why does He let bad things happen to good people? It's not fair."

"Well, I know that He sometimes allows trials to happen our lives, but He also promises to be with us through our trials. He wants us to rely on him for help. He wants us to learn to forgive. You know the Bible says we are to pray for those who treat us bad and ask God to forgive them."

"I can't! I *won't*! She's mean and she's evil. I don't want her to take Mama's place. Papa has to see what she is really like. He just has to!" Martina folded her arms and pouted.

"Unfortunately, we cannot make him see things as they are right now, *Liebe*. We can pray that his eyes will be opened though, and that he will see the truth."

"Why can't he open them now? Doesn't he know that God hates divorce? Even I know that."

"If only it were that easy. You are a very smart young lady for your age. And you know that because you read and believe God's Word. Unfortunately, I'm not sure that your father believes what he is doing is a sin. That's why we have to pray for him."

"I have been, Elsa, but it's not working."

"Well, I believe God does hear your prayers, and that His perfect will was for them to reconcile, but He also gave mankind free will, and up to this point I'm afraid your Papa's will and God's will are two very different things."

"Then God's heart is breaking because of it, isn't that so?"

Elsa nodded in agreement. "Yes, *Engel,* I believe you're right. Just keep praying for them. Don't ever give up."

Elsa said her prayers with Martina, and tucked her in for the night, then went to her room. The whole situation saddened her. She feared for the family's future—especially with a woman like Griselda in charge. She knew Griselda was a veritable Jezebel who had found her Ahab and was manipulating him to do her bidding. Up to now, she had her way in virtually every area, except when it came to Martina. How long would that hope last? Griselda was getting a stronger foothold on Fredric. It could be a matter of time before she would be forced to leave as well. Then what would happen? *Oh Lord, please protect Martina from this woman, and be with Frau Albers. Surround her with your loving arms and comfort her in her time of grief.*

She prayed silently.

* * *

Just as he expected, Martina insisted on going to see her mother once she found out. And just as he promised, Fredric gave his permission for her to visit Katharina for a few weeks. He wanted to be as fair as possible, and even though it meant she would miss some school, Fredric instructed Elsa to keep Martina up to date with her schoolwork.

Fredric took them to the train station, and he hugged his little girl goodbye. He watched the train slowly pull away and looked as his dear beloved Martina pressed her face against the window, waving, her image fading away as the train chugged down the tracks. He felt a pain in his heart, knowing that from this time on there would many more times he would be saying good-bye to his dear Martina, since Kata wouldn't be coming home anymore. This was another consequence of his sinful actions—although he could not make himself face that truth.

The train ride was long, but comfortable. Fredric had purchased first class tickets in the sleeper coach, assuring his daughter and Elsa a comfortable night's sleep. However, Martina did not sleep well on the train. She was struggling with mixed emotions. She was sad to leave her father, but anxious to see her mother. She needed her mother's presence. News of her parents' breakup had shattered her world and her sense of security. She needed to know her mother still loved her, and, in her mind, seeing her was the only way she would be sure. She had written to her mother and even talked to her on the telephone, but that was not the same.

Finally, they arrived at the train station in Vienna and Kata was there to meet them. Her frail and emaciated frame evoked a startled look from both Elsa and Martina. Worry lines etched her ashen face, and she was not the bubbly Kata she had been in the past. She was very subdued.

She hugged Elsa and Martina tightly and began to weep. "Oh, it is so good to see you both!" She exclaimed tearfully, taking Martina's travel case and leading them to a black Benz that Fredric had purchased for her two years ago. Even though women drivers in her day were quite rare, she was quite a good driver. Fredric had made sure of that. They made their way back to her villa and settled in.

Martina caught Kata up with the latest news about school and friends, and Kata told her about her latest opera. After about an hour, Martina's eyes were drooping. It was evident that the trip had worn her out, so Elsa took her to her room and put her down for a nap. Then she returned to talk to Kata.

"Oh, *Frau* Albers, look at you!" exclaimed Elsa. "You have lost so much weight. You need to take better care of yourself."

"I can't help it. I can't eat anything these days, and my nights are fitful. By the way—I think it's time you stop being so formal with me. Please, call me Kata from now on. Remember, you are no longer my employee. Besides, I consider you a friend. Actually, you always have been a friend. I just didn't see it." Kata's eyes filled with tears again.

Elsa smiled compassionately at her. "You have a good heart, Kata, and I have always admired you for that."

Kata could hold the tears back no longer. She sobbed, "What's there to admire about someone who literally sacrificed her family for a career? How could I have neglected them so? Everything that has happened is my fault, Elsa. I caused it!" She buried her face in her hands and wept with such intensity that her whole body trembled.

Elsa took her hand and patted it. "Now, you mustn't blame yourself totally. *Herr* Albers and Griselda had much more to do with this whole situation. They chose to open the door to adultery, with little concern as to the results.

"From what I have learned about Griselda, I wouldn't be a bit surprised if this was her intention from the beginning. She's a very wicked person. It's obvious that she used her looks to lure *Herr* Albers into doing whatever she wanted and unfortunately, *Herr* Albers was oblivious to her plan."

"It doesn't make it any better. I *could* have stopped it." She leaned against Elsa, and Elsa comforted her, saying a silent prayer asking the Lord for words of wisdom to share with this poor woman.

"Many mistakes were made by both of you in this situation, and you can't go back and change the past. Nevertheless, you *can* change the future. There is Someone who wants to help you do that if you just let Him," she said.

"Who? Who could possibly help me through this mess?" Kata looked up with earnest curiosity painted on her tear-stained face.

Elsa put an arm around her friend and former employer. "His name is Jesus." She paused. "If you ask Him to come into your heart, He will be your Refuge, your Fortress and your Comforter."

Kata listened intently as Elsa continued to talk.

"You know, King David in the Old Testament was a man who, even though he loved the Lord greatly, sinned many times. Yet God said David was a man after His own heart. God knows we are going to sin and make mistakes, but He offers us forgiveness and hope if we turn from our sin, repent and ask Him to forgive us. However, you do have to ask Him."

"Oh, Elsa, do you really think He would forgive me? I have been so foolish."

"Yes, of course He will, and I will be very glad to pray with you."

"Oh, yes, I . . . I think I would like that. I certainly have nowhere else to go, or no one else to turn to."

She wiped her face and tried to compose herself. Both women bowed their heads, and Elsa began to pray, "Dear Lord, I lift up my dear friend to you and ask that you surround her with your love and your comfort. I know that you love Kata and her family, so I ask that you reach out to her now and touch her heart and give her your wisdom and guidance from here on."

Elsa's prayer greatly moved Kata. With Elsa's help, she prayed, "Dear Lord, I have been so blind all of these years—I have rejected your Son Jesus, and have been selfish and proud. I am so sorry. Please forgive me of all of my sins, and let me start all over again with you. Thank you so much that Jesus did indeed die for my sin. I ask you, Jesus, to become my Savior and from this day on, I choose to follow you and seek your will for my life."

A peace that she had never before experienced filled her heart. She now had a Savior who had forgiven her sins and past mistakes. She knew that nothing had changed as far as her circumstances, but something had changed in her life. Jesus was now *her* Lord and Master.

Elsa had given Kata a Bible the previous Christmas, and now she had an insatiable desire to read it. Elsa told her to begin reading in the book of John, and that night she did. For the first time since the night Fredric had come to tell her he wanted a divorce, she slept serenely.

* * *

Just before Christmas, Kata had finished another opera and decided she wanted to sell the villa in Austria and return to her homeland, Germany. She wanted to be close to her daughter, and when she made her plans clear to him, Fredric agreed to let Martina visit every other weekend. He also promised she could spend half of her summer with Kata as well. Most likely, she surmised, Griselda put pressure on him to do this. From what Martina and Elsa had told her, she considered their presence annoying. Elsa explained that it was probably the presence of God's Holy Spirit in them more than their presence she resented.

She auditioned with a company that performed in many of the local operas in Berlin, Dresden, Leipzig and surrounding cities. She found an apartment in the southern part of Berlin, about fifteen miles from Fredric and Martina. It was much smaller and less expensive than her villa, but almost as comfortable. The luxuries she had enjoyed during her life with Fredric seemed unimportant now. Actually, she had to admit, they were more a part of Fredric's world than hers. Even as a child, she was more content doing what she wanted—singing in the opera, than living the opulent lifestyle to which her parents were accustomed.

* * *

The early part of 1914 proved to be difficult for Elsa and Martina. After Christmas and the New Year were over, Fredric had to make a business trip to Hamburg. Now that he and Kata were divorced, he promised Griselda when he returned they would get married.

She worked feverishly on her wedding plans. She decided she wanted a very elaborate wedding and she spared no expense—Fredric could afford it, after all. She also insisted that the house be remodeled to fit her tastes and to erase Kata's influence completely in what was now her home. This did not bode well with Martina. Griselda tore down any hint of the Victorian décor that Kata had loved and, while she kept most of the Art Nouveau items Fredric liked, she bought new furnishings that reflected the *Avant-Garde* décor. She brought in paintings by Pablo Picasso and Henri Matisse, artists known for cubism and impressionist paintings. Gone were the warm reds, golds and greens that her mother had cherished. Griselda preferred the more neutral colors. The house took on a colder, less welcoming effect as far as Martina was concerned. "What's wrong with the house the way Mama had it? Mama's house was beautiful. It didn't need to be changed," she protested.

Griselda's eyes narrowed and her lips drew into a thin line. She gave Martina a sharp glare. "That's *enough* of your insolence, *Kinder*! This is *my* house now, *not* your mother's. And *I'll* be the one to determine what stays and what does not. Frankly, she has poor taste in furnishings, and her décor was *very* outdated."

Martina couldn't contain herself. "It was *not!* Our house was *much better* looking 'til *you* came!"

Griselda viciously struck Martina across the cheek, leaving a nasty red mark. Martina held her cheek and looked shocked. No one had ever slapped her before. She remained stoic. This woman would not make her cry.

"I'm telling Papa on you, and then he'll know what you are *really* like!"

Griselda grabbed a large lock of her hair and pulled her closer. "Let me caution you right now, you don't know who you are dealing with," she warned. The corners of her mouth curled up into a diabolical sneer and she raised an eyebrow. "I can have Elsa removed from this house in a split second if you are not careful. If you give me *any more* problems, I will dismiss her on the spot. Then you will deal directly with *me!* So you had better make up your mind right now that you are going to keep your mouth *shut*! Do I make myself clear?"

Griselda's look and the tone of her voice convinced Martina that she was serious, and if she didn't cooperate, things would get much worse for her. Martina looked away, even though Griselda still had her hair, and it intensified the pain. "Yes," she said in a stiff, yet somewhat submissive tone, trying her best to keep the tears from bursting forth and to contain her anger and hurt.

She tugged even tighter on Martina's hair to pull her back. Martina grimaced, but refused to cry out. Griselda's eyes narrowed and her lips thinned. "And if you know what's good for you, you will say nothing to Elsa!"

Griselda released Martina's hair and shoved her away abruptly. Martina quickly turned around and left the room. She was bewildered. Neither her parents nor Elsa had ever treated her like this. Her head ached and her face smarted. But her pain went beyond the physical. She suffered emotional wounds as well. She feared what Griselda might do if she told her mother or Elsa. She couldn't take the chance of losing her precious Elsa. If only her papa had been home. She could show him the red mark on her face as proof. By the time, he returned home, though, there would be no evidence. She had no doubt that Griselda would lie her way out of it, even if she did tell him. She was good at that. Unfortunately, she knew too well that her papa was too blind to see this side of Griselda. She resolved to stay away from her whenever possible. She said nothing to Elsa, and avoided her until the red mark was gone.

At bedtime, when Elsa was helping her get ready for bed, she tried to act as if nothing was wrong around her, and after they had prayed together, and Elsa kissed her good night and left, she knelt beside her bed and prayed: "Dear father, I know I wasn't right to be disrespectful. Please forgive me for that. What my papa and Griselda are doing isn't right either. Please help Papa see what is happening, and also, please keep Mama, Elsa and me safe." She cried herself to sleep.

* * *

April and May of that year proved to be rather calm for Berlin and for the Alberses. Martina avoided Griselda as much as possible and Elsa kept Martina occupied whenever Fredric was not home. After the wedding, Griselda put her efforts into elevating the status she thought she deserved in life. Being the wife of Fredric Albers, the very successful businessman and millionaire, was no small thing. Along with this new relationship, should come certain privileges, she presumed. She spent much of her time planning dinner parties and trying to thrust her way into the social circles that Kata and Fredric enjoyed. To her chagrin, she found it virtually impossible. Despite the cost of the affair, very few guests attended their wedding. Even after they were married, almost nobody, with the exception of a few business associates who felt it was their obligation, attended their social events. The scandal of Fredric and Kata's divorce took its toll. Divorce was rare, and most people neither understood, nor accepted it. Kata and Fredric's friends adored Kata, and most of them quickly realized that Griselda was the reason for their breakup.

Fredric didn't seem to mind the loss of the social invitations at all. He was usually too busy with his business and really didn't care for parties and such gatherings anyway. On the other hand, Griselda fumed over the snubbing they received. She tried to blame it on Kata's return to Germany, claiming that Kata was spreading rumors about her. She insisted that Fredric do something about it.

"What can I possibly do?" he snapped sharply. "Do you want

me to take out an advertisement blasting their actions? Should I go to Kata and beg her to say nice things about us? I know Kata well enough to say she is not vindictive. She is not responsible for the way these people are acting. Remember, they were her friends as well. Be patient."

"You want me to be patient while they sympathize with 'poor Katharina'?" Griselda shrieked in an angry tone. "Can't they see that she brought this upon herself? You can tell her to stop telling lies about us, or you will stop her from seeing Martina. You can also talk to them and convince them that she is the one who left you!"

"First, I am not going to use Martina as a pawn. And, second, I am convinced Kata had nothing to do with this. We have to let time do its work. People will eventually forget the past and then they will change their attitudes towards you."

"All right. I'll give it a little more time, but if things don't change soon, I'll take matters in my own hands," she warned.

He let out a deep sigh. "There's nothing you or I can possibly do about it." He shook his head and walked off from her, in an attempt to avoid any further discussion on the subject.

CHAPTER 22

Leaving the Past Behind

In the early part of June, Martina and Elsa made plans to go spend two weeks with her mother. Fredric and Griselda were going to take a vacation to Heiligendamm, the oldest seaside resort on the Baltic, in Germany. Much of Germany's high society enjoyed vacationing in Heiligendamm, consequently, Griselda was determined that she and Fredric go there as well. What better opportunity to mingle with the upper class would they possibly have? The last thing she wanted was a child going with them on this vacation, so she persuaded Fredric that Martina really needed to spend some time with her mother between her performances.

The time they spent together always sped by much too fast for Kata and Martina, but Kata enjoyed spending every moment she could with her daughter and Elsa. She purposely cut back on her work schedule during this time to be with them. They visited a number of tourist sites, museums and theaters, and often picnicked in a nearby park. In addition, they studied the Bible together, under Elsa's wonderful tutelage. Elsa certainly knew her way around the Bible, and Kata was quick to learn. She had an insatiable hunger for God's Word. Martina delighted in telling some of her favorite stories to her mother, and Kata loved to hear her daughter tell them.

Elsa and Kata found a church very close that they could attend together. It was a small church with about 150 members.

Kata was impressed with the minister, Pastor Johannsen. He was a middle-aged man who had great compassion for his parishioners and whose sermons spoke directly to them. He had sandy hair lightly streaked with grey. He stood about six feet tall and his features were angular. While he was not overly attractive, he had a warm smile and striking blue eyes. His voice was pleasant as he spoke, and Kata enjoyed listening to him.

She was particularly touched one Sunday morning by a message that spoke to her own circumstances. Elsa, Kata and Martina liked to be near the front row. They had established their pew right away. After the singing, the pastor went to the pulpit as usual and looked around at his congregation.

He smiled and began to speak. "Today I want to talk to you all about moving forward and leaving the past behind."

Leaving the past behind. Wasn't that what Elsa had told her she needed to do? How was that even possible? Yes, she had accepted Jesus as Lord and Savior, but her past still haunted her. She was definitely better off spiritually, but many things were still unresolved. She still cared for Fredric. Her heartache was still fresh, and even though Jesus had made it easier, it was like recovering from major surgery; the wound was still painful. How could she bear to think of that woman, Griselda raising her daughter? It seemed hopeless. She was a failure as a wife and a mother. Yes, God had saved her, but how could He turn her life around and give it meaning again?

She turned her focus back on the pastor's sermon when she heard him say, "He knows all about our past and our hurts. He wants to help us leave them behind and live as victorious Christians. My message today comes from Jeremiah 29:11 and Philippians 3:13-14. Read along with me in your Bibles please."

Kata and Elsa opened their Bibles to the passages, and Martina looked on with her mother. First, he read Jeremiah 29:11: "For I know the thoughts that I think toward you, saith the Lord; thoughts of peace, and not of evil, to give you an expected end."

"That expected end is a good one. God has a wonderful plan for all of us. But before we can move ahead, we need to leave our past behind."

Kata's ears perked up. Could God make something good come out of her sordid past? How could He possibly do this? It was such a mess.

Pastor Johannsen gave examples of men in the Bible that had made terrible mistakes in their own lives: Moses, David and Paul to name a few. Yet he showed how God had redeemed each of these men and given them a completely new future.

He explained how God used these men to help others: Moses led the Israelites out of slavery; David became King; and Paul spread the Gospel of Christ all over Rome, Turkey and many parts of Asia. Then Pastor Johannsen read Philippians 3:13-14: "Brethren, I count not myself to have apprehended: but this one thing I do, forgetting those things which are behind, and reaching forth unto those things which are before, I press toward the mark for the prize of the high calling of God in Christ Jesus."

He continued, "Paul tells us that our lives are like running a race. It's important to note that successful runners keep their eyes ahead, focusing on the goal in front of them. They do not look back."

Kata pondered those words. She had been looking back. She knew that she was still dwelling on that fateful day Fredric asked her for a divorce.

"Maybe there are problems and difficulties that could have destroyed you, had the Lord not come into your life." His voice intensified as he exhorted his congregation, "Christians need to walk in victory; however, in order to be victorious, we must learn how to give everything to God. We cannot live in our past, or dwell on how others have hurt us, but rather we must learn to be overcomers. Like Paul, we must have an attitude of winning. We need to keep our eyes on the road ahead. That is, God's road.

"We have to let Him direct our paths and keep us on track. And we can do this by reading the Bible and spending time in prayer. Psalms 119:105 tells us, 'Thy word is a lamp unto my feet, and a light unto my path.' He will guide us through and lead us down that road. Then, as we follow that road, He reveals his purpose for our lives."

God has a purpose for our lives. Kata was intrigued with this concept. She wondered what God could possibly do with her broken life.

"You see, when we go through very difficult trials, God not only wants to help us through them and heal our wounds, but He also wants to use these trials and tragedies to help others. Every circumstance, every trial, and every hurt can be turned around and used for God's glory.

"In Genesis, we see how Joseph suffered injustice even as a young boy. He was sold into slavery and ultimately wound up in a prison after being accused of something he hadn't done." Pastor Johannsen told how God used Joseph's life and raised him up to a position second only to the Egyptian Pharaoh and used him to save a nation from starving during a seven-year famine.

"When Joseph's brothers came to Egypt to buy goods and ultimately learned what had happened to their brother, they were afraid. But Joseph told them what they did actually worked for the good. Look at Genesis 50:20: Joseph tells his brothers, 'But as for you, ye thought evil against me; but God meant it unto good, to bring to pass, as it is this day, to save much people alive.' Paul reaffirms this in Romans 8:28."

Kata turned to the passage as Pastor Johannes read it aloud: "And we know that all things work together for good to them that love God, to them who are the called according to His purpose."

His message struck a chord in Kata. She had accepted Christ as her Lord, but she was still holding on to her past. She had been dwelling on what had happened and what she had done wrong. She was wounded and angry. Those feelings were still there and she hadn't let them go.

He ended his message with a challenge to his congregation:

"If you want to have a victorious and meaningful Christian walk, then you must let go of the past, seek the Lord as to His purpose for your life, then go forward down God's path. Seek His direction and purpose for your life. Let Him use you and your life for His glory."

Then he invited anyone who hadn't given his or her past hurts to God to come forward for prayer. The organist began to play *Leaning on the Everlasting Arms*, and several people went forward. Kata had never seen anything like this in her life, but her heart started pounding. She was riveted. The congregation began to sing:

What have I to dread, what have I to fear,
Leaning on the everlasting arms?
I have blessed peace with my Lord so near,
Leaning on the everlasting arms.

How she wanted to lean in her Lord's arms right now. She wanted him to take those hurts and heal her heart. She started to weep softly. Elsa squeezed her hand.

"I want to go forward for prayer, Elsa. Will come with me?"

"Of course," she said. Elsa put her arm around Kata's shoulders, gestured to Martina to stay seated, and the two women walked slowly to the front.

Kata walked up to Pastor Johannsen. "How can I pray for you, *Fraulein*?" he asked.

She told him briefly her story, and he put his hands on her shoulders and began to pray.

When he finished praying, Kata felt a tremendous weight lift from her chest. An inner peace enveloped her. She started to weep, and Elsa put her arms around her.

"I can't explain it, but suddenly I feel as if all of the pain is gone. I realize for the first time since I accepted Jesus as Savior that God has taken my past and given me a chance for a new beginning."

"He has, but it is up to you now to look to the future He has for you," Pastor Johannsen said. He patted her shoulder and smiled.

She didn't know what lay ahead, but with Jesus at her side, she felt she would be able to get through anything. No matter what, she resolved from that moment on, she would trust Him with everything in her life.

Later that evening, she pondered Pastor Johannsen's words and the way that God had been changing her life. She was so grateful for how God had brought her such hope and happiness. Happiness—yes, but then she thought about her dear friend Greta. All these months, she had forgotten, she had not told her about what had happened to her. She hoped Greta was happy in her new life, yet the one thing she regretted was that she hadn't had a chance to share Jesus with her. She immediately sat down at her desk, took out a pen and some stationary and began to write:

Dear Greta,

Please forgive me for not writing sooner. I trust that you and Karl are settled in your new home by now, and all is going well. You have no idea how much I have missed you since you left and how much life has changed for me. I wish I could tell you this in person, but unfortunately, that is impossible, so I will do my best to convey all that has happened since your departure in my letter.

First, Fredric and I are no longer together. He divorced me last year after telling me about his affair with our new housekeeper, Griselda. I couldn't believe that Fredric would do something like that. Believe me, I agonized over this whole catastrophe for quite a long time. I knew I had to take some of the blame. I felt that I had neglected him and Martina as I allowed my career to take precedence over my family.

It was also very hard on Martina as well, as Fredric insisted on having custody of her and she has had to be in the same household as that woman. Griselda has made life miserable for my daughter, and it tears me up inside to think of that, as I am helpless to do anything about it. It's as though my life had ended. You know, the ironic thing is that it did. At least the life I had before I found out about Jesus.

You see, I learned about the saving grace that Jesus Christ offers us, from Martina's nanny, Elsa. She and Martina came to visit soon after Fredric informed me of all of this. She had tried to tell me this before, but I refused to listen. I was just too busy with my life and thought there was no place in it for such things. But this time I had nothing to lose. I was in utter despair. She told me about how He had come to die for our sins, and that if I just repented of my sins, asked his forgiveness, and made him Lord of my life, He would give me eternal life. It was amazing.

I can't fully explain it, but after we prayed, I felt such a peace wash over me and I felt so clean inside. No, the past hadn't changed, but I had. Since then, I have been reading the

Bible, and God has been helping me pick up the pieces of my life and go on. You see, He takes our past and throws it into the sea of forgetfulness. Today I have chosen to do that with my past. I am leaving it behind me and am going on to build a new future in Christ.

For so many years, you were my dearest and closest friend. And, even though I didn't always agree with the way you interfered with my life, I realize that ever since my parents died, you were just trying to take care of me in the best way you knew how, and to see that I had a good life. You were trying to be the sister I needed. Now, it is time for me to return that favor and offer you something even better than what life has to offer. Salvation. It's a free gift for anyone who just asks. Although I still have lots to learn and I am still growing, Jesus has already made a difference in my life. This could be the greatest role you have ever had in your life. It's there for you if you just ask. I just happen to know the Director personally now, (the roles are reversed,) and I have been asking him to give you the opportunity to accept it.

I wish I could be there in person to share this with you, but first, I recommend that you find a Bible and read the following passages: Romans 10:8-10 and John 3:15-18. In these passages you will learn that Jesus came to this world to save all of us from our sins and to give us eternal life. He made the greatest sacrifice one could ever make. He gave his life for us.

As you read these scriptures, please keep your mind and heart open, then pray a simple prayer (Just imagine that I am with you as you pray, holding your hand, because I will be there in spirit.)

First, confess that you are a sinner (as we all are born into sin when we come into this earth), then, ask him to forgive you of all of your sins (repent), and finally, ask him to be the Lord of your life. I know that if you do this, you will see what I mean. You will never be the same.

I realize that this is somewhat of a strange letter, but I could not go on without sharing this wonderful news with my dearest friend. Nothing would make me happier than to know that, if we don't see each other anymore here on earth, we will be able to spend eternity together.

I do love and miss you, dear Greta, and I hope you will receive this letter with all the love and caring I meant it to contain. You are very important to me.

Please write when you can and tell me all about your life in Milan with your new husband, and hopefully you will follow through with my final suggestion, to accept Jesus into your life as your personal Savior.

Your friend and sister,
Kata.

Kata read it over, then put the letter in an envelope and whispered a prayer: *Dear Lord, I know this letter might seem strange to Greta, but please let your Holy Spirit prepare her heart and let her receive it with an open mind and in the spirit I meant it. I know that, like me, Greta has made lots of mistakes in her life and, well, she hasn't lived the most virtuous life, but I am reminded of the woman in John 8 who had led a very worldly life and was about to be stoned, and how Jesus rescued her. I am so grateful that Greta has found a husband and a new life here on earth, but more than anything, I want her to find out about your son Jesus, and how she can have eternal life. Please help her to learn about your love and forgiveness. Thank you, Lord, for changing my life and helping me to put my past behind me.*

CHAPTER 23

Assassination In Vienna

NOW THAT SHE HAD MADE A peace with her past, Kata was healing emotionally and growing spiritually. She began attending a regular Bible study in her new church. Through this Bible class, she learned more and more about God's love and forgiveness. One particular scripture they studied was from Hosea 2:19-20. It came alive to her:

And I will betroth thee unto me forever;
yea, I will betroth thee unto me in righteousness,
and in judgment, and in loving-kindness, and in mercies.

The first time she read this passage, the vacuum that the divorce had placed in her heart faded away. She knew that the Lord would be her husband and her companion, and she would never have to feel lonely again. She promptly memorized it and kept it in her heart as one keeps a precious gem hidden away in a treasure box.

Kata now had a peace that God was going to be walking by her side and helping her through all of her trials and tribulations. She had a renewed purpose in life.

Pastor Johannes made quick use of her singing talents. "God gives us talents to use for his kingdom as well as in the world," he told her. "So why not use your voice for his glory and be our choir director?"

"I'll be happy to," she said.

She also offered to help with the outreach to the poor in the city. She wanted to serve the Lord any way she could. The people in the congregation loved her, and before long, she had made several new friends—Christian friends.

Pastor Johannes' sermons always had a way of focusing on an area of her life with which she was dealing. She had learned so much about God's mercy and love as well, and she had no doubt that He would show her his purpose for her life. She believed she had grown considerably during her first year as a Christian.

Before she knew it, it was time for Martina's summer break again. Kata was also very pleased that Martina was going to be able to stay with her, as she had a trip of her own planned for June during her break. Francis Ferdinand, the Archduke of Vienna and his wife Sophie had asked her to perform at their palace June 15. They were approaching their fourteenth wedding anniversary and were putting on a gala affair that summer, entertaining delegates from various countries. Kata was asked to be part of it, and she accepted the invitation.

Elsa, Kata and Martina traveled to Vienna the first part of June and stayed in a luxurious hotel near the palace. The Archduke had insisted on covering the cost of her trip, and he spared no expense to see that she and her guests had the most comfortable of accommodations. After seeing her perform before, he knew Kata would be a very entertaining and delightful addition to their celebration.

Kata did not disappoint them. She performed a series of arias for her audience and won the hearts of dignitaries from all over the world who were visiting the royal palace that day. Her finale was an especially beautiful song from the first opera she had performed there a couple of years ago, *Claudine von Villa Bella*. The cadenza at the end of her final song brought an outburst of applause that resounded throughout the palace theatre for several minutes. The audience requested an encore, and she complied.

Princess Sophie took her aside after the performance. "I wonder if I may have a few minutes of your time, *Frau* Albers," the Princess asked.

The Princess was a very gracious lady. She had a deep admiration for this woman who had risen to the top of her career, despite her tragic circumstances. Sophie sensed a strength in her that was almost supernatural.

"I was sorry to learn what happened between you and your husband, but I must say, I am very impressed with the way you are coping with your ordeal. You seem to have an inner peace that one rarely sees. How do you do it? What keeps you going?" she asked.

"Quite honestly, I couldn't have done it on my own. I had help." Kata explained.

"What kind of help?" Sophie's eyes widened.

"Well, you see, right after Fredric left me, I was obviously devastated. Quite frankly, I was almost ready to end my life," Kata continued. "Shortly after that, my daughter and Elsa, her nanny, came to stay with me. . ."

Kata related the whole conversation between her and Elsa that fateful night, while Sophie listened intently.

"When Elsa shared how Jesus could change my life, I realized at that moment that I had nothing more to lose if I accepted Jesus as my Lord. I had lost almost everything anyway. After Elsa and I prayed, and I gave all of my hurts, trials, and sins over to Jesus, He filled my heart with such a peace. I was a new person.

"Over the past several months, as I have been studying the Bible, I've learned to give all of my worries, my trials and tribulations to Him. Now, I go to the Scriptures for guidance, and I get on my knees in prayer for His comfort. He has become my Fortress and my Strong Tower."

Sophie shook her head. "That's a fascinating story, my dear. I don't think I could ever have such faith. I admire your courage."

"My courage comes from God. Trust me, I have my weak moments, but believe it or not, I have learned to praise God for the trials I have been through."

"How can you do that? It seems as if you have lost so much." Sophie asked, raising an eyebrow.

"Well, I realize that had I *not* lost *everything.* Actually, I was the one who was lost before this decision. Had I not taken the step to repent and ask Jesus in my heart, I would have never gained eternal life. I was too proud and independent: too self-sufficient to even consider allowing God to be part of my life."

As Kata saw Sophie's eyes grow larger and fill with tears, she knew that the Lord was at work in her friend, and she was encouraged in her resolve to share her testimony with Sophie. She continued. "I was like the Prodigal Son in the Bible. I came to God after being in utter despair with nowhere else to turn. Then I was able to accept my Father's love and forgiveness."

"The Prodigal *what*?" Sophie asked.

"The Prodigal Son. It's a parable in the New Testament that Jesus told about a young man who was rebellious and full of pride. He asked his father for his inheritance early, then went out and wasted all of his money on things of the world. He wound up penniless, and in a pigpen, eating garbage. He finally realized just how sinful he had been and returned home to ask his father to forgive him.

"His father welcomed him with open arms and had a party for him. That is how our heavenly Father receives us when we go to Him and ask for forgiveness. He welcomes us with open arms and offers us his unconditional love."

"Oh, how I wish I could experience that kind of love," Sophie lamented with a deep sigh. "Ever since I married into Ferdinand's family, I have suffered nothing but rejection." Her expression clouded.

"But you can, and I'd be glad to pray with you to receive it, if you wish." Kata said.

Sophie's face brightened with hope, and she reached out for Kata's hand. "Yes, I—I think I would like to do that."

Kata prayed with Sophie and after they finished, Sophie hugged Kata. A peaceful glow replaced her gloom as she broke into a copious smile and exclaimed, "I *do* feel his love and his peace! Thank you so much for being willing to share your secret with me. I am so very grateful that God brought you into my life, Kata—you don't mind if I call you that, do you?"

Kata stifled a giggle. The Princess of Hohenberg was asking permission to call her by *her* first name. How strange life can be.

"Not at all — considering we are now sisters in Christ," she said with a smile.

* * *

Sophie asked Kata to stay in Vienna for a few more days. She purchased a Bible, and Kata spent several afternoons, along with Elsa, sharing God's Word with her. They quickly formed a friendship. However, Ferdinand announced that he and Sophie needed to make a visit to Bosnia to attend some military maneuvers and to open a museum in Sarajevo.

There had been great tension between the two countries for years. Ferdinand had hoped by visiting this area, he could calm some of those tensions and restore diplomatic relations between Austria-Hungary and Bosnia.

At the end of this visit, Kata hugged Sophie good-bye, and Sophie promised to visit her some time in Germany. She, Elsa and Martina returned to Berlin. Kata was grateful for the trip and the opportunity God had given her to lead Sophie to the Lord. One more person had been won to the Kingdom of Christ, and she had been a part of that.

Early on June 29, after her morning Bible reading, she picked up the daily newspaper and read the headlines: *Archduke and Wife Slain by Bosnian Student.*

She couldn't believe what she was reading. Sophie and Ferdinand *assassinated!*

"No, it can't be!" She cried aloud. She had just spent such a wonderful two weeks with this dear sweet couple. How could this have happened? The article stated that a Serbian nationalist by the name of Gavrilo Princip had gunned them down. She read the major points of the story:

> *Archduke saves his life first time by knocking aside a bomb hurled at his Auto. . . Slain in second attempt . . . Lad dashes at car as the royal couple return from Town Hall and kills both of them. . .*

Kata was overwhelmed with grief and burst into sobs. She experienced a variety of emotions. She agonized over the loss of her newfound friend and her husband, but at the same time, she rejoiced that God had allowed her the opportunity to pray with her to receive Christ. She composed herself, and then read the article below this tragic story: *Austria – Hungary declares War on Bosnia.*

She was even more alarmed as she read parts of related articles throughout the paper:

> *Russia threatens to get involved. She is already moving troops. . . The peace of Europe is now in Kaiser's Wilhelm's hands . . . Montenegrin and Serb armies plan to invade Bosnia and start a rebellion there. . . Czar's forces mass on Eastern border, his capital expects war and counts confidently on England's aid. . . German official says its issue would also mean launching of Kaiser's army . . . Austrian Emperor plan to take command at Vienna headquarters. . . Chain reaction brings panic . . . Outbreak of food riots and prices soar as hostilities are declared and the government steps in to regulate them; Emperor states he may be forced to take up the sword to defend the honor of his monarchy. . . France fears a Great War.*

Kata felt a sense of trepidation as she thought of the repercussions of this horrible incident. She grieved for the loss of her friend, but even more, she grieved for Austria and feared for her own country. She knew that Austria and Germany shared close ties. She dreaded the worst. She worried that Germany would feel compelled to support Austria in this war. The greatest of her fears were soon realized. Austria declared war on Serbia immediately after the assassination, and by July 5, Kaiser William promised to stand with Austria against Serbia.

In August, Germany had declared war against Russia, and France and had invaded Belgium. This was the beginning of what would later be called *The Great War*. It was a time of great devastation and loss, not only for Germany, but also for the whole world.

CHAPTER 24

Tranquility in the Midst of Turmoil

THE WAR BROUGHT ABOUT MAJOR POLITICAL changes, but it also led to social changes in Europe with more opportunities and greater equality for women. As hundreds of thousands of men went to war throughout Europe, women had to fill the vacant jobs they left behind. Germany was no exception. Chemical and agricultural factories were converted to manufacture weapons, necessary supplies, and other war-related products. Over a half million women went to work in munitions factories in order to keep the military supplied with enough ammunition. Women were also needed to work as nurses, secretaries and as general laborers.

As Kata watched the world around her immerse itself in the Great War, she felt that she had to do her part. Her dream had always been the opera, yet her heart seemed to be changing. Was God calling her to do something different to help others during these horrific times?

She remembered the examples Pastor Johannes gave of Moses, a man with a stutter, who was called by God to lead a nation out of captivity. She also remembered the story of the cowardly Gideon, who hid behind the winepress, yet the Lord called him a "mighty man of valor." God used him to rescue Israel from their enemies with only 300 men. These thoughts encouraged her. She knew in her heart that the Lord could use anyone who was willing to serve him and trust him. She talked to Elsa about it during one of their visits.

"Oh, Elsa, I want so much to help others get through this horrible war."

"Do you have any idea what God is calling you to do?" Elsa asked.

She shook her head. "No, I'm not sure, but I do know that I have to do something. I don't agree with the aggressive actions our government has taken in this war. There are innocent people who are being hurt because of it. I just can't sit back and do nothing; yet all I've ever known is the opera. I don't have any other skills, I'm afraid." Kata sighed, and frustration shrouded her features.

"I know that I want to help our men who are on the front somehow. Many of them are just boys and don't have any idea what they are really fighting for. I fear if the hostilities continue, hundreds may never reach adulthood, and thousands may come home blinded or crippled in this godless war. I have heard that many of them just want to die. They need to know that we care and will support them when they are wounded for a cause they may not even agree with. They need hope. Above all, they need Jesus."

Elsa's eyes glistened, and she looked at Kata with admiration. "It sounds like the Lord is tugging at your heart, Kata. He's trying to get your attention, and if you pray and let Him guide you, He will show you what to do."

"Do you think so?"

"I know it. The Lord has done this many times in my own life. When I have felt a desire in a certain area, I have always taken it to God, and almost every time, I knew that He was directing me to do something specific. That is how I came to be with your family. It was God who laid it on my heart to apply for the position of nanny for Martina."

Kata looked surprised. "Are you telling me that you asked God whether you should apply for this job?"

"Yes." Elsa told Kata the whole story of how she prayed for the Lord to use her after she lost her husband. Then she told her about how a friend gave her the ad she and Fredric had put in the papers, and how she prayed for the Lord to open the door if she was to be their nanny.

Kata's eyes widened. She grasped Elsa's hands in hers. "That is amazing. You have had such faith, Elsa. You could have easily taken the path I did after losing my son, or have given up hope just as I was about to after losing Fredric, my home and my daughter. Instead, you ran to the Rock. In the midst of your tragedy, you sought God's direction. And now, look how the Lord has used you to bring Martina and me to Christ."

"God will readily show us what He wants us to do. We just have to learn to listen," Elsa explained.

"I really want to find God's purpose for my life. I want to do something that is going to have an impact in this world. I don't want to entertain people any longer. I want to win them to Christ."

"You've come a long way in a short time. I'm so proud of you. I've no doubt that you will win many for Him."

"I believe that He's leading me to leave the opera. I never thought I would say that. It's funny how God can really change our hearts and our desires, isn't it? Since I was a little girl, I always dreamed of being on stage and performing, despite my parents' objections. I was driven by my desire to sing my way to fame. I used to live for finding the biggest, most important role possible, and now that desire is gone.

"I want to be free of this—this weight around my neck that cost me my family. Oh Elsa, how could I have been so blind? If I'd only have listened to you the first time you tried to talk to me about God. I could have stopped all of this from happening. I could have been serving the Lord in some way and *still* have had my family. Maybe I could have even helped Fredric find God," Kata said remorsefully.

Elsa smiled and patted Kata's hand. "I'll be happy to pray with you, if you'd like. The Bible says that God gives us the desires of our heart, but more than that, I also believe that He puts that desire in our hearts," she mused. "I think if we pray together, God will surely let you know His will in this."

"Yes, I'd appreciate your prayers," Kata said. Together, the two women got on their knees, joined hands and prayed.

Elsa prayed first: "Dear God, I am so grateful for my dear friend and sister in Christ. I know that you have done a great work in her life. I ask you to give her clear direction as to what you want her to do. Then please make a way for her to walk in that direction. Open doors wide and provide for her in whatever it is you want her to do. We thank you so much for that direction and guidance. In Jesus' precious name I pray."

While she was praying, Kata began to weep softly. She saw herself floating above a battlefield. It was as if she had wings. Bones and limbs were projecting through muddy clumps of dirt. Acrid smoke permeated the air. Bombs were exploding all around the trenches. Wounded soldiers cried out in pain. She felt their terror and agony. The more the Lord revealed to her in this vision, the more she cried and began to shake.

Then she looked down and saw herself dressed in white, reaching down and holding the hands of many of them. In the midst of the terrible scene before her, waves of peace filled her heart and she knew that the Lord was revealing a new purpose for her life.

She squeezed Elsa's hand and continued the prayer Elsa had started, "Dear Father, I believe You hurt when your people hurt. You cry when your people cry. Now Lord, I am crying. I am overwhelmed with compassion and I want to do whatever you want me to do to help. Please open that door wide and help me to walk through it. Fill me with your wisdom and guide me in your way, Oh Lord. I thank you."

When they finished, she hugged Elsa. She smiled, and her tear-filled eyes sparkled.

"And thank you, for helping me to come to know the Lord, and for teaching me so much about Him."

She grasped Elsa's hand. "I think God has made you *my* guardian angel. I don't know what I would have done had you not come into our lives. It just amazes me how when God shuts one door, He opens another. For years, Greta and I were so close—and then she married and moved out of my life. Now He has brought you to me, not only as a nanny to my daughter, but also as a close friend. Greta was the earthly sister I never had, but you are my sister in the Lord." She smiled at Elsa and wiped her tear-filled eyes.

Elsa put her hand on Kata's shoulder and nodded in agreement.

"And I believe that Lord is going to show you clearly what to do, my dear sister."

* * *

As the wounded were being transported by the thousands back to Germany, the need for more help in the hospitals grew at a tremendous rate. The call was going out all over Germany for volunteer aids in the over-crowded hospitals. Kata couldn't escape these pleas. She went she ran into people everywhere, talking about the overcrowded hospitals and the ravaged, mutilated victims being delivered in ambulances like massive bundles of raw meat.

The number of casualties was accelerating daily. Hundreds of thousands of soldiers were convalescing in hospitals, but too few doctors and nurses were available to take care of them.

Kata occasionally had the opportunity to talk with men who had come home on leave. She heard horror stories of brave soldiers holed up in dirty, damp and foul-smelling trenches, many of which would cave in, causing injuries or at times, even death.

Sickened by the details, and filled with overwhelming compassion and sadness, Kata finally knew what God wanted her to do. He wanted her to leave the opera and to help with this atrocity of a war. He was calling her into the nursing field. She had no medical skills, but most hospitals were desperate for help. Yet, if God could equip David, a mere shepherd boy to become a mighty king, couldn't He equip her to become a nurse? Most new nurses gained their experience through on-the-job training as aides. *How ironic; here I am giving up the very thing that actually cost me my family. It's amazing that the things we think are so important at the time, can suddenly become trivial in the presence of God's plan for us,* she thought.

* * *

Kata's application to be a nurse's aide-in-training was accepted without question. Because the need was so great, any able-bodied woman who merely showed some interest was immediately considered. After filling out all the necessary papers, and going through a series of interviews and tests, she began her first day of training at one of the major hospitals in Berlin.

A matronly German head nurse greeted her when she reported for duty. Kata guessed she was in her mid-forties. She had brown hair streaked with grey. She was not an attractive woman, but she had a kind face. She had brown eyes and a light olive complexion. She looked worn and tired, but spoke with great determination. "Good morning, *Frau* Albers." She greeted Kata with a firm handshake.

"Pleased to meet you, Nurse Hemmler," she said with a smile.

"It is so good to have you join us," said Nurse Hemmler.

"I am looking forward to working with you and the staff here," replied Kata, returning her shake.

Nurse Hemmler's smile faded in to a grimace. She took a deep breath. "Don't get your hopes up just yet. You might not make it through the first day, once you see what we're up against here. We have had many well-meaning ladies who came to us thinking that they wanted to help, but after seeing the horrific shape that so many of the soldiers are in, the conditions they have to work in, the pressure we are under, they literally become nauseated, and many leave us before completing even one day of work." Nurse Hemmler said, shaking her head sadly.

"I don't think you have to worry about me. I believe that God has put me here, and He is the one who will help me get through anything I might encounter," Kata assured her confidently.

Nurse Hemmler smiled at her approvingly. "It sounds like you have great faith, Kata, but I'm guessing we'll soon find out whether it is strong enough to endure what you are about to see."

She took Kata into a large room filled with about fifty other women who were beginning their first day of training as well. In the front of the room were a large black board and a table with a variety of utensils and medical paraphernalia. After Kata and the other ladies had been sitting for a few minutes, Nurse Hemmler introduced another nurse and a doctor who had just walked in the room. The nurse was slightly younger than Nurse Hemmler, probably in her early thirty's. She was about five foot seven inches, had blonde hair, blue eyes and was very slim. She was attractive, but like Nurse Hemmler, she looked worn and weary.

The doctor was approximately six feet tall. His brown hair was graying at the temples. She guessed he was in his mid to late forties. He had green eyes, a long, slender nose, and a rectangular-shaped face. While he was not particularly handsome, he had a pleasant appearance. His eyes were his striking quality. Elsa noticed that his eyelashes were very long for a man.

"I would like to introduce you to the two people who will be responsible for your training over the next several weeks," said Nurse Hemmler as she faced the audience, then looked over at the couple. "This is Doctor Otto Fleischer and his assistant, Nurse Helga Kaufmann." Both of them nodded and smiled briefly at their trainees.

"I am going to turn this session over to them, but please know that I will be around throughout your training and will be glad to assist you any way I can. I hope to see many of you out on the floor very soon." With that, Nurse Hemmler turned and left the room.

Dr. Fleischer faced the new trainees, nodded a greeting, offered a cordial smile, and then began talking. "First, I want to thank you all for your willingness to volunteer your time to help with those who have put their lives in danger to defend our country. I do want to warn you, though; this will not be an easy task. It will take a great deal of patience and stamina not only to complete the training, but also to be able to continue to in this work.

"The sights you will see and the stories you will hear will be enough to break your hearts and turn your stomachs inside out. Many of you may even be traumatized as you listen to the terrible woes of war."

He paused and studied the new recruits for a moment, as if he was looking for signs of hesitation, then continued. "We are going to put you through a very rigorous, but expedited training program that should normally take months. Because of the urgency of the problems we are facing, we have no choice but to train you in a matter of a few weeks.

"You will put in an average of ten to twelve hours a day, six days a week, and you will go home exhausted every night. You will wonder many times why you are here and whether you are doing any good—especially when you watch men die that you have been caring for, sometimes for weeks. There will be days that you will be extremely discouraged, overwhelmed and very depleted, but I also want you to know that you are working for a tremendous cause. Despite the deaths you will witness, you *will* be saving lives."

Kata was impressed with the frankness of his speech. She wasn't daunted in the least, however. After all, it was important to present the harsh reality of the situation and perhaps even trying to discourage those who were there for the wrong reasons. She also thought he was trying to encourage those who knew they were called to this profession. She was sure that she was one of the latter.

"Now I will give my assistant a chance to say a few words. She will actually be spending more time with you than I will, so I want you all to have a chance to get to know her," Dr. Fleischer concluded.

Nurse Kaufmann reiterated much of what Dr. Fleischer said, then explained the training program briefly with them and gave them the necessary forms they needed to complete for the training. She then took them all on a brief tour of the hospital.

While Kata had some idea of what was happening on the front, she was not prepared for the scenes she encountered as they walked through the hospital. The floors were crowded with hundreds of war casualties, which ranged from minor injuries to life-threatening wounds. Men groaned and even shrieked in pain. Blood was everywhere. Several had lost limbs, eyes, or had half of their heads blown off. Many were suffering from rat bites and sores from head and body lice, along with war wounds.

The smells were sickening, a mixture of blood, carbolic acid and other odors she couldn't identify. Nausea consumed her. Several times she wretched and put her hand over her mouth, but she determined to continue. Her heart surged with compassion for these men, and wanted to do whatever was humanly possible to help them. She would need to pray and ask God to help her overcome her fears and weaknesses.

The next few weeks of training went quickly. Amidst all of the turmoil and the tragedy of war, Kata's spirit remained tranquil. She knew that she was in the right place, and that the Lord was her guiding force.

CHAPTER 25

The Angel with a Mission

BY THE MIDDLE OF 1915, THE war was still raging. Kata had finished her training in March, but her days were long and very difficult. At forty-one, her body rebelled from the harsh treatment to which it had been exposed ever since she became a nurse. Kata often came home fully depleted, just as Dr. Fleischer said they would be. Her feet ached from pain and her limbs cried out for mercy. Her head throbbed. There were times she felt discouraged.

"It just seems almost impossible to keep up with all of the wounded," Kata bemoaned to Nurse Hemmler, in the staff lounge one afternoon during a short, but much-needed break.

Nurse Hemmler, who was sitting on a small divan across from Kata, stretched her legs, and rotated each ankle one at a time. Standing for long hours on their feet often caused swelling. She exhaled deeply. "Actually, my dear, this is luxury compared to what the wounded have to endure in the hospitals at the front." She straightened and re-pinned some of the graying strands of her hair and pushed them up under her cap.

"Oh? What have you heard about them?" Kata inquired."

"Well, one of my best friends is a field nurse. I get letters from her occasionally. You can't even imagine what they go through. It's almost unbearable for the poor men." Nurse Hemmler leaned forward and she lowered her voice so as not to alarm some of the new trainees sitting in the room.

"Before they come here, most of the wounded are sent to field hospitals called "clearinghouses." She tells me that they're not much more than a tent or hut. The wounded receive only very basic care by medics before being sent here, to hospitals in the city, poor souls. There are no antibiotics or X-rays, and heaven help the men if they have to have emergency surgery." She winced as she described the conditions.

"Why is that?" Kata asked.

Nurse Hemmler lowered her brown eyes, and a painful expression washed over her face.

"Well, it's not the fault of the medical personnel, I can tell you that. They have no choice. Unfortunately, because of a shortage of anesthetics, the doctors are often forced to perform surgery while these men are fully awake. Sometimes they're lucky enough to have a little laudanum or whiskey, but that doesn't happen very often. Thankfully, many of them pass out from the pain."

"That is just unfathomable!" Kata remarked with consternation. "Isn't there anything that can be done about it?" Kata's eyes widened and her eyes filled with moisture as she pictured these men having to endure unspeakable pain.

"No, it's a sorry situation all around, I'm afraid. We are doing all we can to keep up here. You know that." Nurse Hemmler sighed deeply again and continued. "What makes it even harder for these soldiers to recover, are the conditions the doctors have to operate under. Poor lighting, not enough staff, and filthy conditions make the treatment in those places well below standard to say the least."

Kata shook her head in disbelief as she listened to Nurse Hemmler's grim description of the front. "It's a wonder any of these men make it here alive under the circumstances, then."

Nurse Hemmler appeared to be staring far off and shook her head in dismay. "Not only the soldiers, but many of the doctors and nurses on the front suffer from a form of shock themselves and have to be sent home early because they cannot endure what they see. Most have little or no experience in war and are unprepared for what they have to face out there."

"I see now why so many of these of the men have such terrible surgical scars when we get them." Kata lowered her head and shifted uncomfortably." She resolved even more to pray for a quick end to this atrocity of a war.

Nurse Hemmler's face brightened a bit. "On a more positive note, I do have to say the other staff nurses and I are amazed at the remarkable way you apply your faith in caring for your patients. The rather unorthodox manner in which you pray and repeat scriptures over those who are still unconscious or in a coma, seem to make a difference in most cases. And medically, I'm quite pleased at what a quick learner you've been. It's hard to imagine you had no training before you came here." Nurse Hemmler smiled approvingly at her.

Kata blushed. "Well, it's also the remarkable training program you and the staff here provide for us. I have learned so much from all of you. And I believe God had a great deal to do with it as well."

"Your faith is a definite plus, Kata, that's for sure," the pleasantly plump nurse said. "You know I was raised in church, and I am a Christian, but I never gave much thought about using my faith in my profession." The creases around her eyes turned into smile lines as she grinned at Kata. For a moment, it made her look younger than her forty-plus years.

She continued, "I have a new appreciation for ministry because of you. Actually, I think you could teach all of us a few things about faith. Maybe what we need is a Bible Study for the nurses here, during some of our free moments."

"That might not be a bad idea. I think we all get discouraged watching so many come back maimed, crippled and hurting. And so many of these men are dying because there is not enough medical help. At times it even shatters my own faith." Kata wiped a tear from her eye.

Nurse Hemmler looked at her and took her hand. "Kata, you're a pillar of faith as far as I can see, you would be a good person to start it. I, for one, would be glad to be a part of any Bible study that you lead. Give it some thought."

"I'll certainly pray about it and see what God tells me to do. I'm very grateful for the opportunities I have to pray for the injured; to not only tend to their wounds, but also to tend to their spirits. However, I'm still relatively new in the Lord, so I'm not sure I'm ready to. . . "

Nurse Hemmler interrupted her. "I don't think that'd stop God from using you. You obviously know more than the rest of us. I must confess, I haven't spent all that much time reading the Bible. I've just been too busy since this war started." She sighed heavily and shook her head.

Kata paused and pondered the idea for a moment. "Well, I find that without starting the day in the Scriptures, I am just depleted. So it definitely would be good to share the Bible with other nurses and give them the same opportunity I have had. It would certainly help me as well, and I'm sure that knowing more about God's Word would be just what we *all* need to help us get through this terrible war. On the other hand, we will *definitely* have to ask God to build in some extra time in our already overloaded day to make time for one." With that, the two nurses went back to work.

Kata continued to share the Lord with her patients every opportunity she got. She was bold in her witness. She realized that many of these men had no guarantee they were going to make it through another day and she was concerned for their very souls. While she wanted to see them make a complete recovery, the condition of their spiritual recovery was even more important.

One particular incident, which deeply affected Kata, was that of a twenty-one-year-old young *unteroffizier* named Eric Drescher, a member of the National Guard. While he had been fighting in the trenches, a bomb exploded just a few yards from him. It killed several of his comrades and left him in very serious condition. He lost an arm and had multiple lacerations on his face, neck and chest. The damage also left him in danger of losing an eye. Shrapnel from the bomb entered his chest and lodged dangerously close to his heart. At first, the doctors had given up on him. However, Dr. Fleischer did not. He was committed to saving this young *unteroffizier's* life, if possible.

He performed surgery on Eric. The young man remained unconscious most of the time, and when he did wake up, he merely looked around, groaned, and then slipped back into a fitful, pain-ridden sleep.

Kata took special interest in this young man. She was convinced he could make it with God's help. She watched the way Dr. Fleischer worked feverishly on the young soldier to try to save his life and she prayed for both Dr. Fleischer and Eric with great fervor. She asked to be assigned to his case, and whenever possible, she knelt by his bed and prayed. After four days, and major surgery, he finally woke up. Kata happened to be at his bedside when he began to stir. He looked over, saw Kata, and said in a very weak voice, "What . . . happened to me?"

Kata quickly came to his bed and patted his remaining arm. "It's all right, Eric, you are safe now. You are in God's hands. He's looking after you."

He looked around the room, then looked at his bandaged body, and noticed the missing arm. He screamed, "No! Not my arm!" He began to wail loudly. He started to try to get up, but Kata restrained him. "Please, lie still, Eric. You cannot move yet."

"Let me up! I won't stay here!" Eric insisted.

"I'm sorry, but you're not in any condition to go anywhere right now. You must stay here for a while." She placed a compassionate hand on his shoulder.

"The doctor was able to save your life, but you are not out of danger yet," Kata informed him.

"What do you mean—I'm not 'out of danger'?" He glared at her angrily.

She gave him a grim, yet sympathetic glance. "Well, Eric, the shrapnel penetrated several parts of your body, and although Dr. Fleischer removed as much as possible, a few small pieces were too close to the heart and . . . he thought it best if . . . he left them alone."

Grimacing with severe pain, he attempted to get up again.

"Please, don't. You will only make matters worse," she said, sounding as comforting as possible.

His anger turned to hopelessness as he agonized with great emotion, "Just let me die. I hear most men do after losing limbs in this bloody war. I can't live without my arm. How can I tell my fiancée?" He tried one more time to get up, but again she held him down gently. He was too weak to resist her.

"You are really are more fortunate than you realize. You will be able to do much more than you think you can with one arm. Besides, we're not like most hospitals you hear about. We have a very knowledgeable and dedicated staff, and our recovery rate is much higher. And they are doing amazing things with artificial limbs today.

"Don't give up, Eric. There are many more souls out there who have been injured far worse, I assure you. Some have come back with *no* arms or *no* legs. Several men have even lost both eyes. Others have had their lungs or bodies severely burned by poisonous gas. Most of these soldiers will be scarred for life. As far as your fiancée, if she really loves you, she will look beyond your loss and love you no matter what. Just trust God to see you through this," she said.

"God?—God? God let this happen to me!" he lamented. How can I trust Him with *anything* after this?"

"God didn't make this happen," she continued calmly. "He loves you—He made an even greater sacrifice for you by allowing His only Son to die for you. He knows what loss is and He knows what it is to hurt and feel pain. If you let Him work in your life, He will carry you through your valley of despair."

Eric didn't say anything more. He just looked at her for a moment, and then he turned his head away, whimpered with pain, and drifted off to sleep.

A few hours later, after Kata made her normal rounds, she came back to his room. She found him lying there, staring at the ceiling.

"I would be glad to come after work and read to you if you would like, Eric," she offered.

"Suit yourself," he said in a bitter tone and turned his head away from her.

Kata refused to give up easily. "Very well, I get off at 6:00. I will be back at 7:00," she said.

He did not respond.

She came back with the book, *The Pilgrim's Progress*, sat down in a chair by his bed and began reading. Still no response. For the first couple of days, he didn't seem to pay much attention. He just stared off quietly as she read.

She continued to visit him, undaunted by his obvious rebuff. She always brought him a small gift of some sort: a paper, candy, magazines, or sometimes a pastry from the local bakery when she came. He accepted her gifts, but said little other than to occasionally grunt a weak 'thanks'. One day, however, after a week of her consistent visits, he looked at her curiously and asked, "Why do you keep coming to see me, even after I treat you so badly?"

"It's not because I need your affirmation or approval, but rather it's because God has put you on my heart. He loves you and is very concerned about you. Whether you want to believe it or not, He has good plans for you."

"Good plans for *me*? A one-armed man? What can *I* do for *him*?" Eric sneered sarcastically.

"Look around you. Many men here are much worse off. You can still walk, you can still see and you can still do many things with one arm. If you let Jesus work in your life, you can be so much to help others, instead of laying around feeling sorry for yourself," she said.

Eric lashed out in an angry tone, "What do *you* know about pain and loss? You have the nerve to come here every day in your immaculate uniform, and preach to me about God? You couldn't possibly imagine what it's like see friends of yours die all around you! How can you know what it's like to lose something valuable to you?!" He was practically screaming at her now, with fire in his eyes.

Kata patiently listened to him rant. She understood his hurt. His remarks rekindled the memory of the painful tragedies she had experienced in her lifetime. "I have lost more than you realize," she said evenly. "You may not be able to visibly see my loss, but it is more than just an arm or leg."

She hesitated for a moment and looked down. Then she faced him again and bit her trembling lip. "You see, I have lost my parents, a son when he was only four, dear and close friends, my husband and the custody of my only daughter. Unfortunately, I didn't know God then."

She paused and suddenly felt emboldened to share her testimony with him. "I have since learned that despite all that I did, and all that I lost, God sent His Son Jesus to die for me and to give me life. I learned that He loved me, and He wanted to walk with me daily and to help me get through all of my trials. I just needed to give him *my* life.

"Like Pilgrim, I put my burden at the cross, and although I still face obstacles in my life, I know that I am heading towards that Celestial City." A glow enveloped her face. Her eyes glistened and her trembling lip transformed into an angelic smile.

She continued, "I gave up a promising career as an opera singer to serve the Lord for the rest of my life. I see death all around me every day, but I have *never* regretted my decision to follow Christ. Yes, I *do* understand what loss is, but God understands it better than any of us."

He just looked at her; his mouth opened. He didn't say anything for a moment. Finally he said, "I-I'm sorry. I didn't mean to. . ."

"It's all right," she interrupted him and patted his hand. "I do understand. I have felt the bitterness you are feeling today. Above all, though, please remember, Eric, an arm can be replaced, but a family cannot." She gave him an understanding smile. "I'll let you get some rest." She put the book on his nightstand and walked out.

* * *

"Fascinating book, that *Pilgrim's Progress,"* Eric remarked the next time he saw Kata.

"You read some of it?" she asked.

"All of it," he said. "I haven't quite got it all figured out yet, but this man Christian ran into many obstacles along the way, didn't he?"

"Yes, his walk wasn't easy," said Kata as she checked his vitals and changed his bandages. "He encountered characters such as Pride, Despair and Vanity along his journey."

"He faced death, too, didn't he?" Eric continued.

"He went through the Valley of the Shadow of Death; yes," she said.

"Of course, it's Faithful who accompanies him through this valley, and then there's Hopeful, who keeps him from drowning and helps him to reach the Celestial City. The book is full of very interesting characters." Eric said. His mouth formed a tight frown. "I think I was trapped in the 'Castle of Despair,' after being in the 'Valley' for so many months."

"Remember, Eric, it is in the Valley that Christian heard the words from the 'Twenty-third Psalm'."

"And those words gave him comfort and helped him get through," Eric concluded. He turned his head towards Kata and nodded as though he had a new revelation.

"King David wrote that Psalm when he was going through trials in his own life. Even though he faced danger, persecutions and war, he learned to put his trust in God, and the Lord always saw him through. The Shepherd that he talks about is Jesus," Kata explained.

"You know your Bible; I'll say that, *Frau*. . ."

"You can call me Kata," she said. She wrapped the last of his bandages and straightened his covers. "I have spent a great deal of time in the Bible. It has helped me so much in my walk, and it helps me to get through every day of this abominable war that has taken the lives so many men—on both sides." She stiffened slightly. No matter how much faith she had, she still could not reconcile in her mind such meaningless bloodshed.

"Look, *Frau*—Kata, I'm sorry for the way I treated you and for the things I said to you. I had no idea. . ."

"Don't worry about it," she interrupted, gently patting his hand and giving him a comforting smile. "I understand fully. When we are hurting, we often get angry and want to lash out at someone or something," she said, trying to put his mind at ease.

"Well, I know you only meant to help me. I—I'm not sure about this Jesus, but I'll make a deal with you. If you want to teach me more about him, I'll listen. After all, I have nothing but time on my hands."

He returned a smile and reached out his hand as a sign of a truce. She accepted it and said, "I'll agree to that. I'll give you a Bible of your own as well."

Over the next three weeks, during his recuperation and when

Kata had time, she read parts of the Bible to him, especially the passages dealing with how the Lord helps and carries His people through times of trial. He loved to hear the Psalms. She also read the book of John to him. Here he learned more about God's love and ultimate sacrifice.

One particular evening as she was discussing Jesus' crucifixion, she could tell that he was visibly moved.

"I don't understand how someone could do that for anyone. That has to be incredible love. I am not sure how He can possibly forgive me. I have killed so many men during this unspeakable war." Eric sighed heavily and lowered his eyes. "In fact there were times I think I . . . half enjoyed it—especially when I saw friends of mine being slaughtered. I wanted revenge. His face darkened and filled with remorse. "I don't think I can forgive myself, let alone ask God to forgive me."

"It is called unconditional love," Kata said. "He loves us in spite of ourselves. Take the case of the thief on the cross next to Him. Here was a man wanted for crimes against others. He was probably very deserving of his punishment. Yet, when he asked Jesus to remember him, Jesus told him that he would be in paradise that very day. Jesus knew that even though He had to go through so much pain and suffering, it was worth it for the salvation of just one person—not matter what that person did. He wipes our slates clean, Eric."

There were tears in Eric's eyes as she continued to talk about others in the Bible who had committed unspeakable sins, yet many of them were in Jesus' lineage. She shared about Rahab the prostitute who had the faith to hide the Israelite spies. She told him how David had committed adultery and even murder, but when he repented, God forgave him, and even called him a man after His own heart.

"I—I think I am ready to ask Him into my life. I'm not sure what he can do with this ole' cripple, but I'm willing to give my life to him and let him try." Eric said as he lowered his head.

"The possibilities are endless, Eric. Just turn your life over to him and let him use you for his glory."

With that, Kata prayed with Eric and he asked Jesus into his heart.

"I feel like a ton of bricks has been taken off of my chest," Eric said, smiling after the prayer. Peace replaced the fear in his eyes and a glow washed over his face. Kata sensed that Eric was a new man that night.

"Speaking of your chest, I'm going to pray that the Lord supernaturally remove that shrapnel from it," she said.

Eric shook his head in unbelief. "Now, that might be asking a bit too much from God, I'm afraid."

"Nothing is impossible with Him."

She put her hand on his chest and began to pray that the Lord reach down and heal him completely.

The following week, Eric was up and walking around, talking to other injured soldiers and telling them about Jesus. He was a different man. He paid little attention to the missing limb, and the scars on his face were healing nicely.

Dr. Fleischer stopped by to visit him one afternoon and commented on the change in him.

"It's that Nurse Albers. I have to admit at first I didn't know what to think of her, but now I am beginning to think that she is really an angel with a mission from heaven," he said.

"That may very well be, Eric." Dr. Fleischer mused and nodded in agreement. "She certainly has a unique way to care for patients here. I have heard from more than one of them that she is a real encourager. And she certainly loves to tell them about Jesus.

"Now, let's talk about you for a few moments," Dr. Fleischer said. "You're making great progress, and I'll be sending you home soon. First, I need to schedule you for some final tests. I've been particularly concerned about that shrapnel around your heart."

"You know, I haven't had a lot of chest pain lately, so I am wondering whether that prayer of Nurse Albers could have made a difference," Eric said.

"What are you talking about?" asked Dr. Fleischer.

Eric told him how Kata had prayed for him, and how he had accepted Jesus. Dr. Fleischer looked surprised.

"Nurse Albers did that?"

"Yes, Doctor. She is an amazing lady. Maybe God did perform some kind of miracle."

"Well, I don't know that much about miracles, but we'll take a look. Thanks to a fairly new technology, we can take a picture of your chest and see inside."

"A picture? How do you do that?" Eric asked.

"It's called an X-ray. It will actually penetrate through the walls of your chest and give us an image of what's inside. I'm sure we'll soon find out what is going on."

* * *

"I can't believe it!" Dr. Fleischer exclaimed, after speaking with the radiographer and looking at Eric's X-ray. "There's no sign of the shrapnel anywhere! Do you think there's something wrong with the machine?"

"No, Doctor, it's working perfectly." We have it checked regularly, and the results are always satisfactory."

The doctor stroked his chin and shook his head in astonishment. *Maybe there was something to Kata's prayer after all,* he thought to himself. *There's no other explanation—is there?"*

He shared the news with Eric. "That's incredible. I wouldn't have believed it before I accepted Jesus, but now I guess I understand so much better his love for us," Eric said, shaking Dr. Fleischer's hand.

"I—I think maybe God might be calling me to preach—ever hear of a one-armed minister, Doctor? I guess I don't need two arms for that, now do I?" Eric grinned.

In his remaining few days at the hospital, he spent most of the time reading the Bible and sharing his newfound faith with other soldiers throughout the ward. By the end of that week, Eric was fitted for an artificial arm and released from the hospital. Before he left, he shared with Kata his plans for the future.

"I believe God is calling me into the ministry. Actually, since I was a child, I think I had this empty feeling that I was never able to satisfy. Since I really didn't know God, I had no idea what this desire in me was. Now, thanks to you, I have an excitement about the future that God has for me. I owe you my life. You know . . . if I didn't know better, I'd think you were an angel sent by God."

Kata laughed at the idea. "No, Eric. God saved your life. He just used me as an instrument. But I don't think it is an accident that you came here, and I believe you are right about one thing. He may have had a plan for you to preach, but you had to meet Him as Savior and Lord first."

Then she looked at him with a more serious expression. I do believe in time, God will use you to save the lives of thousands. I feel so blessed that He chose me as the means for you to come to know Him." Kata's eyes filled with tears, and she took Eric's hand.

"Well, I will never forget the day I met an 'angel with a mission from heaven', he said as he hugged her goodbye. "I'm going home and as soon as I heal up, I'm enrolling in the seminary—believe me, that's the last thing I'd have thought I'd have done with my life . . . that is, until I met you."

She hugged him back firmly and replied, "I hope one day I get to sit in on one of the sermons of the 'one-armed preacher' who is fully armed with the Spirit of the Lord."

CHAPTER 26

Lunch with Dr. Fleischer

KATA'S NURSING SKILLS WERE FLECKLESS. SHE learned very quickly. She was a credit to the nursing profession. She treated every one of her patients as if he was the only one. By the spring of 1916, Kata had become one of the lead nurses at the Berlin Hospital. She continued to share the love of Jesus with her patients, and Eric was the first of many she prayed with to receive Him as Savior.

One afternoon, while she was eating lunch in the hospital cafeteria, Dr. Fleischer walked in. He noticed Kata sitting by herself. He ordered a cup of coffee and a sandwich, and walked over to her table.

"Do you mind if I join you?" he asked as he stood in front of the chair across from her.

"Not at all. Please, sit down," Kata said, gesturing towards the chair.

"I want to tell you how pleased I am with your work here, Nurse Albers. You have done very well with your patients. They seem to love you."

"Why, thank you, Doctor, but at times I don't feel that I do enough for these poor souls." With her elbows resting on the table, she took a sip from her cup of coffee and looked straight ahead. "When they come here, so many of them are in such bad shape that it is a wonder they ever walk out of here."

"Yes, war has certainly taken a great toll on our men, I'm afraid," he replied with a sigh. “I have to admit, though, you do have a unique way of helping these men. I was very impressed with the way you handled that young *unteroffizier,* Eric, a few weeks ago. You sure changed his life. I am still trying to figure out what happened to the shrapnel in his chest. I understand you prayed with him before I took those X-rays. Something tells me you had a little to do with that miracle.” He shook his head in amazement.

Kata replied humbly, “I did nothing. God did it all.”

“God used you, but you had to step out of the boat, so to speak, and be willing to share the truth of God’s Word with that young soldier.”

“God put that desire in my heart when He called me out of the opera into the field of nursing. More than anything, I long to see those who come from the front lines make Jesus Lord of their lives.”

Dr. Fleischer studied her. For the first time, he noticed how attractive she was, despite the weariness she tried hard to conceal. He admired her inner strength and her faith. Warmth tugged at his heart. He had been very professional in his dealings with Kata and the other nurses, but after watching her for the past several months, observing the way she cared so compassionately for her patients, he found himself very attracted to her.

The more he listened to her share the Gospel with her patients, and the more he observed her grace and her love for Jesus, the more he was convinced that Eric was right about her. Perhaps she was an ‘angel with a mission’.

He observed a glimmer of optimism in her beautiful hazel eyes, and enjoyed the way they sparkled when she talked about God. He loved how her ruby lips curled up in a slight smile. He couldn’t miss her auburn hair, even though most of it was neatly tucked under her nurse’s cap. It complemented her creamy complexion. He found it difficult to take his eyes off her. An ineffable feeling stirred within him. He hadn’t felt that way since he had met his late wife many years before.

Suddenly, he caught himself and tried to appear more detached and professional, despite the emotions welling up in him. He shook his head and chuckled.

"You are something else, Nurse Albers. You know, I have a great deal of faith in God as well, but I don't think I would have taken on such a challenging goal as you did with Eric. It probably is a bit idealistic, but I do admire your persistence. You helped to bring another soul to Christ."

"Are you a Christian, then, Doctor Fleischer?" Kata asked as she ran her finger around the rim of her coffee cup.

"Yes, but I'm also half Jewish. My mother was Jewish and my father was a Gentile—a Baptist."

"That's very interesting. When did you come to know Christ?" Kata queried.

"My father was very strong in his faith. When my parents married, he was not really a Christian. It was about three years after they were married that he decided to visit a church with a Christian friend of his, and that is when he gave his heart to the Lord. He tried to get my mother to go with him, but she would not at the time. For a few years, he was content to go to his church and let her go to her synagogue.

"When I was about five, he started to take my older brother and me to church every Sunday. At first, Mother was not very happy about it, but Father insisted. He told her that she was still free to attend her synagogue, but his children were going to learn about Jesus. Even though she did not necessarily agree with his faith, she was an obedient wife, so she went along with his decision. When she learned that my brother and I had come to accept the Lord as our Savior, she protested at first, but she soon realized our conversion was real. She finally decided to our visit church. She came a few Sundays after that out of sheer curiosity, then one evening the Pastor preached a message from Isaiah 53."

"And had your mother never read that chapter?" Kata asked. "It is part of the Old Testament."

"Well, in the Jewish faith, it is often overlooked, because it contains a detailed description of Christ's crucifixion. Some rabbis even refuse to read it in the synagogue—I've even heard some refer to it as 'the forbidden chapter'."

"'The forbidden chapter.' I had never heard that expression

before," Kata said, listening intently. Dr. Fleischer continued. "Consequently, our mother had never heard this passage before. That night, as she listened to the description of how Jesus suffered and died on that cross for our sin; how He was beaten and rejected, how He suffered; how He carried our sorrows, was pierced for the transgressions, and was crushed for the iniquities of *all* mankind, she was greatly moved.

"That night, when the minister gave the invitation to accept Jesus as Lord, Mother gave her heart to Christ."

"What a wonderful story, Doctor. So then you have the best of both worlds. You are part of God's chosen people and you are also a part of the body of Christ," Kata mused.

"I was very young then, but I will never forget the look on her face after she came back to her seat. God's peace and joy were radiating from her."

The Doctor's eyes glistened with tears as he recalled the event that had finally brought his family together in the Lord. He continued. "From that day on, our family grew together in the Lord. My parents became missionaries and eventually moved to India, and my older brother became a minister. I contemplated it, but I loved medicine and had a deep desire to help the sick, so I chose to become a doctor."

"That's very admirable," said Kata

"Like you," he continued, "I do try to encourage my patients, and when I have the opportunity, I do talk about the Lord. I have to admit, though, I haven't had the *chutzpah* to share the Gospel as boldly as you have."

Kata chuckled at his use of the Jewish colloquialism, *Chutzpah;* however, she shook her head vehemently, and then refuted his remark.

"It's not me, but the Holy Spirit in me who gives that boldness. I do know you can have that boldness as well. If you just trust Him, the Holy Spirit will do the same for you. When I see so many of these young men on the verge of death, I realize that I could not live with myself if I didn't share the plan of salvation with them—to let them know they can have eternal life if they just give their hearts to Jesus."

"You are really an inspiring lady. I admire that."

Dr. Fleischer looked at his watch and said to Kata, "I didn't realize that we have been here so long. I need to get back to work." He had been a widower for five years and never considered seeing anyone else, let alone marrying again. He had been very much in love with his wife. Something about Kata, however, reminded him of her. Could he entertain the idea of finding love again?

"Before I do, though, I was wondering—I hope you don't think I am too forward, but would you consider having dinner with me sometime?" he asked.

Kata lowered her eyes. "I don't know if that would be a good idea. You see, I . . . well, I am divorced. I still am trying to put my life in order. I don't think I am ready to see anyone."

Dr. Fleischer saw that she was uncomfortable about his request. He tried to put her at ease. "You don't have to explain. I would never do anything to make you feel uncomfortable. I enjoy talking to you and want to learn more about your faith and your life. I would just like to be a friend."

"Well, perhaps we could have lunch in the cafeteria again," she smiled and added, "—on the condition that I buy my own lunch."

"Agreed." He got up, shook her hand gently, and walked away leaving Kata to finish her coffee. He was pleased, and at the same time, somewhat relieved that she wasn't too eager to develop a serious relationship. Perhaps he was not quite ready either.

Chapter 27

The Wages of Sin and War

OVER THE NEXT TWO YEARS, THE war became even more intense. Conditions worsened and morale was slipping even deeper into the abyss than could possibly be imagined. The winter of 1916 had brought in some of the bitterest cold that Europe had experienced.

Kata listened to the horrors of war every day as the injured shared their terrifying experiences at the front. Trying to keep their clothing warm and dry was extremely difficult for the men on the front. Water supplies froze and dugouts were so unbearably cold that the soldiers built fires to attempt to keep warm, but these acrid fires caused such thick smoke, that some men suffocated in their sleep. Because of these almost unbearable conditions, most men only got an average of about two to three hours sleep at night.

She heard about their almost intolerable living conditions in the foul-smelling and unsanitary trenches. Some men, who merely dared to lift their heads above these repugnant dugouts, trying to get a little fresh air, literally had their heads blown off by sniper fire. She heard the cries of so many men reliving those scenes repeatedly in the form of paralyzing nightmares. She heard about the horrifying effects of gas warfare. The scenes of terror never left her. There had never before been a war of this magnitude in terms of destruction.

Each night she returned to her comfortable apartment, she brooded over those tales. They found their way into her own nightmares. She often dragged her worn out body to bed, then drifted off into a dismal sleep, only to be transported to the front. She experienced the same nightmare many times. She often saw herself in a trench filled with mud mixed with skulls, bones and body parts scattered all around her. Looking down at her feet she saw blood pooling around her and rising to her ankles. Some nights she would imagine herself eating a piece of stale bread, only to have it snatched from her hand by a rat, the size of a terrier. When she tried to take it back, the monstrous rodent attacked her fingers.

Her dreams often ended with someone screaming out, *gas masks!* She would grope around in the fog trying to find hers, but before she could find it, the deadly chemicals would seep into her nostrils, and fill her lungs. She could feel the caustic gasses eating away at her body. Just as she was about to strangle in a choking fit, she would wake up, often screaming out in terror and gasping for air: her body soaked in a terrible sweat and her heart pounding rapidly against the walls of her chest. She would put her hands over her heart, wait for it to calm down, and then she would pray for the men who were at the front. She believed that the Lord allowed her to see these things so that she would intercede for those still in battle.

* * *

In Berlin, the wounded were coming in by the hundreds. The hospital was very large, but it did not seem to be able to hold all of the wounded and those suffering from other effects of the war such as typhoid fever, trench foot, tuberculosis and pneumonia or even rat bites. Several of the hotels in the city had to be converted into auxiliary hospitals to accommodate the injured.

Kata now had her own team of nurses. She tried to keep them encouraged. Most of them felt overwhelmed, but Kata knew that with God's help, they could endure. As Nurse Hemmler had suggested, she began a Bible study for them during their lunchtime whenever they could fit it in. She had asked Pastor Johannes' wife to volunteer a couple of hours a week to help her with this, as she did not feel she was ready to lead one on her own just yet. Mrs. Johannes was very eager to help. She wanted to do more for the cause, and thought this was an ideal way to build the nurses' faith and to keep them encouraged that what they were doing was a service to the Lord, as well as to the wounded and the sick. Many of them had come to know Jesus as a result of their efforts.

The war had affected so many areas of life for Kata and for the whole country. During their visits, Elsa could see that the war was wearing Kata down, as she had little energy to do anything when they were together. "Kata, when are you going to take time off? You are *killing* yourself," Elsa remarked during one of her visits. "I take my Sunday mornings off, and when you are here, I try to just work part of the weekend, six hour shifts—from 12 midnight to 6 a.m. That's enough for now," she reasoned.

"But you come home so exhausted. You are not eating right and you're neglecting your home and your health. You can barely keep your eyes open during dinner. Why, yesterday, when I was reading to you and Martina, you were nodding off! You really need—"

"I am quite aware of what I need," Kata interrupted with an air of defensiveness. "However, my salary doesn't allow for such luxuries as housekeeping any longer. With the economy the way it is, even Fredric's stipend isn't enough to make ends meet these days. And I certainly don't have the time to cook. I eat what I can and when I can."

"I'll try to help you more when we visit," Elsa offered. "Perhaps I can make a few dinners for you to have during the week. You can keep them in your ice box."

"Oh, they won't keep more than a day or two at best. I just cannot afford more than one good block of ice a week. Besides, I do get at least one good meal each day I am working, you know. The cafeteria does have fairly good food, and it is free for the staff."

"I am sorry, Kata. I didn't mean to criticize, but I am very concerned about you. You have deteriorated so since our last visit. You need your rest and to take better care of yourself."

Kata wilted a bit. "I know you're right, but you don't understand! We have so many wounded to take care of and not enough nurses to care for them. This war is taking its toll, not only on the wounded, but also on those of us caring for them—not to mention their families. I have to do what I can to help. There's no other way."

Elsa did not argue with her any more. "I know that God is using you, Kata. I can see that when I have visited the hospital with you. You have such a ministry with your patients, and it is evident that they admire you. It just upsets me to see you this way. This ugly war is destroying our nation, I'm afraid."

"I agree. It is terrible the way food has to be rationed now," Kata said.

"Thank goodness you saw fit to have a garden and stock up on supplies early enough, Kata."

"I believe that was the Lord's prompting. After all, didn't he warn Joseph about a future famine?" Kata asked.

"Quite true." Regardless, you have prepared well for this time of famine in Germany."

Kata smiled and said, "The famine isn't just about food. Just look at women's fashion. Why, dresses are nothing but mere coverings—a hodgepodge of fabrics thrown together with no fashion to them whatsoever."

Elsa nodded. "They are almost immodest—they don't even cover our ankles anymore."

"The shortage of fabric definitely has affected our dress. Some days I do miss the satins, the velvets and the beautiful silks, but I wouldn't have time to wear them even if I did have such a dress. I am in my nurses' uniform almost every waking hour. Besides, I feel blessed just to have a home and a career. There are many today that don't even have that."

Elsa nodded. "This war has certainly put a strain on every aspect of our lives. Everyone has had to make such terrible sacrifices."

"You are quite right. I have even had to put my car away for the time being. There are such shortages of fuel.—Thank goodness I live close enough to the hospital to be able to walk most days. And when it's cold, I can get a taxicab."

"Yes that is a blessing for you, Kata, but please be careful. With the rioting going on in the city, over this war, walking can be dangerous."

"Oh, I don't worry about such things. They seem to be taking place closer to the center of the city. Besides, I trust the Lord to protect me and to provide for all of my needs. He has never let me down. I may not be living in the opulence that I once did, but He has met every need. For that, I am thankful. And, believe it or not, I am actually much more content now than I ever have been."

"It's amazing how you've grown since you have come to know the Lord. I am very proud of you."

"And I am so grateful for the day that God brought you into our lives, Elsa. You changed my life."

"No, it wasn't me. It was God," Elsa insisted.

"Well, you had more to do with it than you realize." Kata's face clouded as they discussed the effects of the war. " We really need to pray that our Kaiser will put an end to this war and that our men will be able to come home for good."

* * *

Fredric had also suffered greatly and found no peace during this time. The Great War had affected industry as well. Much of the industry switched to producing war-related items such as weapons and chemicals. Fredric found it very difficult to find workers for his factories. So many men had gone to the front, thus cutting production almost in half. He managed to find women who were willing to work in place of men, but it still did not meet the needs of production as the German unions fought the hiring of women. He had to shut down a few of his factories temporarily, which cut into profits.

These hardships did not deter Griselda from being demanding. She still expected to live in the lavish luxury to which she had grown accustomed before the war. She had no compassion for what was happening. Her greed and shrewish nature put great pressure on Fredric. He found himself working longer hours in order to avoid confrontations with her.

He now regretted his decision to leave Kata for this fishwife. He wished he could undo his past. He thought about the wonderful life he had enjoyed with Kata, despite her career. Worst of all, he saw how his little Martina agonized over having to put up with Griselda's continuous carping. She did not care at all for her stepmother. His problems seemed insurmountable. Griselda had such a hold on him. She seemed to know how to manipulate him. Martina's life had changed so much since he had divorced Kata. The consequences of his sin had taken a tremendous toll on both of them, and he did not know where to turn. He had sold his soul for a moment of pleasure and now he was miserable.

CHAPTER 28

Though I walk Through The Valley

By the fall of 1918, it was evident that Germany had lost the war. Germany's Kaiser Wilhelm II, who was the grandson of Queen Victoria, fled to the Netherlands. The war finally ended in June 1919, with the signing of the Treaty of Versailles, but not without major consequences for all involved. Thousands continued to die even after it was over. Germany alone lost almost two million men during the war, and an additional four million were wounded.

The country's troubles were not over by any means, though. A battered Europe and war-torn Germany suffered severe hardships of every kind. A new democratic government, the Weimer Republic, was proclaimed in November 1918, and there was great political unrest. Many Germans opposed the new government.

To make matters worse, a severe pandemic of influenza broke out in Europe and spread all over the world. Millions succumbed to this dreadful disease. Hundreds of thousands died. The hospitals barely had a chance to recuperate from treating the war casualties when Germany was affected by this terrible illness. It did not discriminate. It permeated all areas of civilization from the children to the elderly, from the very poor to the very rich. Many of those stricken died an excruciating death.

The hospitals were once again deluged with patients. This time, though, it was not just young soldiers; this time it included children and the elderly. It was almost more than Kata could bear as she saw little children, their lungs filling up with fluid, coughing up blood, or women and the elderly drowning in their own body fluids. Many of her patients died after dehydrating or losing control of their bowel functions.

One little boy, who was only about five years old, was brought in during the latter stages of the illness. He reminded her so much of her little Max. Kata stayed with him as much as she was able. His condition struck her so fiercely. She prayed diligently for him.

As he lay there, struggling to breathe, Kata watched his mother agonize over her little boy. She relived the illness and ultimate death of her son. God filled her heart with great compassion for his mother as she empathized with her pain.

"I know what you are going through, *Frau* Klein," she confided to the young woman as she sat by her son's bedside, weeping.

"Please, Nurse Albers, call me Hannah," she requested.

Kata related the story of her own experience with Max, and then tried to comfort the woman by telling her about Jesus' love and concern for her son.

"But how could God let this happen to our children?" Hannah's reddened sleep-deprived eyes met Kata's as she looked up at her.

"God does not *cause* this to happen. There is also evil at work in our world. It is not God's will for little ones to suffer, but He gives us strength to endure any trials we may have to go through. He does not leave us comfortless."

"How did you make it through the loss of your son?" the young woman asked, looking at Kata as if she were searching for hope.

"Unfortunately at the time, I didn't know the Lord, so I had a very hard time coping with my son's death. I didn't handle it well, I'm afraid. It was only many years later, when my husband . . . left me, that I realized I needed divine help. I needed Jesus in my life. It was with His grace that I was able to get through the incredible pain of such a loss. I don't know how I would have made it without Him," Kata shared. "I do know that God understands the agony we feel when we lose our children more than anyone can imagine."

She told her of the great sacrifice God had made when He sent His son Jesus to die. Then she invited the woman to make Jesus her Lord and Savior.

Kata's testimony was so effective that Hannah accepted the invitation and asked the Lord into her heart. Kata then asked Hannah to join her as she prayed for the young boy. Finally, Kata felt a real peace.

"You know, coincidentally, there is a story of a lady in the Bible also named Hannah who prayed fervently for a child, and God heard her prayers. God gave her a son," Kata explained. "Somehow, I believe that your prayer was very similar, and that God is going to give you your son back."

"Do you really think so?" The young woman asked. Her eyes grew wide with hope.

"Yes," said Kata. She did not understand fully what would happen, but a burst of faith and expectation surged inside of her. She left the room to give the young mother time alone with her son, and to see to her other patients.

The next morning when she came back to check on them, she was jubilant to see the boy sitting up in his bed, eyes open and color in his cheeks. He was smiling and talking to his mother. Hannah was beaming. "He's so much better today. I can't believe it! I think he's been healed. God really did hear our prayers!" she exclaimed. "He is truly a mighty and wonderful God. I will always be grateful for what He has done in my son's and in my life."

Kata's countenance expressed awe and amazement.

"I am so happy for you as well. As long as I have been a Christian, I never cease to marvel at God's goodness and mercy," Kata added, shaking her head and smiling at the boy and his mother. She was overwhelmed with love for her Lord and Savior, who had been with her through all of her trials and had helped her to share with others about his love and mercy, through her own testimony.

* * *

Two weeks later, while Kata was at home resting after working a twelve-hour shift, she received a call from Elsa.

"Oh Kata, you must come to the hospital quickly. Something *terrible* has happened," she said.

Kata heard the tremble in her voice.

"Is it Martina?" Kata asked nervously.

"No, Kata. It's Fredric," she said in a sober tone.

"Fredric? What has happened to him?" Kata asked. "Has there been an accident?"

"I think he has the influenza," Elsa told her. Her voice quivered. "He—he's been sick for two days now, but wouldn't admit it. He looked so bad when he came home this evening." She paused briefly, took a deep breath, then continued.

"He passed out and I called for an ambulance. Martina and I had a taxicab bring us here to the hospital. He's not doing very well, I'm afraid. Martina is quite upset."

"I-I'm not so sure it's a good idea for me to come, Elsa. Why call me? Where's Griselda?" Kata asked.

"She's away on another one of her trips. He's been sick for some time, but Griselda was oblivious to his symptoms. As long as Fredric keeps her in fine jewelry and clothing, she doesn't seem to care about anything else."

"Why not just contact her?"

"We can't," insisted Elsa. "No one seems to know where she is for sure. She never tells me where she is going."

"Well, I'm not sure it's the right thing for me to do—after all, I'm no longer his wife."

"But Kata, you must come. There's no one else who can look after him like you can."

"Look, I'm not trying to be unsympathetic. On the contrary, I'm very concerned. I'm afraid that if Griselda finds out that I interfered, though, she might take it out on you and Martina."

"Griselda did not leave word as to when she would be back, and besides, if nothing else, you need to be here for Martina. She needs her mother right now," Elsa said, adamantly.

"All right, I'll come, then," said Kata. *Of course, Martina would need me. She must be frightened, seeing her father in his condition. I must go, at least for Martina.*

She quickly dressed and rushed back to the hospital. When she walked into Fredric's room, she turned pale. His face had a bluish cast to it. He was very weak and coughing up blood.

Martina and Elsa were standing close to his bedside. Martina's eyes were red and tear-filled. Kata tried hard to hold back her own tears. The memories of this man she had loved dearly, flooded back into her heart. She thought she had finally let these feelings go, but looking at his fragile body lying on the brink of death stirred her emotions. Nevertheless, she had to be strong for Martina's sake.

Elsa hugged her. "Thank you for coming, Kata. He's been in and out of consciousness."

Martina clung to her mother, sobbing violently. "Don't let him die," she begged. "Please, Mama, do something!"

She put her arms around her daughter and held her tight, then lifted her chin and looked into her swollen eyes. *"Liebe,* it is in God's hands. We have to trust Him in this." She kissed her daughter's forehead, and walked up to Fredric's bed. She read his chart, walked over to his bedside and took his pulse. She looked over at Elsa. A wave of alarm swept over her face. "He's very weak," she said shaking her head soberly—as if resigned to the fact that he was not going to make it.

"But Mama, God can't take Papa. He just *can't*!" Martina insisted.

"We cannot tell God what He can and cannot do, *Schatzi.* We can pray and believe, he's in God's hands."

Kata had seen miracle after miracle; on the other hand, she had also seen many people die in her care. She didn't know what would happen with Fredric, but deep in her heart, she knew that God was sovereign, and no matter what, everything was in His control.

She fought back the tears and tried to quell the heartache that was attempting to overwhelm her. Even though they had been divorced for some time, and despite the fact that he had left her for another woman, her feelings were still strong for this man. She looked down and addressed him in her thoughts. *How could I have spent so many years with you and not still care, Fredric?* She gently grasped one of his hands. Fredric opened his eyes to see Kata standing there, holding his hand. He was too weak to raise his head.

"Kata, I. . . " he said faintly.

"Don't strain yourself Fredric. You are too weak to talk," Kata insisted, patting his hand.

"No, no, I need. . . to. . . talk. . . to. . . you," he insisted breathlessly.

"It's all right Fredric. You don't need to say—"

He interrupted her. "I have been so wrong. . . I . . . threw away-- true love. I—sold . . .my . . .soul . . . for . . . I'm so. . .sorry. . . Kata."

"Please—don't say any more, Fredric. I forgave you a long time ago. The Lord has taught me so much. I was as much at fault in our marriage as you were," she admitted, patting his hand and smiling fondly at him.

"I—I—don't. . .deserve . . .your . . . forgiveness," he said remorsefully, gasping for air between words.

"None of us deserve forgiveness, Fredric, but Jesus died for us so that we could *all* be forgiven. I have no right to hold on to *any* bitterness. Please, accept my forgiveness and that of the Lord's in your own life, Fredric. He can give you a new beginning."

"But. . . He. . . can't possibly. . . forgive what. . . I have. . . done to. . . you. . . and . . . our daughter," he continued in labored breaths.

"Yes, Fredric, He can and He *has,*" she insisted. "If you just repent of your sins and ask for His forgiveness, He'll give it freely. Can I pray with you?" she asked.

He was in pain and very weak, but she could tell that he had grasped the concept, despite his condition.

"If He . . . will accept someone. . . like me, then . . . yes. I'd. . .like. . .that," he said, smiling weakly. "I. . .need . . .God's. . . forgiveness."

Martina looked with great emotion while they were talking. Tears trickled down her cheeks and her lips trembled. She moved to the other side of his bed, took his other hand and kissed it.

"Oh Papa, I know He will forgive you. He loves you and has been waiting for you to open your heart to Him—and so have I."

He nodded, closed his eyes, and Martina bowed her head while her mother led her father in the sinner's prayer. He repeated after her slowly and with great difficulty, but when they had finished praying, he opened his eyes and smiled. His whole body relaxed. A profound peace filled his countenance. "I. . . feel. . .His. . . presence. . .He's here . . . I know He's . . . forgiven. . . me. Thank. . . you," he said, and then drifted into a deep, comatose sleep.

Martina burst into grateful sobs. Kata's eyes streamed with tears as she drank in the events that had just unfolded. Fredric had finally accepted the Lord, and she had been able to witness it. She took Elsa and Martina into an adjoining waiting room.

"Try to rest a little while, *Engel.* I will keep an eye on your papa," she said to Martina.

Elsa stayed with Martina and Kata returned to Fredric's room. She sat beside his bed and said silently prayed while he continued to sleep.

The evening wore on very slowly, but Kata did not leave. She had no idea when, or if Griselda would arrive, but she decided that she would stay with Fredric as long as she could. She tried to convince herself that what she was feeling was "the love of the Lord", but deep inside, she knew she never had stopped loving this man. As he lay there, barely clinging to life, a variety of emotions filled her heart as she allowed past events to dominate her thoughts.

She recalled their first meeting, and how he had eventually convinced her to marry him. She remembered their early years, and then how she chose to return to the opera. She had sacrificed her marriage for the sake of fame. *I was so blind. I threw him to that woman!* She thought of the sad irony of the situation. The thing that she had tried so hard to hold on to—her career, she eventually gave up for the Lord anyway. *If only I would have come to know God sooner—maybe we would have had a chance.* Then she remembered the words of Pastor Johannes, and the day she had prayed to leave her past at the cross. God had turned her life around and had given her a new mission in life. Since she had become a nurse, He had used her to witness to so many patients who might have died without knowing Him. She thought about others who had come to know Christ, such as Eric, Princess Sophie and Hannah, because of her testimony.

Although she was content with her life now, it took tragedy and loss for her to realize her need for Christ. It was in the valley that she had found true happiness. God had taken her shattered life and had turned it into something beautiful. He had made Romans 8:28 a very real part of her existence. *You have taken the foolish mistakes I have made and turned things around for your glory*, she confessed.

Now she saw the Lord doing that same thing in Fredric's life. He, too, had been a "victim" of affluence and pride. He was a self-made man. Until he actually faced death, he had taken life for granted. She looked down at his emaciated frame. How pitiful he looked lying there. That robust, self-confident man she had loved so deeply was no more. Instead, the man lying in the hospital bed next to her was helpless—dependent totally on God's mercy and grace.

It was in this state that he finally gave his heart to the Lord. Now, no matter what their future held here on earth, she knew that they would meet again in heaven. She lowered her head and said a silent prayer, *Thank you, Jesus, for what you have done today in Fredric's life. I only pray that one day Griselda can come to know you as well."*

She shocked herself with these words. Had she just prayed for Griselda? Yes. She did pray for his wife. That had to be the Lord. Only He could fill her with that kind of love. A deep sadness for Griselda pooled in her heart. How lost this woman really was. How much she, too, needed God. *Help me to be a witness to Griselda,"* she added with a sigh, realizing that would take a real move of God. Her eyes became heavy, and she began to nod . . .

* * *

"Nurse Albers—Kata," she heard a voice and looked up to see Doctor Fleisher standing in front of her, patting her shoulder. "You really need to go home and get some rest," he advised. "*Herr* Albers is still sleeping, and it's after midnight."

"Where are Martina and Elsa?" she asked after she was a little more alert. "They're asleep in the waiting room. They should go home with you as well. I can call a taxicab for you, if you wish," Dr. Fleischer said.

"I-I don't think I should leave him."

"There's nothing more you can do here. Besides, you won't be able to care for any of your patients if you don't get some rest," he argued.

"All right, then," she conceded reluctantly. "I will for now, but please notify me *immediately* if there is *any* change."

He agreed and helped Kata, Martina and Elsa get a taxicab. Kata slept fitfully that evening, waking up frequently. In the morning, the three of them hurried through a light breakfast of *brötchen*, coffee and fruit, and then promptly returned to the hospital.

When they entered Fredric's room, Doctor Fleisher had just finished examining him. He asked Martina and Elsa to step out of the room for a few minutes while he talked with Kata.

"How is he this morning?" Kata asked Dr. Fleischer.

He shook his head somberly. "It doesn't look good for him, I'm afraid."

Kata looked searched his eyes for any glimpse of hope or encouragement. "Is there nothing else we can do for him?"

"I wish I could give you some positive news, but I think he let this go much too long. Has anyone been able to locate *Frau* Albers?"

"No. Her staff believes that she is visiting relatives in the country and could be gone a day or two more. They do not know how to get hold of her."

Dr. Fleischer frowned. "I hope she returns before. . ."

"Before *what*?"

"Well, I'm afraid his condition has worsened. His lungs are filling up with fluid. He is literally drowning, and there's nothing I can do to stop it." From his tone and demeanor, Kata sensed that Dr. Fleischer was very frustrated and worried. The wrinkles on his forehead, the stress lines on his face and the dark circles under his eyes concerned Kata, but right now, she had to concentrate on Fredric.

Kata looked over at Fredric's face. Impending death announced itself on his countenance. His face and skin had a yellowish cast to it. Kata knew this was a bad sign.

"How much time do you think he has?" She faced the inevitable that lay ahead for Fredric, yet she knew that she had to be strong for her daughter's sake.

"If he makes it through the day, I will be surprised," he sighed.

Kata hugged her arms desperately, bit her lip, and in a trembling voice asked, "How am I going to tell my daughter?"

Dr. Fleischer reached out and took her in his arms to comfort her. How tender and loving they felt. She allowed him to hold her for a moment, then suddenly pulled away and faced the door.

"I have to go to Martina," she said as she tried to compose herself. She brushed away tears, straightened up and stiffly walked out of the room. She wrestled with the feelings she had allowed to overtake her briefly. Had she enjoyed the comforting feeling and warmth of Dr. Fleischer's arms? No. Her despair and his understanding just came together for a moment. She could never feel anything for another man—ever. Even though Fredric had deserted her for someone else, her love for Fredric was unconditional—and unending. He had been her first and only true love. He may belong to someone else now, but she would always love this man. She did not have to be here for Fredric. She could have just left him in the care of other nurses, but she didn't. And, she admitted, it was not just for her daughter.

Kata found Martina sitting on a bench right outside of his room, huddling against Elsa. Kata sat on the other side of her and took her hand.

"He just can't die, Mama. He can't leave us!" Martina leaned over to her mother, buried her head in her mother's lap as they sat on the waiting room sofa. Kata ran her fingers through her daughter's hair and tried to console her.

"I know how it feels to face the death of one you love, *Liebe.* I lost my parents at a young age. And, remember, your papa and I lost your brother, Max, before you were born. I almost let his death destroy me. No matter what happens, though, *Engel*, we know we will be together again in heaven now." She did her best to encourage Martina, but Martina was inconsolable.

"It's not fair, Mama. It was hard enough to see you and Papa get divorced, but the thought of never seeing one of you the rest of my life is almost more than I can bear! I'm not ready to let him go." Martina buried her head in her mother's arms and cried even harder.

"Sometimes we have to let go of the things and people we love the most in order to let God really work in our lives."

"Are you telling me that God is making me give Papa up so He can work in my life, Mama?"

"No, *Engel*. I don't believe God is the reason your father is dying. There is a devil that causes bad things to happen in this world. Things like war, disease and divorce are all part of this world, but God promised us that He would *always* see us through. This is a time when you must really trust him to hold your hand as you walk through this valley."

Martina calmed down a bit, looked up at her mother and nodded in agreement. "I need His comfort and strength, so I can face this," she said.

Elsa looked on in silence. She was so proud of Kata as she listened to her counsel Martina. She knew that no matter what lie ahead of them, these two women had the faith to face it. *Thank you so much, Dear Heavenly Father for allowing me to be a part of their lives.* She prayed silently. She also marveled that perhaps in God's infinite wisdom, Griselda was unreachable through this time, which had made it possible for Kata to lead Fredric to the Lord and allowed the Lord to work forgiveness and healing in their lives. That *definitely* would not have been possible had Griselda been there. However, at the same time, she grieved for that poor unfortunate woman who did not know God.

At that moment, Dr. Fleischer entered the room. He walked up to Martina and Kata and placed a hand on her shoulder. His face clouded as he spoke and he gave Martina a sympathetic glance. "I'm sorry, but . . . he's gone."

Martina burst into a torrent of tears once again, and Kata held her daughter close as she stared at Dr. Fleisher for what seemed like an eternity. Her mind and her spirit waged war within her. For a brief moment, time seemed to have broken barriers. A part of her wanted desperately to go back in time and fix all of the mistakes she and Fredric had made in their marriage. Her flesh wrestled with her faith. Yes, she had faced tragedy and loss before, but this seemed different somehow. She had shared so much with this man for so many years. Why couldn't she turn back the hands of time and make it right? Why couldn't they have shared a life together in Christ? She wanted to rescue the past and change the future.

She quickly caught herself and came back to the reality of the present. God was with them right now, and He would give Martina and her the strength they needed to face this tragedy as well. Psalm 23:4 formed in her thoughts: *Yea, though I walk through the valley of the shadow of death, I will fear no evil: for thou art with me; thy rod and thy staff, they comfort me.*

She allowed the Lord to soothe her frazzled mind with these words and ultimately resolved that she needed to be strong for her daughter. She bit her lip, set her face like a flint, looked Dr. Fleischer directly in the eye and said evenly, "He is with the Lord."

* * *

Before the influenza epidemic was over, it had taken a tremendous toll on the world. It had become a pandemic, affecting virtually one-third of the world's population and killing over fifty million people worldwide. It was one of the deadliest viruses that man had ever experienced in history. Between this pandemic and the Great War, the world witnessed the deaths of more people in a single era than had ever been known to mankind.

CHAPTER 29

This My Last Will

"WHY WASN'T I NOTIFIED?" GRISELDA SHOUTED at Helga, the housekeeper who had been in charge while she was gone. She returned home two days after Fredric passed away. Fury consumed her when she learned that he had actually died in her absence. She became even more incensed when she learned that Kata had made the funeral arrangements without waiting for her. She dismissed the fact that she had failed to let anyone know where she went, which was normal for her. Helga knew she would still be blamed even if she reminded Griselda of that fact, so she stood in silence while her employer flayed her with her words.

Griselda had her driver take her to the funeral home, where she assailed the director next. "How *dare* that woman handle *my* husband's funeral!" she screamed when she found out that Kata had already carried out all of Fredric's funeral arrangements.

During his illness, Fredric must have had some concern about, or premonition of his death and regrets about his marriage to Griselda. He had dictated his wishes to his longtime friend and lawyer, *Herr* Klaus Schmidt. Since Griselda could not be located, and since Martina was a minor, *Herr* Klaus had consulted with Kata, and together they had complied with his directives. Fredric had instructed that he was to be cremated, and his ashes were to be scattered over the Danube, near the Iron Gates National Park.

"We merely followed his wishes, *Frau* Albers. I apologize, but we had no choice," said the funeral director, attempting to calm the irate woman.

"You haven't heard the last of me over this. You will hear from my lawyer!" she threatened, and she dashed furiously out of the funeral home. This of course was an empty threat, as everything had been done legally. How dare everyone assume Katharina was the logical choice to handle Fredric's affairs, even if no one had been able to contact her? They should have waited for her return. This only infuriated Griselda more. A few days wouldn't have made that much difference.

Her jealousy and rage quickly turned to fear. What was to become of her now that her main source of income was gone? How had he provided for her in his Will? How long could she remain in the house she and Fredric had shared before she would have to leave it or be responsible for its expense? She assumed her husband had made provisions for her. On the other hand, she knew that they hadn't been getting along so well, and he had voiced his regrets so many times during their quarrels. She wouldn't know for sure until his Will was read, and that wasn't going to take place for several days yet. One thing had to change right away, however. She did *not* want the burden of a child—especially one that was not her own.

"I want you and Martina to pack your things and get out of this house as soon as possible!" she told Elsa soon after she had returned.

"But . . . this is Martina's home, the only place she's known her whole life," Elsa protested. "She should at least have time to get over her father's death before being forced to leave it."

"That's where you are wrong. This is *my* home, now and I'm not going to put up with that insolent vagabond any longer. You can both go to live with Katharina for all I care. As a matter of fact, you can leave immediately. I certainly have no need of your services anymore."

Elsa stared at Griselda in disbelief. "At least give her time to get her things together. Surely you'll give her that. You can't be so heartless as to put her out of her home so quickly."

"All right. You have forty-eight hours—no longer. And don't think she can take just anything she wants. She may take her clothes and items in her room, but she'll not take anything else in this house. Everything here belongs to me. Do you understand?"

"Oh, I understand perfectly well, Griselda." Elsa gave her a look of disgust. "You are nothing but a greedy, vicious, self-centered—J"

Griselda cut her off. "I suggest you stop right there, Elsa, or I may take back my generous offer to give you the forty-eight hours, and have you both leave immediately with just the clothes on your back!" A sinister expression of satisfaction washed across her face.

Elsa turned around, bit her lip and walked away before she allowed anything else to come out of her mouth.

She entered Martina's room and found her little charge packing her belongings. It was almost as if the Lord had prepared this young lady for the inevitable.

"I won't stay under this roof any longer, Elsa. Griselda has made living in this house impossible. Without Papa here, who knows what she'll do. I just want to go to Mama's." Tears streamed down her cheeks and she leaned into Elsa's welcoming arms.

How intuitive, my little kinder is. She knows Griselda would have made her life if she stays. Elsa felt relieved and said a quick prayer under her breath: *Thank you, Lord, for preparing her heart.* "We'll leave tomorrow if you'd like. I will call your mother and let her know."

The next several days passed slowly for Griselda. She attempted to play the part of the grieving widow by dressing in black, looking forlorn, and taking every opportunity to shed a tear or two as she related her side of the story to anyone who listened. She told acquaintances how Kata and Elsa had deliberately kept her husband's illness and death from her. She grasped for anything that would sway a sympathetic ear her way. It was easy to blame them now. They weren't around to defend themselves.

She claimed that she had left a contact number for Elsa, but Elsa must have destroyed it so that no one would be able to find her. Few people however, swallowed her tale. Most people who knew Kata, Elsa and Griselda saw through her lies. She received no sympathy or support for her claim.

Two weeks later, Kata, Griselda and Martina were summoned to *Herr* Schmidt's office for the reading of the Will. When Kata and Martina arrived, Griselda was already there. She was waiting in the room just outside the office when Kata and Martina walked in. She stared at them coldly.

"Good afternoon, Griselda," said Kata, cordially. She was determined to be gracious and to try her best to be a good witness for the Lord.

Ignoring her greeting, Griselda replied in a bitter tone, "If you believe I am going to allow you to take *anything* that Fredric has left, you had better think again!"

"You can put your mind at ease. I want *nothing* from Fredric, but I do expect that he has provided for his daughter, and that, my dear, is what I intend to see her receive," Kata said with even determination.

"That may be, but he had *better* have sufficiently provided for his wife first. I'll get my *own* lawyer if I have to," Griselda retorted.

Kata did not respond. She and Martina quietly took a seat across the waiting room and ignored Griselda's hard stares.

In a few minutes, *Herr* Schmidt invited them into his office. Griselda once again tried to look like the grieving widow, but as the lawyer began to read the Will, her expression of grief morphed into one of greed and optimistic expectation.

The lawyer read the preliminary legal details. Next, he proceeded to inform them of the more relevant terms of the Will:

"*Frau* Albers, you may remain in the home you and he shared. He has given it to you along with a sizeable stipend on which to live. It amounts to one third of his estate."

Griselda looked at him in disbelief. "One third? That can't be right. I'm his wife. The bulk of his estate should be mine!"

"No, he has also provided for his daughter and for his first wife."

Griselda's face turned red and the veins in her neck stood out. She jumped to her feet and shook her finger at the lawyer.

"I don't believe for one minute that this is really what Fredric wanted!" she argued. "This is a travesty! I understand his logic in leaving something to Martina; but Katharina? Never! I'll not have it! I'll *not* settle for one third of his estate. I will contest this—this outrageous attempt to steal what is mine!"

Klaus responded calmly, "This is a legal document, drafted by me according to his wishes and signed in my presence by *Herr* Albers. I am merely carrying out his wishes," he said in a very stern voice, peering at her over his reading glasses. Now, I suggest you take a seat and let me proceed, or I shall have to ask you to leave my office immediately." He stood up and continued to divulge the remaining details.

"A trust has been established for Martina. She will receive a monthly allotment from the estate until she turns twenty-two."

He turned to Katharina and continued. "Until that time, she is to remain in your care and custody. Then, she will inherit the remainder of his estate. He has also left a sizable sum to you, as well as two of his factories."

Katharina looked surprised. "For me? I wasn't aware that I was even a consideration. We've been divorced for so many years."

"Yes, and it should be enough to help you to live quite comfortably, assuming that the economy does not grow worse."

Griselda said nothing. She sat back down, and tapped her foot impatiently. She looked as if she was ready to explode.

The attorney continued. "He has left instructions that Martina is to attend a finishing school and after that, a university. He has set up a fund for both.

"He has also stipulated that if something should happen to Martina before she turns twenty-two, then the remainder of her inheritance would be evenly divided between both of you, *Frau* Albers and Katharina."

Griselda could hold her tongue no longer. Once again, she ranted. "This is *outrageous*!" She stood up and marched over to Kata and Martina, who were sitting on the other end of the *Herr* Schmidt's desk and looking at Griselda in astonishment. She shook her fist at the Kata.

"I think you had something to do with this. I wouldn't be a bit surprised if you coerced him into making this Will while he was dying. I'll get to the bottom of this, and if I have anything to say about this, neither of you will get a *single mark!*"

Kata said nothing. She merely tightened her grip on Martina's hand. The lawyer looked at Griselda and shook his head in disbelief.

"This has all been done legally. I'm afraid there is nothing you can do about it. *Herr* Albers left you well provided for. I don't see why you are upset with this arrangement. You will have a sizeable sum on which to live, as well as the house. It makes perfect sense. After all, he was married to Katharina for several years. All the papers are in order and I don't think there is one court who would question it.

"*If* you chose to sue, I think you would waste a great deal of your inheritance on legal fees, and speaking professionally, I believe you would lose your case."

Griselda ignored his warning. She continued to rage on.

"We shall see, *Herr* Schmidt! I will *not* give up that easy," she replied angrily.

Kata also attempted to reason with her. "Griselda, I understand you are upset, and I assure you this was *completely* Fredric's doing. I had *no* knowledge of what was in his Will."

Griselda stormed over to Kata and shook her finger in her face. "You haven't heard the last of me!" she threatened and then angrily charged out of the room, leaving Kata and *Herr* Schmidt staring at one another in silence for a few minutes. Martina clung to her mother tightly.

As Kata and Martina were getting ready to leave, Herr Schmitt stood up, walked around to them and shook Kata's hand. "I am terribly sorry for the way *Frau* Albers assailed you, Katharina. There was no call for it."

"It's not your fault, *Herr* Schmidt. We will be quite all right. Thank you so much for your services. I know you and Fredric were quite good friends for years, and that you followed his instructions to the letter." She returned his handshake, and she and Martina left his office.

While she never doubted that Fredric would have provided quite well for his daughter, she was still astonished that Fredric had been so generous with her in his Will. Even though she planned to continue working, she now had the peace of knowing that they could live quite comfortably.

"Mama, I was so frightened that Griselda was going to try to take me back with her," said Martina, still holding firmly on to her mother as they walked to the car. "I never, ever want to go back with her, I am so glad the lawyer said I can live with you for good."

"Yes, *Mausi,* you and Elsa can stay with me forever."

Kata was also relieved that the question of custody had been firmly established. Not that Griselda would have fought her for Martina; on the other hand, she knew how cruel the woman could be and had no doubt that she would use Martina as a pawn, if she thought it possible. She knew Griselda made Martina's life miserable when she married Fredric.

She also had the ominous feeling that they hadn't seen the last of this woman. Griselda would attempt to steal the entire estate, if she could. She had no idea what she might try in the future. She did not trust Griselda, but she *did* trust the Lord and recalled Psalm 91. She believed that God would protect them no matter what happened.

CHAPTER 30

Post War Trials and Triumphs

THE LATTER PART OF 1919 BROUGHT even more political and economic change to Germany and major changes in the lives of Kata, Elsa and Martina as well. First, they realized that Kata's small apartment was too cramped for the three of them. She enough from Fredric's estate to buy a comfortable house; therefore she decided with the political and economic problems plaguing the country, it would be best to buy something quickly.

Kata also wanted to be out of the city where rioting and unrest was increasing. The hospital where she worked was about a mile inside the metropolis, and now that limited driving was permitted once again, if she purchased a more economical car, they could easily live on the outskirts of Berlin.

She bought a modest, but comfortable three-bedroom house about fifteen minutes from the hospital, and just a couple of miles outside the city. It was nice to have her own home once again. The house was a twenty-year-old brick, two-story Victorian style home, which had recently been remodeled and had indoor plumbing, a garage and a large back yard.

Mail was flowing smoothly again, and she was surprised one day by a letter from Italy. She recognized the handwriting as Greta's and anxiously tore it open:

My dear Kata,

Please forgive me for not writing sooner, but with the war and everything that has been happening here, I found it nearly impossible to do so. I have so much to share, so please bear with me.

First, let me say how sorry I am to hear of what happened between you and Fredric. I dare say that he will pay a heavy price one day for what he did. You have truly been in my thoughts and prayers.

And I am happy to tell you that Karl and I also have a little girl. I found out that I was going to have a baby soon after our honeymoon, and believe me I was shocked! I had no idea that would happen at ***my*** *age. Nonetheless, she was born healthy, and we named her Katharina Margarethe. She is a lovely young lady now, and I have told her all about her "Tante Kata" in Germany. She is looking forward to the day she can meet you.*

You would probably be surprised to hear that yes, after all those times I cajoled you about working and having a family, I am now a housefrau and loving every moment of it. I enjoy being home with my lovely daughter and being a loving wife to Karl. I cannot believe how much God has changed my heart. (Yes, I mentioned God.)

You see, Kata, when I got your letter telling me about Jesus, at first I was a bit put out with you—preaching to me like that. I knew you had good intentions, though, and that you were "only looking out for my best interests." Of course, that is how you must have felt about me for years, isn't it? How ironic.

I did get a Bible, and started to read those verses you gave me. Then, one day, I asked Karl to take me to church. Well, he was very surprised that I would want to go, but we did. There was a little church not far from us here in Milan, so we decided to attend a service there. You will never believe it, but that very day, the minister just happened to be teaching out of Romans 10. Then he brought up John 3:16 and explained, just as you did in your letter, that anyone could have eternal life if they gave their lives to Christ.

If I didn't know any better, I would have thought that you followed my example; that you contacted that minister and told him about my needing a Savior in my life. I had to laugh at your comment about knowing the "Director." It brought back such memories.

Well, God really worked in my heart during his sermon and right after the service, I asked Christ to come into my life. Karl was also impressed with his message, and just a few weeks, after several interesting discussions with the minister, he also accepted Jesus as his Savior.

I can't thank you enough for your obedience in writing that letter to me. Despite Karl's very busy schedule, we have both been singing in the choir.

During the war, we volunteered time to help with the cause, even though neither of us was in agreement with the war. I cannot help thinking, that even though Italy eventually sided with England, we were united in our thoughts about the whole thing.

Anyway, I have so much more to share with you, but I'm afraid it would take a book, so I will close for now and write more later. I'm anxious to send this letter and hope to hear from you again.

I do miss you so and pray we will be able to see each other soon. It is amazing to know that since we are both Christians now; we are really sisters in Christ.

I am anxious to hear from you and learn what is going on in your life. I am sure Martina is quite a lovely young lady by now.

Please write to me very soon and tell me everything that is happening with you.

Your friend and true sister in Jesus.
Greta

What a wonderful surprise! Greta was now a Christian. *And* a mother! Yes indeed; what irony. God certainly has to have a sense of humor, Kata thought as she mused over how she had "meddled" in

Greta's life. She was so happy for her friend. She had now found real happiness, not only as a wife and mother, but also as a true believer in Christ. God was so good. Kata decided to sit down and respond to her letter immediately. She also knew she had to tell her about Fredric—the good news and the bad.

* * *

Now that the war was over, the threat of the flu had waned somewhat, and her patient load had lightened, Kata took some much needed vacation time to settle into her new home. She and Elsa, with the help of Dr. Fleischer and a few of her nurses from work, moved the contents of her apartment to the new home. She had most of the furniture she needed, but she added a few more chairs, a gas stove and a Kelvinator, a more modern refrigerator than her icebox.

She found a 1917 Ford in quite good shape for an incredibly good deal. It had been owned by an older couple who had taken very good care of it. When she told them that she was a nurse, they decided to give it to her for half their original asking price.

"Our son served in the Great War," the wife said. "He was severely wounded. Had it not been for the diligent care of a kind nurse who didn't give up on him, even though many thought he was not going to make it, he may not have lived," she said gratefully.

Kata and Elsa started a vegetable garden early in the spring to help defray the cost of food. Martina loved to help them and became quite the little gardener.

The German mark was still holding its own at this time, but Kata had heard troubling rumors of pending hyperinflation. She was concerned that the mark might be headed for trouble. Her lawyer advised her to sell the factories that Fredric had given her and pay off her house. She put the remainder of the money in a savings account. She was very frugal with her budget. She also continued to tithe, and was amazed at the faithfulness of the Lord to meet their every need.

Dr. Fleischer often visited Kata and Martina after Fredric's death. He knew Martina was very close to her father and that she was having a hard time coping with her loss.

"You know I do appreciate your spending time with Martina, Otto," Kata told him late one afternoon as the two of them sat on her porch after he had taken them to the zoo.

"She's a precocious young lady. She seems to be very interested in medicine, and I don't mind answering her questions about it. Besides, you know that I enjoy being with both of you, Kata."

"Well, you are very kind, but we don't want to take advantage of you. Your time is valuable, and I'm sure you have more to do than to just be at our disposal. Besides, I'm not too sure you should take her interest in medicine that seriously at this point. Martina's very young and could change her mind a dozen times before deciding on a career, you know."

"Kata, you and Martina are like a breath of fresh air in my life. I can't tell you how much I look forward to spending my days off with you." He reached for her hand, but she did not offer it. Instead, she rose and walked towards her front door.

"Thank you very much for a wonderful day, but I am very tired and should be going in. I will see you tomorrow. Good afternoon, Otto." She smiled briefly, then turned and went inside, leaving him standing on her doorstep.

She walked into the living room where Elsa and Martina were discussing the day's events. Elsa was working on some needlework and listening to Martina with great interest.

"We had such a wonderful day at the zoo, today. Dr. Fleischer is a very interesting man. I can talk to him about almost anything. He is a quite fun to be around, as well. Wouldn't it be something if him and Mama—"

"Martina, don't you have some school work to finish?" Kata interrupted with a hint of irritation in her voice.

"No, Mama, my work is all done. Besides, I'm telling Elsa all about our day at the zoo."

"Well, you can tell her all about it later. I wish to talk to Elsa for a bit. Please give me a few minutes with her, *Schatzi.*"

"Yes Mama." Martina obediently got up and went to her room.

"I can see you are a bit uneasy about Martina's conversation, Kata."

"I just don't want her getting too attached to Dr. Fleischer—or getting any ideas about him and me."

Elsa peered up from her embroidery. "I think it's a bit late for that. She's quite taken with him, and he does seem to be genuinely interested in you both." She continued her work.

"That's what concerns me. I don't want to encourage anything. He is a good man, but I don't think there can be anyone else in my life—after Fredric."

Now Elsa put her work aside and gave Kata her full attention. She looked at her intently. "What are you afraid of, Kata—falling in love again? Do you think that the Lord can't bring another man in your life just because of what happened between you and Fredric?"

Kata grimaced. "Why, yes—no. . . oh, I don't know what I think, but I'm not ready to be serious about anyone. Love is just too perplexing of an emotion. I don't want that complication again." She threw her hands up in frustration.

"So that's it. You never stopped loving Fredric, did you?"

Kata exhaled deeply. "Please Elsa, not now. I'm just too tired to discuss it further. Will you excuse me?" She didn't wait for Elsa to respond, but quickly retreated to her room.

A veritable storm erupted inside of her mind. Her emotions were at war. She knew Elsa was right. She had never stopped loving Fredric. She knew that Dr. Fleischer cared deeply for her, and she cared for him—as a friend, nothing more. He was a wonderful, kind man, and a Christian, but she fought any desires that stirred up in her for this man. She resolved to spend the rest of her life serving the Lord. There was no room in her life for love or marriage again.

On the other hand, feelings of loss and even guilt, and unexplainable loneliness shrouded her. Hadn't she thought the same thing about Fredric so many years before? She was wrong then. Was she wrong now? No, this was different. Her marriage didn't work out. She couldn't take the chance of it happening again.

She determined to thwart any feelings she had for this man by burying herself in her work, taking on more hours, all the while taking great care to avoid Dr. Fleischer when possible.

He caught up to her one evening when she was working very

late. “Kata, what are you trying to do, be an army of nurses? You don’t need to be here so much,” he said.

“I’m fine. There’s work to be done here. We have a new batch of nurses to train, and there are reports to take care of, and there—”

He didn’t let her finish. “And there’s your health to think of. You need to take better care of yourself.” He patted her shoulder and looked into her eyes. She looked away quickly.

“There’s a wonderful *Singspiel* tomorrow evening at the Friedrich-Theater. Why don’t you come with me to see it?”

“I’m sorry, I can’t. I will be busy tomorrow evening.”

“Doing what?”

Kata gave him a look of irritation. “That’s really not your business, is it?” Her voice was sharp, and it clearly wounded him by the look on his face.

“I’m sorry. I didn’t mean to pry. It’s just that lately it seems as if you’ve been avoiding me. Have I done something to upset you?”

She looked at his hurt expression and softened her tone a bit. “No, I’ve just had a lot on my mind and haven’t been up to socializing much. Maybe some other time.”

Before he could respond, she turned away and began talking to one of the other nurses about a patient.

Kata came back to him later and apologized. “I realize that I treated you quite unfairly. Please forgive me.”

He shrugged his shoulders. “There’s nothing to forgive. I just wanted to take you away from all of your work and help you enjoy life again. Look, Kata, I know that Fredric’s death was hard on you and Martina, but you need to get on with your life. I think you’ve forgotten that.” He smiled, but kept a reasonable distance.

“You forget, I went through the loss of my wife, and even though our circumstances are different—your being divorced from Fredric; I do know what it’s like to lose the one you love. I understand the hurt and pain that goes with it.”

Kata looked up at him and smiled. “I appreciate you and your willingness to help Martina and I get over these times. And you’re right. I know that I have to put it behind me. It seems that God sometimes has a hard time getting my attention about these things, doesn’t He?” Her mood was a little lighter.

"I understand that feeling. Believe me it has taken me quite a bit of time to—"

"To what?" Kata asked, looking at him curiously.

He hesitated, looked at his feet for a moment, and then looked back at Kata.

"To notice anyone else. These last few years of working with you; I have grown to admire and respect you. Your love for God and your dedication to serve others is amazing. I have watched you grow in your faith so much since you first came to work here. I guess I. . . well, for the first time in years, I find myself . . . falling in love again." His eyes met hers and he put his hands out to take hers. She grasped his, but she kept him at a distance.

"Please, don't say any more. You are a wonderful man, and perhaps if the circumstances were different; I mean, if I had never married Fredric . . . It's just that I've done a lot of thinking. I know you have been a kind and caring friend, and I appreciate that. I don't think I could ever feel the same way about anyone else again, though." She looked at him with such sincerity, that Dr. Fleischer dropped his eyes and lowered his head sadly.

Then he looked up and added, "I won't bring the subject up again. But please, promise me that we can go on being good friends."

Kata smiled and kissed him on the cheek. "Of course, you will always be a good friend to me."

* * *

One morning soon after their discussion, she didn't get out of bed. Elsa thought it strange that she hadn't come down for breakfast. Kata was supposed to be at work within the hour, so she went to her room. "Kata! . . . Kata! . . . It's almost time for you to go to work. Are you awake?" No answer. Now Elsa was concerned. She burst into the room and found Kata, still in her bed, covered up with her blankets, shivering and moaning almost as if she was having delusions. She was talking, but not making sense.

Elsa felt her head. She was burning up with fever, and shivering at the same time. "Kata, I am going to call Dr. Fleisher. You need medical care right away." Kata did not respond. She just kept murmuring unintelligibly.

Dr. Fleischer was there within fifteen minutes of Elsa's call. He examined Kata, and looked at very alarmed. "I think she has the influenza, but I need to run some tests to be sure. I am going to take her to the hospital," he told Elsa. "Can you get some of her things together?"

"Influenza?" she queried in a concerned voice. "I thought we were over that," she remarked nervously.

"The pandemic seems to be mostly over, but we have had waves of it occasionally. We never really have been able to eradicate it totally yet. And considering the way Kata has been working, lately, I am not totally surprised by this," Otto stated with equal concern for her. "I have been warning her for weeks to slow down, but she wasn't listening to me." He shook his head.

He ordered an ambulance to Kata's home, and she was transported quickly to the hospital. He had her admitted, and then ran the necessary tests. To his chagrin, she was positively diagnosed. Now the wait began.

CHAPTER 31

Putting on God's Full Armor

For days, Kata lingered between life and death. She was normally healthy, but this strain of flu had a nasty reputation of attacking the healthy and young, rather than the elderly population and children. It was a strange phenomenon.

She hovered between fitful sleep, and semi-consciousness. Dr. Fleischer was at her side every possible moment he could spare. Martina and Elsa stayed in her room day and night as well. Martina was beside herself. She could not believe she was reliving the same scenario she had been through with her father. For her fifteen years, she had experienced so much tragedy and devastation. Yet, once again, her faith was being tested.

"What is God doing? First my father, and now my mother?" she asked Elsa on the fifth day of her mother's illness. She was emotionally whipped. She had no tears left. She looked for promises of her mother's recovery in the Bible, in a "still small voice" within, and from Dr. Fleisher, but she was getting nothing at this point. She hugged Elsa, who was the closest person to a relative that she had at this moment. Elsa kept her arms around her little Martina, attempting to comfort her.

"I—I am not sure, Marti. The only thing I can think of is that He wants us to trust Him and have faith."

"I can't imagine life without her, Elsa. I need her so much. I can't lose her now."

Elsa embraced Martina and calmly assured her, "I have watched the way God has used her to bring so many others to Jesus. Somehow I don't think that He is ready to take her home yet—she still has work to do, and she still has a beautiful daughter to take care of."

Elsa stepped out of the room for a few minutes to give Martina some time with her mother. It just didn't make much sense to her, either—but then not too much *did* seem to make sense these days. If Satan had ever come close to shattering Elsa's faith, this was about as close as he could. Nevertheless, she stood firm.

She shut her eyes and looked up towards heaven: *Lord, I need your strength more than ever right now. Kata and Martina need me to be strong, but I know I can't do it without your help. Like Martina, I find myself questioning you in this, and I don't want to. I want to believe you are not going to take Katharina from us. I want to know in my heart, beyond a doubt, that you are taking care of things and that I can trust you to heal her, but I am having trouble trusting. Please—help my unbelief.*

Her lips trembled and her eyes glistened with tears. She was trying to be brave for Martina, but it was very difficult. She loved her little family and couldn't stand the thought of losing them. Had she not suffered enough loss? She remembered that David had moments of doubt as well. She thought about how he would just tell his soul to praise the Lord: *God, give me a scripture to help me to overcome this raging battle going on in me. I don't want to doubt you. You have always helped me through difficult times. I know you can help us now,* she prayed. Suddenly she recalled the words of Ephesians 6:10-18 that exhorted his people to put on his full armor. Her heart rejoiced, because it reminded her that God was listening to her. She had to put on that armor and take on the battle, even more fervently, in the Spirit. She walked back into Kata's room with renewed faith.

"Marti, do you remember how we prayed for your parents to come to the Lord, and even though we didn't see the answer right away, God eventually did answer us?"

Martina sniffled and looked up at Elsa. "Y-yes, Elsa, I do," she whimpered.

"Well, *Schatzi*, I believe in my heart that right now that we need to put on *all* of his armor, just like we read about in Ephesians."

Marti sniffled again, wiped her nose and calmed down slightly. "All right," she replied obediently.

"Well let's pray again. And we'll pray and pray until we have a peace in our hearts that we have done all we can do on our part," she continued.

They did just that. They prayed and read Ephesians 6 and several psalms from Elsa's little pocket Bible that she always carried with her in her handbag.

* * *

Later that evening, after he convinced Elsa and Martina to go home for the evening and get some rest, Dr. Fleischer returned to Kata's room. He was struggling with his emotions as well. He stood beside her bed, ran his hand over her head and caressed her cheek. A tear fell from his eye to her pillow. Despite her resistance to the idea, he had grown to love Kata more than ever. Regardless of what Kata had told him previously, he believed that the Lord had brought Kata in his life, not only to help him in the hospital, but also possibly to be a helpmate to him in the future. He desperately wanted to pursue the conversation they had earlier and tell her she was mistaken, but he was willing to be patient and give her more time to get over Fredric's death.

Now, he was on the brink of losing her, just as he had lost his dear wife years before. How could this happen again? He believed that God had good plans for him and for Kata together.

He knelt down, put his elbows on the edge of the bed, lowered his head, folded his hands and began to pray inwardly. *Dear Lord, I have been so blessed to have this veritable "Florence Nightingale" working by my side for the past few years. She has been such a gift. I even think you spoke to my heart about making her my wife and working together with her for your purpose and for your glory. I find it hard to believe that you would take such a gift back, but I want to be open to your complete will, so please, Lord, show me if I have been wrong, or please heal my little "angel from heaven.*

For the first time since his wife's death, he broke out in sobs. His sorrow came from deep within. He couldn't picture life without

Kata any longer. *Dear, dear Kata. Would she ever know how much she meant to him? Would he ever be able to tell her how deeply he had fallen in love with her?*

At that moment, he heard a still small voice within him: *Be at peace, my son. I have a plan and a purpose for both of you. It is not finished yet.*

Was God letting him know He was going to heal Kata?

CHAPTER 32

A Hope and a Future

Elsa and Martina rose early in the morning. They had been praying into the night. Even though she was exhausted, Elsa felt a peace envelope her.

"Let's go see Mama now, Elsa," Martina said after they finished breakfast. "I want to see if God answered us yet."

Elsa agreed. "All right, we'll go right away, then." They caught a taxicab and arrived at the hospital just before visiting hours. As soon as they were allowed to see her, Martina took Elsa's hand, and together they entered Kata's room.

There, they found Kata with her eyes open and Dr. Fleisher holding her hand. She had a faint smile on her face.

"Mama, you are awake!" exclaimed Martina rushing to her side and lightly laying her head on Kata's chest, taking care not to make her breathing any more difficult.

"Yes *Leibe,* thanks to all of your prayers." Kata wrapped her fragile arms around Martina.

"Oh, Mama, we've prayed for days!" Martina lifted her head to take a good look at her mother's face. It was still very ashen, but there was a subtle glow about her that encouraged Martina.

Dr. Fleisher motioned to Elsa to come closer as well. "She is still very weak, but I think that the worst is over. She said that God spoke to her heart and told her not to worry, and that she would get better."

Kata didn't speak, but she nodded her head in agreement and offered a feeble smile.

"That's *wonderful* news, Dr. Fleisher!" Elsa exclaimed. "I just knew she would be better. When we prayed last night, I felt a great peace. I think the Lord was giving us all assurance."

"I'll give you and Martina a few minutes with her, but I can't stress enough the need to let her rest. The next few days could be critical. I don't think she is totally out of the woods yet, but she is showing some signs of improvement." He looked back at Kata and squeezed her hand, then left the Elsa and Martina alone with her.

Dr. Fleisher walked back to his office and sank into his chair. Tears filled his eyes, and his heart swelled with thanksgiving. He put his head down on his desk for a moment and thanked God for answered prayer.

Later that day, he stopped in to check on Kata's progress. "It's so wonderful to see you awake!" he exclaimed and kissed her hand.

"Yes, Otto, I. . . I am awake," she said in a faint but audible voice.

"You have been in and out of consciousness, and we were worried that you wouldn't come back to us." He gazed at her as she lay there. Despite the fact that she had been very ill, her beauty never waned. Her complexion was still pale, but he admired its smoothness. Her eyes, though not as bright as usual, still had a slight sparkle, when she opened them and looked up at him.

"Thank you . . . for your care . . . and . . . your prayers," she said, and she closed her eyes. "I'm. . . sorry," she said. "I've been praying, too . . . I'm not sure if I had a dream or a vision . . . but I distinctly remember seeing the Lord. The room suddenly got very bright . . . and I heard a voice. I can't fully describe it . . . but I knew that it was . . . Jesus." She paused for a few minutes, and when she had regained enough strength to talk, she continued, "He spoke . . . to me. . . He said, *'My daughter . . . your past is over. . . You are to move into the future and possess the land'."* Then she closed her eyes and rested again.

Dr. Fleischer sat down beside her and took her hand. "Take your time, Kata. Don't try to talk too much. You are still very weak."

"No . . . I must go on . . . while I remember." Kata took a labored breath and continued. This time it was as though the Lord was giving her supernatural strength to share the vision God had given her. An angelic brilliance seemed to radiate from her face, and the corners of her mouth allowed a faint smile.

"I thought of Jeremiah 29:11: *For I know the thoughts that I think toward you, thoughts of peace, and not of evil, to give you an expected end.* He was making it very clear to me . . . that it wasn't my time yet, and that there was more to do."

"Of course, Kata. I believe that. You have been a veritable angel to all the sick and wounded here these past few years. It was hard for me to imagine that God would take you home yet, either." He took her hand and stroked her forehead. Kata smiled and closed her eyes.

"Rest, now. You need to get better. Everyone has been very concerned about you." Otto stood up, bent over and kissed her cheek, then left her to ponder the meaning of her vision.

Kata nodded in silence. Sharing her dream had depleted what little energy she had mustered. She reached up and touched his cheek. Then she let her mind drift back to her dream. Had she been wrong about things? Each time she heard that scripture, she could make him out, standing in the distance, nodding in agreement. She saw herself slowly moving in his direction.

Was the Lord telling her that Otto was to be part of that future? Her heart filled with warmth and a strange new desire permeated her body as she contemplated that possibility. She began to see him in a new light. Had she been so blind not to see this dear man—not only for the wonderful, caring Christian he was, but also for the blessing he could be in her future?

* * *

Over the next few weeks, Kata made slow, but steady improvement. At first, she could barely sit on the edge of her bed without feeling dizzy and weak. Under Otto's consistent care and watchful eye, she slowly gained her strength. He, Elsa and Martina spent a great deal of time reading to her and keeping her updated with the latest events. Nurse Hemmler, who had also spent time taking care of Kata during her illness and recuperation, also came in to visit her as often as possible. She, Elsa, and *Frau* Johannsen kept Kata's Bible study going while Kata recovered. With each passing day, Kata grew stronger and stronger. On one of her visits, Elsa brought her a letter she had received from Eric, the young officer she had nursed back to health during the war. She was so surprised.

Dear Nurse Albers,

I hope this letter finds you well. I have never forgotten my dear sweet nurse who helped me through the most difficult time I had ever experienced. If it hadn't been for you, I know I would have given up and ended it all. Anyway, I wanted to write and tell you what God has been doing in my life since then.

After I left the hospital and traveled home, I encountered so many obstacles in my path. I often thought about that book, Pilgrim's Progress, and Christian's struggles. Believe me, it would have been easy to give up, having only one arm. My fiancée tried to accept my condition, but in time, she broke off our engagement. I was crushed, to say the least. Also, several of my friends tried to discourage me from going into the ministry. Then I met a young lady in the church I had been attending who reminded me of you in some ways. Her name is Ingrid. She was so strong in her faith, even though she had lost two brothers in the war. She kept telling me so many of the same things you did—including how God takes our circumstances and turns them around for his glory. We began an outreach in our church, with the blessing of our pastor, to men who had returned from the war, wounded, or emotionally scarred from the war.

She was planning to be a missionary, and she encouraged me to pursue my dream. We attended seminary together. As time went on, we fell in love and were married. God has been so good to us. Once we graduated from Seminary, I was offered a church of my own in a nearby town.

Through all of this, one great lesson I have learned is that losing a limb is nothing compared to losing eternity. Had I not lost that limb, I may never have known about Jesus. Romans 8:28 has become one of my favorite scriptures.

My wife now serves at the local hospital, and assists me with our church as well. I cannot believe how happy we have been, and I owe it all to God, and a certain "angel" with mission from heaven.

Sincerely,
Eric

Kata was elated. She had no idea how much she had influenced this young man's life. She praised God for that opportunity, and for the fact that now he was ministering to others. She shared the letter with Otto.

Once she was strong enough to walk the halls of the hospital for at least half an hour, Otto began taking her for short walks through the hospital grounds when the weather was warm enough. His nearness made her feel safe and secure. She looked forward to their personal time together now. Desires she hadn't known for years stirred in her. She was drawn to this man in a new way. A way that she didn't dream was possible ever again. Were these desires put there by the Lord? Could she even dare to think—was He going to give her a second chance in marriage? Was it even possible?

* * *

As fall approached, the winds grew stronger, so it was difficult to go out more than a few times. Otto wanted to be sure that Kata didn't have a relapse. However, he couldn't let time escape him any longer. He felt in his heart that the Lord was bringing Kata and him together for a specific purpose.

He realized that she was also beginning to see this, and that she was drawing closer to him. He sensed her desires were as strong as his were. One afternoon as summer was about to bid its farewell, and the mild breezes announced autumn's pending debut, Otto decided to express his feelings for Kata again. They strolled through the hospital garden together, admiring the array of purples, reds, oranges splashed across the grounds, and discussing how the Lord had blessed them through all of the trials they had experienced during the war.

"Kata," he began, as he held her arm to aid her walking, "I know it's no secret to you that I care for you very much."

Kata stopped walking, turned and looked up at him and smiled. Her complexion quickly regained its rosy hue, and the sparkle in her eyes brightened once again. "Yes, Otto, I know."

He continued. "When I thought you were slipping away from us, I prayed so hard that God wouldn't take you home yet. The thought of losing you was more than I could bear. I did not want to lose . . . " His eyes moistened and he looked straight ahead. "I mean, I didn't want to lose such a wonderful friend and nurse."

"You were going to say something else, weren't you?"

Otto lowered his head. "Yes. I never told you this, but my first wife, Lisette, was ill for several weeks. She . . . died of pneumonia. Watching you in that hospital bed those first several days . . . brought back those difficult memories. I . . . couldn't face losing you, Kata, and I asked God for a miracle. I . . . promised Him, that if He would heal you, I would serve Him in any way that He wanted for the rest of my life . . . even if—" He stopped again.

"Even if what, Otto?" Kata's expression held anticipation.

"Even if you walked out of my life forever."

Otto stopped for a moment, gazed affectionately into her eyes, and tenderly held both of her hands. She held his gaze and welcomed his touch. When she didn't draw back, he decided to open his heart to her. Taking a deep breath, he said a bit nervously, "Kata, dear Kata, I . . . I have fallen in love with you. I think I must have loved you ever since that first day we talked in the cafeteria. I just couldn't move on from my past."

"I believe I understand how you felt. I could not see beyond my past, either. I wasn't letting go. I couldn't allow myself to even consider another man in my life. I was quite satisfied with just being friends."

"I want our friendship to be more than just that. I would like to . . . to see you. I mean . . . I would like to court you." He held his breath for a moment. He wanted to reach out, caress her in his arms and kiss her passionately, but he restrained himself.

Kata smiled. "You know, those days, lying there, realizing how close I came to death, yet knowing God gave me a second chance at life, gave me lots of time to think. I've been doing a lot of soul searching, and thinking about the future. That dream kept coming back to me. I know now that God has a new direction for my life."

She paused and looked away briefly, but then turned back to face him. "You are a very kind and loving Christian man . . . and I am blessed to have you as a friend . . . and somehow, in some way, I think you are part of God's new direction for me."

"Oh, *Mien Leipschen*!" Otto's heart began to pound, and he pulled her closer.

"Let me finish, I have more to say." She pulled away slightly, but still stayed in his embrace.

"I . . . I didn't know the Lord when I married Fredric, so of course I hadn't sought God's will first. But now that I do know Him, I have been giving a lot of thought to the possibility of someone else in my life. And, yes, I would be honored for you to court me . . . that is, with proper boundaries, and with chaperones, of course." She said with a mischievous smile

"If by chaperones, you mean Martina and Elsa, they are welcome to join us anytime for dinners and evenings at the theatre, if you wish to invite them."

His face was aglow with love and happiness and his heart was full. Her actions calmed the tension in him. He now felt that he could be more at ease with her and freer to share his feelings, and he resisted no longer. Gently, he bent down and kissed her lightly on the lips. His heart raced as he felt her softness and her body close to his. In time—in God's time, he knew that he would ask her to be his wife.

They strolled back to her room and Otto kissed her on the cheek and reluctantly left to make his rounds. Kata settled back in her bed, but she could not sleep. She felt alive once again. She knew this was right. God *was* blessing their relationship. A peace and warmth washed over her. She recalled how God had brought Ruth and Boaz together. Was Otto *her* Boaz? She was willing to find out. . .

* * *

Katharina sat in her favorite chair reading her Bible in her upstairs study. Her forty-sixth birthday had come and passed. A hint of grey at each temple splashed her thick auburn hair, now pulled back in a loose bun. Her creamy skin almost void of wrinkles, with the exception of finely etched smile lines around her mouth and a few faint crows' feet notched the corners of her hazel eyes. Even though she was middle-aged, her beauty had not waned. She was wearing a white silk blouse, with a square box collar and a simple blue and beige striped wool jersey skirt, which flowed easily to her ankles. War had depleted society of the elaborate Edwardian styles. It had virtually snuffed out the era of *The Belle Époque.*

She put her Bible aside and rose to gaze out the large three –panel window, which overlooked her spacious, fenced-in back yard. The morning was clear and crisp. March was almost over, yet the days were still rather cool. This particular morning the sun was breaking through the clouds and casting its golden ribbons onto the earth, creating a magical glow across her flower garden. Her blossoming daffodils, irises and hyacinths painted the garden with colorful pinks, purples, oranges and yellows. She pondered seriously the birth of this new spring season: how quickly this year was already passing, and how the wheels of time seemed to be accelerating.

She thought about her beloved homeland and the way that the Great War, as well as political and economic turmoil, had taken a great toll on it.

She dared to recall the heartbreaking trials and tragedies she had gone through, yet she was grateful for the grace that had sustained her through these times, and she believed in her heart that God had begun to restore the years that the locust had eaten. She realized that despite the way her life had gone, the many roads she had traveled, God had put her on the right road now.

* * *

"Mama, Mama! Hurry! We're waiting for you!" Martina burst into the room and grabbed her mother's hand, pulling her towards the door. She left her memories and returned to the present. Today was her precious daughter's sixteenth birthday. They had a big day planned.

"Oh! I am sorry *Liebes.* I confess I was daydreaming. Oh dear, are Elsa and Papa Otto waiting downstairs? She quickly felt her hair to make sure it was still together, looked in the mirror, straightened her skirt, and followed her daughter downstairs to the drawing room.

Otto pulled Kata close and bent down to kiss her.

"Good morning, *Meine Liebe Frau,* he said softly with a grin. They had been married two months now, and the magic was still there. She looked up into his eyes. "Good morning to you, too, *Liebe Ehemann."* Her eyes were shining.

"All right, you two," said Elsa, smiling as she attempted to cajole the newlyweds. "Enough. Let's begin this great celebration! Our little girl is growing up."

"Yes, she is. Today she is a young lady and ready to join the ranks of young adulthood," Kata added, turning to Martina and putting her hand on her daughter's shoulder. Martina was almost as tall as she was now, and she looked so much like her, with the exception of her deep blue eyes. They were definitely her father's eyes.

"Yes, you are a grown up young lady. I am so proud of you. Let's have some tea and cake and then we will do whatever you want to do today on this, your special day." She hugged her daughter and gave her a kiss on the forehead.

Martina was all aglow. Her life was so different today, but she was happy. She had a family again. Even though her own father had passed on, in the short time they had been together, Otto proved to be a loving and caring stepfather. He had made her mother very happy and treated her as if she was his own daughter.

"Yes," she said excitedly. "I *am* grown up now. And I want to go to see that new film with Rudolph Valentino. He's such a *dream!"* She hugged herself as she said his name.

With the introduction of silent film, movie stars were becoming very popular, and now the world was in love with this new idol. Martina was no exception.

"Really, *Liebe,* can you contain yourself?" Kata lightly chided her with a chuckle. "We'll go see that film *The Sheik,* later this afternoon, but right now, let's have some birthday cake and open your gifts."

The newly formed Fleisher family gathered around the dining table, now adorned with gifts and a huge birthday cake with sixteen candles. They joined hands, began with a prayer and sang "Happy Birthday" to Martina. Despite the disconcerting political clouds looming over their beloved Germany and many parts of the world, this was a wonderful new beginning for all of them. God had blessed them with new hope and a new future, and they were going to set aside the cares and worries of the day, and celebrate together.

Epilogue

GRISELDA ALBERS STOOD BY THE WINDOW watching the rain pelt against the windowpane. The grey, dismal sky and the crashing sound of thunder reflected her mood. She was often in dark spirits since she learned the details of Fredric's Will. Even though it had been almost five years since Fredric had succumbed to the influenza, she was still miserable.

No, she was not mourning the loss of her "beloved" husband. She was mourning the loss of his *total* assets. Griselda had ice water running through her veins. She had no concept of love. She was void of compassion.

She expected to inherit virtually everything and to have a greater say in his business after his death. She was shocked to see that Katharina was even a consideration. Although Griselda expected Martina would inherit some of his estate, she assumed it would be an insignificant amount. Nor had she expected the Great War to take such a toll on Germany's economy. Her greed and ambition blotted out any possibility of contentment. In the standards of the day, she was still a wealthy woman, but it was not enough. She worried about the economic disaster that was plaguing Germany. After its surrender in 1918, and the signing of the Treaty of Versailles, Germany was forced to make reparations of billions of British pounds for causing the war.

Hyperinflation also dealt a major blow. The incredible devaluation of the mark affected every aspect of Germany's social, economic and cultural life. Had it not been for the impeccable business practices Fredric's lawyer and Fredric's trusted assistant, Deiter Zimmermann, whom he had named as general manager in the event of his death, Frederic's companies might have gone under during all of this. Griselda was not a bit grateful for this fact. Instead, she constantly harassed Deiter and the companies' lawyers, and cajoled them for not bringing about a quick and complete financial recovery. Deiter had tried his best to assure her that if they just tightened their belt for a time, made some sacrifices, they would see the business' recovery. Griselda would not accept this. She did not want to sacrifice anything. She wanted to continue to live in the fashion to which she had grown accustomed. No, that was not the solution. Somehow, she needed to get hold of Katharina *and* Martina's shares. She had to come up with a plan to secure their assets. It was *not* fair that Katharina should have one mark from the estate. Fredric had divorced her. *She* was the rightful heiress, and that brat daughter of hers, Martina, didn't deserve anything either. She had been nothing but trouble for Griselda since the first day of their marriage.

Griselda contemplated the possible ways to get what was rightfully hers. She already knew that going through the legal channels would not work. The Will was legitimate. No. There would have to be another way. She would be patient. She had waited five years already. She would come up with something. A morbid smile crossed her lips. To what lengths would she dare to go in order to claim what was rightfully hers?

Author's final notes

KATA'S CHARACTER IS BASED SOMEWHAT ON the life of my maternal great-grandmother, and many of the events of this book such as the Great War, the pandemic influenza outbreak in 1918, the sinking of the Titanic, and the assassination of The Archduke Franz (Francis) Ferdinand and Princess Sophie are all true events. However, please keep in mind, that the stories surrounding these historical facts are fiction. History teaches us a great lesson. It teaches us that we live in a world full of sin, sickness, tragedy and death. Yet the Bible teaches us that in this world we are also given a great Hope. His name is Jesus (See John 16:33).

My purpose in writing this story was to entertain, to inform and to inspire. It was also to share Christ and His marvelous plan for our lives. Kata's story is like so many of our own. She experienced the pain of losing loved ones. She faced the pain of losing a child; the pain of losing a husband to another woman; the pain of rejection; and the pain of tragic world events around her. But she also learned that despite all of the tragedy in her life, through Jesus she could have a new beginning and hope for the future. She discovered that through a personal relationship with Christ, she could put the past behind her and face the challenges ahead. She embraced his forgiveness and salvation. She learned that no matter what had happened in her life and no matter what she was to face, Jesus would not leave her nor forsake her.

Like my heroine, I too have experienced the pain of loss and rejection in my own life; however, over forty years ago, I found what Kata did. I found Jesus. I learned that God had good plans for me. Did I still face hurts, tragedies, suffering and pain? Yes. However, the difference is that after receiving salvation, I had Jesus to hold my hand and walk beside me, no matter what came my way.

Each of us can have the very same thing that Kata received. Virtually all of us have a past full of sin, sorrow and suffering, but every one of us can receive God's forgiveness and salvation. God's word tells us that *all have sinned, and come short of the glory of God*, (Romans 3:23). Many of my readers may already know this, and have given their lives to Christ, but perhaps you are one who has never heard this very important message. Just as Elsa shared with Kata and Martina, I want to share some life-changing scriptures with you. John 3:16 tells us that *God so loved the world, that He gave his only begotten Son, that whosoever believeth in him should not perish, but have everlasting life.*

Romans 10:9-10 also says *that if thou shalt confess with thy mouth the Lord Jesus, and shalt believe in thine heart that God hath raised him from the dead, thou shalt be saved.*

The main message of my book is this: No matter what your past, you can have a future in Jesus. It is a simple three-step process:

1. Confess that you are a sinner and repent of those sins, (Romans 3:23/ Acts 3:19)
2. Believe that Jesus died on the cross for you to take your sins away, (John 3:16)
3. Ask Jesus to come in to your heart.

Once you do this, you will be made "righteous in Christ (See Romans 2:13), and you will be a "new creation in Jesus (2 Corinthians 5:17). So now, Dear Reader, if you have not yet accepted Jesus as your Lord and Savior, I would like to invite you to do so now. Simply pray this prayer with me:

Dear Lord, I confess that I am a sinner. I come to you and ask you to forgive my sins. Just as your Word says, I believe that Jesus is your Son and that He died on the Cross and rose from the dead so that I could be forgiven and have Eternal Life. I Thank you that I am now a new creation in Christ and I will worship you all the days of my life. In Jesus' name, Amen.

Dear friend, if you prayed that prayer and meant it, you have experienced what Kata did when she gave her life to Jesus. The next step is to start reading the Bible and find a church that believes and teaches God's Word. Most importantly, seek the Lord and ask Him to show you His plan and purpose for your life, and I assure you, you will not be disappointed.

Yours in Christ,
Donna Boddy

Sources

Most of the details concerning historical events in this book are based on general knowledge and my own study of historical events over the years as well as stories my maternal grandmother and my paternal great-grandfather used to tell me about World War I. In addition, I took verses from the *King James Bible.*

German phrases & words used in this book:

Ehemann / husband
Engel /Angel
Frau /Mrs. /Wife
Fraulein/ Miss
Herr /Mr.
Kinder / Child
Liebe/ Dear
Liebling / Darling
Mausi / Little Mouse
Mein Gott / My God
Meine Liebes / My dear
Prinzessin / Princess
Schatz / Sweetheart
Schatzi/Schätzchen Little Treasure
Tante /Aunt
Unteroffizier/ Corporal
Wunderbar / Wonderful
Liebe *Frau* / Dear wife

About the Author

Donna Boddy teaches English and Spanish. A mother of three and grandmother of six, Boddy lives and works in Kansas, where she and her husband are active in their local church.